W9-AXV-658

On The
Divinity of
Second
Chances

On the Divinity of Second Chances

Kaya McLaren

DayBue Publishing

First DayBue Publishing Edition 2004

DayBue Publishing, design, and logo
are trademarks of DayBue Publishing.

Design by Lisa Schulz Elliot / Elysium.
Cover illustration by Jody Hewgill.
Printed in Canada.

10 9 8 7 6 5 4 3 2

Library of Congress Catalog: 2003108689
ISBN 0-9668940-7-3

DAYBUE PUBLISHING
Illuminating the mind and awakening the heart.

PO Box 4961, 100 Lindsay Circle
Ketchum, Idaho 83340
www.daybue.com

to Tasha Good Dog

On the
Divinity of
Second
Chances

The Moon on the Magnificence of Change

THE MOON ABOVE sees it all, and since she is an orb that appears to come and go, the moon understands the cycles of second chances. Yes, change is inevitable, she understands, but it can be done with some grace. She does not cling to last month's trip around the Earth, and she does not project herself into next month's. She shows us a slightly different expression each time we see her. She is both the same moon and an infinity of different moons.

The moon sees Anna and Phil, like Uranus and Neptune, seemingly sharing aspects in common, but definitely in their own enormous orbits. Anna would be the colder of the two. It sees their youngest, Forrest, much like Mercury in retrograde. Sometimes what is actually moving forward appears to move backwards as it corners a bend. It sees Olive, Anna and Phil's oldest, like a nebula, the source of new creation. Phil and Anna's middle child, Jade, much like the sun, radiates energy wherever she goes, bringing things to light and transforming that which wishes to be transformed. Pearl, Anna's mother, much like Jupiter, takes up a lot of space and has a spot that is prone to irritation.

From above, the moon watches this family as they show their dark sides and light sides, as they orbit and reinvent themselves. She remains in the sky, reminding those below of the power of illumination in darkness, reflection, and the magnificence of change.

Jade on the Laundromat

THERE'S NOTHING LIKE the hypnotic sound of washing machines. I fold my T-shirts, still stained on the sides from where I wedge the oily arms of my clients above my hip to get a better grip. I find the sound of the Laundromat so soothing. I have effortless moments of that emptiness for which all those who meditate strive. Yes, Laundromats sound a little like the ocean in a way—nothingness. Just emptiness. I love losing myself in the low rumbles of Speed Queens and Maytags. I don't even care about my massage sheets going rancid and the little bits of kleenex all over my personal laundry. I have yet to get a load of laundry through without a kleenex hiding in a pocket. None of it matters.

"I like these Laundromats better than church," my spirit guide, Grace, says, pulling me out of the emptiness. "More meditation, less fear." We nod together and look around. Three other customers also appear to be in the emptiness— one, a young man who rode in on a skateboard with his bag of laundry thrown over his shoulder like Santa, and the other, a Mexican couple, also folding laundry.

Olive doesn't even say hi to Aretha, my husky-rottweiler who waits for me outside the glass doors. She just storms in with her pink plastic laundry basket and a small red plastic bag on top. She drops her basket in front of the washing machine closest to me and picks up the plastic bag. "It's over," she announces. "Matt left." I watch her dig in her bag. As her announcement sinks in, I try to figure out the appropriate reply. Anything supportive I say now could be used against me if they get back together later.

"Wow," slips out. "Are you okay?" Good. That was a good thing to say. That was the right thing to say.

Olive pulls out six pairs of new cotton bikini underwear, rips off the tags, and throws them in the washing machine. "Oh, I'm fine," she says with residual anger around the edges. "I'm fine and I'm through with wearing uncomfortable underwear." She spikes the underwear tags in the garbage, then puts her quarters in the machine and scoops out some detergent from her box.

Okay, I'm really not sure how to respond to that . . . *Amen sister!* perhaps? "Well, cotton is king," slips out. Jesus! Where is my self-censor mechanism?

Olive walks to the other side of the Laundromat and, as usual, starts digging in the lost and found box. "What does a person have to do to keep a mate? Half my sock drawer is full of singles!"

I look at my own bare feet. Yeah, not my problem. "Why

don't you donate them to the kindergarten so kids can make sock puppets?"

"Then what happens if I find the mate to one of the socks I've given away? I don't want a Romeo and Juliet ending in my sock drawer. God, where do you suppose they go?" She begins to sort her laundry into two machines.

"I think the Laundromat is a portal to other dimensions, and that's where the socks go—other dimensions," I joke. She gives me that look. She doesn't get my humor. Never has. I swear everything I say irritates her. I've learned there's really nothing I can say or do about that.

Suddenly, Olive's eyes bulge and she pukes right there in the garbage, just like that. I jump up, put one arm around her and with the other hand, pull the garbage closer to a bench so she can sit and let it all out. She pukes again. "The smell in here is too much for me," she tells me as she starts to run for the door. I quickly push in the quarters to start her machines, then run out to help her into her car and drive her home.

Grace sits in the backseat with Aretha. "She doesn't know it yet, but you're going to be an aunt."

Olive on Crossroads

CROSSROADS. I THINK about them a lot—why we go one way and not another. To what degree is our life dictated by fate and to what degree is it a choice?

I ask because last night something happened that would have looked like a choice had someone been there to watch it, but it felt predetermined, as if I was there only as a formality.

When I try to remember last night, I can't put the events in order. I can't even recall most of what I said. I remember thinking. I remember thinking in that way you do in those five long seconds it takes for your car to slide off an icy road once it begins to spin, where time slows down and you find yourself with enough time to figure out the meaning of life, although you don't actually figure it out because instead you're thinking about what your dad's reaction will be when he sees your smashed car.

In a way, what happened last night is not so different from sliding off the road. In the same way Dad always told me not to hit the brakes on an icy road, he also told me Matt was never going to amount to anything. In both cases, I had to see for myself that Dad was right. He was. I hate that.

I remember thinking *oh, here we go again.* I remember looking at his face, noticing it wasn't nearly as handsome as I had thought it was these last four years, watching his mouth move even though his jaw was clenched. I remember wondering how he could think living in a tipi year-round was the answer to our problems. I remember picturing myself showing up at my job at the bank in un-ironed clothes, muddy shoes, greasy hair, and reeking of body odor and menses— then envisioning myself unemployed in the tipi. I remember seeing myself in a smoky tipi with a sick baby and a pile of dirty diapers. All day long, I melt snow so I can wash the diapers by hand. I'm angry—too angry to be a wife or a mother. Above all, I remember envisioning myself feeling trapped. It was as if I left a concert just for a minute so I could run outside and get something from my car. But when I tried to get back into the show, I couldn't—because the ticket said "No Re-Admits." And I'm begging the bouncer, but he's not budging. "No Re-Admits"—he just keeps saying it over and over. I know that's what it would be like trying to get back into mainstream society after having lived in a tipi. Matt's mouth was moving, but I wasn't listening. I was seeing my future.

"It's not forever," he said. "It's just for a couple years so we can save a down payment." I knew that was a lie. I had seen my future. It was forever.

I remember thinking that if he had made a different

choice at a crossroads earlier in his life, we wouldn't be in this position now. He had chosen to snowboard instead of going to college, and now he wanted me to pay the price. I wasn't going to do it. I had paid my dues for a better life than that.

I remember looking at his face and realizing I had stopped loving him—just like that. How do you love someone who wants to sentence you to the life I had just previewed? That's not love. I don't know what it is, but it's sure not love.

I submerged myself in a hot bath and listened to him pack. I didn't want to watch; instead, I sat there thinking about how my hot water and his backpack were indicative of the separate paths we had just chosen.

He barged in near the end to get his shaving kit, his vitamins, and a few miscellaneous toiletries. I felt naked in his presence for the first time in years. I wanted to cover myself, but I didn't. I acted like everything was normal. He took one last look at me, scanning my naked body. I didn't recognize the look in his eyes. Finally, he barked good-bye and left. I felt nothing but relief at his departure. I felt the promise of a greater peace in my life, though anger still hung in the air. Even though I knew someday I'd praise Jesus this didn't work out, right then I just felt used up. Plus, it's harsh to have any man walk away from you when you're naked. We all know that's just not nature.

When Matt was still trying to take my hot water away, I felt panic about the threat of losing something so vital. Stepping into the hot, steaming water soothed something deep inside me. After Matt's departure, the threat of losing this vital steaming water was gone. Once the threat was gone, the bath was just a bath again and suddenly felt significantly more tepid.

I felt overwhelming grief and had trouble sleeping. Four years is a long time. It's a long time to have someone in your life, and it's a long time to dream the same dream. I sifted through my memories and I sifted though my grief. I realized my greatest grief was for the loss of my own picture of my future. That picture was pretty detailed, and I had to accept my future wasn't going to look like that anymore. For me, there is no grief more devastating than the grief for what could have been.

For the first time in my life, I found myself with no vision, no dreams. My heart sank, taking the rest of me with it.

Pearl on Sunflowers

Dear Anna,

I have just planted another crop of sunflowers. An orange cat showed up at our door. We've taken her in. Beatrice has taken a shine to her. I figure these old farmhouses can always use more mouse patrol. The weather is getting warmer. We've had a few days in the high 70's. It's supposed to rain today. We could use it. I haven't shot at Dean in a whole week. Hope all is well in Cottonwood. Give my best to Phil and the girls.

Lovingly, Mom

I PUT MY letter in an envelope and leave it by the door so I will remember to take it with me to the post office tomorrow.

For now, I sit on my porch in the old rocker my mother used to shuck peas in, and look out onto my freshly planted fields. Soon, little sunflower seedlings will sprout their first leaves, and shortly thereafter, bright sunflowers will shine their cheery faces at me. They will be a sea of sunshine. Sunflowers have been such a welcome change after those decades of corn. My parents grew corn on this land, and then my husband followed in their footsteps. Not sweet corn, mind you, but feeder corn. At last, this farm is mine, and the corn siege is over. And at last, my life is mine, and the husband siege is over.

I suggested sunflowers to my husband once. I was only proposing a few acres of it at the time. He chuckled at me and told me women didn't know anything about the business of farming. Shortly thereafter, the sunflower oil market boomed.

"What do I want to grow this year?" is a great question, one I love mulling over, even if I do make the same choices year after year. Each year, it's *my* choice. This year, I decided to grow sunflowers, a new dress, and some groundbreaking choreography integrating my two favorite things: guns and tap dancing. In the garden, I decided to grow more of those Fort Laramie Strawberries. I don't make preserves anymore. I just stick everything in ziplock bags in the freezer. I think I might like to grow a braided rug made out of all my husband's old wool suits. Next winter, maybe. I have always wanted a pair of red cowboy boots to wear on special occasions. Yes, this just might be the year I grow a pair of red cowboy boots.

But at this moment, I watch an early summer storm come in to water my freshly planted sunflower seeds and simply grow satisfaction. I watch Beatrice return from her brisk walk along the west fence, noticing the way she kind of swishes and her cropped hair bounces, the way she stops to study a flower through her cat glasses. I love everything about her. My heart feels so full, like it might just burst.

"Dean's cows made it through the fence again," she informs me. "I chased them back."

My heart no longer feels like it just might burst. Anger boils up inside me. "That's six times in the last month. Dean isn't learning," I say. I think he's hoping I'll shoot one of them; he knows that in order for me to avoid legal trouble, I'd have to cough up a compensation price for it higher than what he'd get at the auction. I have a plan for Dean and his cattle, but timing is everything.

"Dean is such a special man," Beatrice says in the way only she can. She sits next to me and sighs. I put my arm around her, and she pats my leg. "What would you like for dinner?" she asks.

"One of Dean's cows," I answer.

Anna on Growing Old in Cottonwood

DON'T GET ME wrong. Cottonwood, Idaho, is a beautiful place to live, and after growing up in South Dakota, I am thankful for the elegant life I've had here. Cottonwood is a ski resort town, nestled in a long valley that runs north-south, where the Cottonwood River winds through the valley floor, lined, as you might imagine, with ancient cottonwood trees. The hills and mountains are arid on the south sides—just sage and yellow grass, but the north slopes where the snow does not evaporate in the high-altitude sun, host handsome groves of aspen, pine and fir. The residents of Cottonwood are a mix that seems to work. Most are rich, athletic, and beautiful in a way you expect to see only in California. The majority are friendly and genuinely caring. Residents pass each other on the Rails to Trails doing or training for some sport modified with either "power" or "extreme."

It is both a good place and a hard place to grow old. It's

a good place to grow old in that there are many people in their eighties who do their yoga every day and are still among the first on the ski slopes on powdery winter mornings. Old age is not equated with inactivity, boredom or poor health, with the exception of knee replacements, which are a given, of course. It is, after all, a ski town. It's a hard place to grow old in the way that it's a place where many women have made the pact, "I'll be beautiful, if you'll be rich." The men continue to hold up their end of the bargain as they age and good investments continue to pay off, while women begin to struggle and grasp to maintain their only idea of beauty—the youthful beauty they knew at twenty. Plastic surgeons do very well in Cottonwood.

I sit in my breakfast nook, the only place in the whole house where I truly feel comfortable, and paint a raisin using black and white acrylics. With my smallest brush, I add more white highlights to a wrinkle, bringing it out. A colorless raisin—it is exactly how I feel.

I take a break to prepare a cup of jasmine tea. My earlier paintings of emerging fruit still hang in the breakfast nook and in the kitchen. I began painting when I was first pregnant with Olive, and that half-flower, half-fruit was exactly what I felt like then. Apples, pears, cherries, plums, apricots, peaches —my paintings were sensuous, luscious, and succulent. They were all about maternity and femininity. Sometimes, in the kitchen, I stop and study one of these old paintings. Gone are those days. That era is over. It's strange really, to wake up one day and realize that your youthful kind of beauty is *gone*. Your tight skin and smooth legs are gone, and they are never coming back. Never. Another kind of beauty awaits, but it's not the same. It's not a beauty associated with the sense of still having an unlimited life ahead. It's not a head-turning kind of beauty, but rather a beauty more rooted in the expression of one's eyes. It has something to do with love, grace, and wisdom. Actually, it has *everything* to do with love, grace, and wisdom. It's a beauty people have to take a minute and look for. It may even be more of a feeling people experience in your presence than an appearance. I don't know for sure. But I know I don't have the peace of mind and heart to pull off that kind of beauty. I'm caught between two kinds of beauty, falling through the cracks.

I study a photograph of my mother that sits on a shelf in a silver frame. I always thought she was so dowdy in her farm clothes and plain hair, but as I study her eyes now, I see her beauty exceeds mine. She has attained the phase two kind of beauty.

My kettle whistles, so I put the photograph down and pour my hot water into a pot. While I wait for the tea to steep, Phil's newspaper catches my eye. Words jump out at me: *Invisible. Ignored. Unseen. Grief. Irreversible.* I take the scissors from the junk drawer and cut out these words to collage onto my raisin painting, maybe in the background, maybe in the highlights. Maybe I'll cover them with a thin layer of paint or two so people will have to look closely to see them.

I return to the window in the breakfast nook with my tea

and continue to paint my raisin. Crone. I roll the word around in my mouth like an awkward jawbreaker. When I think of the word crone, I think of raisins. Crone. I think that's what I'll call this painting.

I don't paint to sell. I used to paint to celebrate, but now I simply paint to process. I can't even chew on the crone jaw-breaker without hurting myself. I can't swallow it. I can only suck on it for a while until it dissolves into something I can deal with.

I caught a glimpse of my reflection in a window yester-day and saw my grandmother's face. Not my mother's, which I had always heard would happen. No, I saw my grandmoth-er's face.

I wear black. Sleek, black, tailored clothes and trendy shoes. My hair is cut very short, and my eye make-up is dark and dramatic. I always thought of myself as sleek, but how does one go about being a sleek raisin? Nature is cruel, giving you an identity you get used to, only to have it transform into that of your grandmother. My grandmother was not sleek; she was severe, angular, and mottled. The only soft thing about her was the downy hair on her chin. I look for my reflection in the window. Yes, I'm on my way to becoming hollow and bony, just like my grandmother, sunken and mot-tled just like a raisin.

Forrest on Lightning Bob and Self-imposed Solitary Confinement

I WAS FOURTEEN and in shock, horrified by my own capabilities and terrified by the way my life could change in an instant. A rash impulse that felt so right in one moment, now felt so wrong. I felt betrayed by my instincts. After hitching back from South Dakota, I wandered aimlessly in the sage and pine covered mountains beyond Cottonwood. At some point, I just started walking up. In retrospect, I was trying to climb out of the depths of Hell.

I spent my first night on a hillside, hungry and dehydrated. After burying myself in pine needles to stay warm, I listened to the wolves and wailed with them as it hit me how truly and irreversibly alone I was. It struck me that my innocence was gone. My virtue was gone. Anything that connected me to God was gone, and I grieved for it. I was in Hell now. My existence no longer had worth. I wailed and the wolves wailed with me. A chorus of grief.

I awoke to the sound of sniffing and opened my eyes to see not a wolf, but a German Shepherd. Behind him stood a man in a Forest Service uniform with black hair and a moustache. He took a few steps closer to me and squatted down. His nametag read "Lightning Bob."

"Are you okay?" he asked.

I shook my head.

"Are you injured?"

I shook my head.

"Do you need water?"

I nodded. He handed me a small canteen from his belt. I knew I didn't deserve the water. I deserved to be left to die. I drank half his water anyway, and then felt guilty about it.

"Do your parents know where you are?" he continued.

I shook my head.

"I imagine they're pretty scared by now."

I shut my eyes. Not only was I a murderer now, but a source of torture for my parents as well. I hung my head and let my tears fall.

Lightning Bob didn't ask any more questions. He led me to his tower and fed me bacon and eggs. I felt so unworthy of his concern and limited rations.

"Do you play cribbage?" he asked. When I shook my head, he proceeded to explain the rules. I tried to concentrate, but my mind was filled with fire. He coached me through our first game. In actuality, all I did was hold the cards.

Next to me was a calendar. The July 5th square had five

tally marks and the number five hundred thirty-seven scribbled on it. I pointed to it and looked at Lightning Bob.

"I've been struck by lightning five hundred and thirty-seven times now, five times that night. Oh, don't worry—it hits the lightning rod and doesn't hurt me, but boy, let me tell you, all my hair stands up. One of my friends who also works in a tower thinks it keeps us young. Look," he said as he lowered his head and began to part his hair in different places for me to examine. "No gray. I'm forty-nine and I still have all my hair. Look for yourself—it's all there. All my other friends are bald and gray, but I've still got a full head of hair, not a trace of gray."

I tried to give him my best fascinated look.

"Yeah, five strikes on July 5th—weird, huh?"

I raised my eyebrows and nodded my head without looking at him.

"Yeah, that was a wild night. I wrote a poem about it. I like to write poems. I always have. It's a gift." He stood up, took two steps and grabbed a notebook from under his cot.

"The Storm . . ." He glanced up from his notebook at me. "Most of my poems have that title." I nodded. "The Storm," he began again dramatically.

The sky rips open
The sky, it cracks
It almost gives me
Heart attacks.

Truthfully, I was not particularly moved by the poem, but I was genuinely fascinated by Lightning Bob. He was unmistakably different.

When he excused himself to go to the outhouse, I bolted.

Jade tracked me, but not in the way you usually think of tracking. She used to do this when we were little. No one ever wanted to play Hide and Seek with her. I guess I should have expected her, but I didn't. She brought me a backpack with nuts, oats, a first-aid kit, a water purifier, a sling shot, a sleeping bag and a tent. She also gave me a twenty-dollar bill, a spiral notebook, and some pencils. When I saw her walking toward me, I ran to her and flung my arms around her. "What am I going to do?" I asked her over and over. "What am I going to do?" It was the first time I had heard my own voice in a week. I broke away from her and dropped to the ground. She looked at me with such deep concern, I knew she didn't have any answers either.

"What have I done?" I asked.

She looked so sad as she shook her head.

We sat side by side for nearly four hours, neither of us talking, each deep in our own thoughts. A couple times I saw her cry. I needed her to come up with answers, for her to help me undo what I had done—I knew if there was someone who could, it would be Jade.

"There are no answers," she finally said in the same way she would have said, "There is no hope." She looked at me matter-of-factly. I was crushed. "Write Mom and Dad a letter," she said. "I'll put it in the mail so they don't know I know where you are. They need to know what's going on."

I had no idea what to write to my parents. I couldn't bring myself to write the words "kill" or "murder." Eventually, I settled on keeping it simple: "Dear Mom and Dad, I have done something very bad. I can't come home, but I want you to know I'm okay. I love you, Forrest." Jade handed me an envelope. I wrote the address that used to be mine, but would never be again. I slipped my letter in the envelope and handed it back to Jade.

"I'll be back," she said. Then she gave me a big hug and rocked me a little, back and forth, back and forth, like the aspens around us, swaying in the breeze. And then she left. As I watched her walk away, I realized my life as I had known it was over. My self, as I had known me, was gone.

Thirteen years later, here I am two ridges away from Lightning Bob in my primary tree house, still in my self-imposed solitary confinement. I wonder about setting myself free sometimes, but it still doesn't feel right.

Jade on Childhood

IN MY OLD room at the parents' house, there's a crayon picture I drew when I was five or six. Mom framed it. It's of Grace and me dancing to "Soul Train." Both Grace and I have our hair in cornrows. Grace's hair is black, and her skin is brown; my hair is orange, and my skin's fuchsia. I must have had one of my many sunburns when I drew it.

A memory of returning from school rushes back to me. I was six years old. I passed Olive, then eight years old, who was playing on her Donny and Marie drum set. "Hi, Olive. Hi, Chief," I said to Olive and her guardian, Walks Far.

"Stop that! There's no one else here!"

"Yu-huh," I argued. "He's sitting right beside you drumming. Good thing too, 'cause you white girls aren't known for your sense of rhythm."

"You're a white girl! You're a white girl, too!" Olive yelled as I walked away down the hall.

Mom was playing Barbara Streisand in the living room

while she ironed. I winced at the sound of Streisand. Forrest, four years old, was playing with blocks near Mom. "Hi Mom," I greeted her.

"Hi, Sweet Pea," she replied without looking up from her ironing.

I walked back to my room and shut the door. Pictures I had drawn of Grace hung on my wall.

"Oooh. Look at you, girl. You got to be better about wearing that sun block," Grace said.

"Grace, how did I end up in this white girl body?" I asked.

"It's good to experience a lot of things, child." Grace did her best to comfort me.

"I don't know if I'm going to make it," I told her. "I think my momma's white girl music just might kill me. How could Donna Summer do a duet with that Barbara Streisand?"

"Turn on your radio, child. I'll play you some Sly." Grace knew this always lifted my spirits. I turned on my radio, and Grace made Sly and The Family Stone come on with "You Can Make It If You Try." We sang along and got down.

Now I study the picture I drew as a child. "Jade and her imaginary friend, second grade," Mom had written under it. Imaginary friend. Around the time my second grade teacher suggested I get a schizophrenia screening, I stopped talking to anyone about Grace. Grace told me it would probably be best if I kept quiet about that which others did not understand.

When I was even younger, some members of my old congregation from a previous lifetime used to show up and play chase with me. They would run through walls though, and I would smack right into them. I'm pretty sure my parents thought something was wrong with me then, too.

I had called my congregation "ghosts," but Grace corrected me. "They aren't ghosts! They are spirits! Nothing offends a spirit worse than being called a ghost! A ghost is a soul that is too confused to leave the Earth dimension and go to Heaven just yet. A spirit is a soul that has gone to Heaven, but has come back for a quick visit to check on you. You see the difference?"

I look at myself in the mirror. I don't look much different than I did in my second grade self-portrait. Like Grace, I still have cornrows, but now I wear them in a ponytail to keep them out of my face. My skin is not as fuchsia now. I couldn't get waterproof SPF 40 in the seventies.

Phil on Being Benched

THE BMW HAD an oil change a thousand miles ago, and the Mercedes fewer than three hundred miles ago. Neither needs new oil. I study the spiral notebooks I keep in each car where I record every maintenance and repair, every oil change, every fill-up. I calculate the mileage to make sure the cars are still running efficiently. The mileage shows no change. The cars are spotless. This task did not take up much time. I take out my daily list of goals and cross off "Check cars for anything."

I look around for something to do. I rummage through immaculate cupboards for something to organize better. Garden tools. I can put nails in the cupboard on which to hang each tool in alphabetical order. Shovel comes before spade. Then comes trowel. Rake comes before shovel. But what do you do with tools that have a modifier? Should the bamboo rake be under B, or should I phrase it "rake, bamboo," which would precede, "rake, metal"? And should the flathead shovel be under F or "shovel, flathead," which would come before "shovel, spade"? I decide to go with the latter system. I know, though, that it really doesn't matter much.

I used to be an investing genius. Yes, genius. How do I know? Millions and millions of dollars—that's how I know. Do I flaunt it? No. Sure, I have a BMW and a Mercedes (parked in alphabetical order), but that's because they're the best-made cars in the world. Heck, I've had the BMW since 1978 and the Mercedes since 1972. They're still going strong. They were sound investments.

My family doesn't know how much money I've made. Best that they not. They know I've done well, but they don't know the details. I'm very protective of my wealth. Wealth is like a delicate orchid few know how to keep alive and healthy. I, for one, never want to be poor again. I grew up poor. Hated it. I like nice things, and I like to share them with Anna, sure, but I don't like waste. I don't like the feeling of my wealth slipping away. Plus, I want my kids to find their own way in this world. It's important to a person's character to overcome obstacles. It's also important to learn the value of a dollar. Yes, some could argue that I hoard my wealth, but from my perspective, money in the bank is simply a report card, something to prove that my judgment is superior to most—something to show my epic success. Why would I want to invite my family to spend my report card? Sure, I have some trusts just for tax purposes, but no one will know about them until I'm dead and gone. You know, I got in on the ground floor of some big ones. Big. Wal-Mart, for one. Wal-Mart has made me very wealthy. Most of my wealth was made in futures though. Do you know how many people can pull that one off? It takes an investing genius to do so.

Now, at Anna's insistence, most of it sits in Sallie Mae and Freddie Mac, where I can live very comfortably on dividends and not have to watch the stock market. She wanted me to put it all in a regular old savings account. Can you imagine? A savings account! Millions of dollars not earning jack squat in a savings account? She threatened to leave me if I didn't, saying that she did not wish to watch me kill myself with my bond market addiction. We compromised on these stable, federally insured bonds, where it earns higher interest than it would in a regular savings account, but where I don't have to worry so much about the economy going to hell.

It was corn that did it to me. When it hit the press that genetically-engineered Star corn contaminated other American corn, no country wanted to import American corn. I found myself in bad shape. Didn't see that one coming. For a while, it looked as though an obscene number of bushels of corn would be delivered to my house. I had to unload this corn, even if I had to give it away. I felt the pain in my chest shoot down my left arm. I knew what was happening. Three decades ago, when I was a young hotshot living in Chicago, I saw at least twenty men drop dead right there in the Mercantile Exchange of the same thing. Still, I couldn't afford the luxury of a heart attack until I unloaded that damn corn. If I was going to drop dead, I wasn't going to trouble Anna with an obscene amount of corn delivered to our house by default.

Now, here I am, like a racehorse that injures his leg and never races again. I'll never play the game like I used to. My genius is going to waste because my body can't stand the stress any longer. I'm lucky to be alive; Anna insists on pointing that out to me all the damn time. Do I need someone to remind me of my mortality all the damn time? Do I need my wife to remind me that I have passed my prime and am now degenerating rapidly? No. I hated those weeks following the heart attack when Anna was nursing me. Indignant, to say the least. I had always been in charge. I had always been on top. I had been a man my family could depend on. Then, one day, I woke up to find she was stronger than me, and I was dependent on her. Where do I go from here? How do I get my pride back? By organizing garden tools in alphabetical order? No. How pathetic! What kind of man am I now? Worthless as all that corn. Sometimes I wish someone would just plow me under.

I reach into one of my tool boxes for the latest *Forbes* magazine, take a good look around, and confident that Anna is immersed in her painting, crack the magazine open. Ahh.

Pearl on The Neighborhood

I OPEN MY front door and greet the cool morning with a smile. My hair is pulled back in my favorite red scarf, the one that matches my bright red pedal pushers I wear so that my pants don't get caught in my bike chain. I step out onto my porch, survey the sky around me, walk down my steps, and take the old Schwinn cruiser from where it was leaned against the porch. I drop my letter to Anna and some dog cookies in the flower basket on my handlebars. I walk my cruiser down the path from my house until I reach the driveway. I adjust my handgun holster so that my piece rides a little more toward my back and doesn't get in the way when I pedal. I spot Beatrice, that early bird, out in the garden.

"Beatrice! Would you like to ride to town with me?" I call to her.

"No thank you!" she calls back. "It looks like rain!"

"Chicken!" I call to her as I hop on and begin the three-and-a-half mile ride down the smooth clay road. I like the hum of my tires on the clay and enjoy seeing the pattern my tires leave in the silt-clay dust as I weave down the road, creating a giant serpent from my house to town.

I pass the Hildebrand's house. Erika Hildebrand has taken to collecting small livestock lately. I study her two pygmy goats and miniature donkey as I pass their pasture. As I make my way down farther, the Anderson's dogs run out to greet me—Amigo, a Blue Heeler, and Kiva, an Australian Shepherd. I stop my bicycle and give them both a dog cookie, then begin to pedal again. The dogs try to herd me by running circles around my bicycle. Julie Anderson, mowing the little lawn around her house, looks up and waves. She whistles at her dogs, and they leave their unsuccessful attempt at herding to run back home. At least ten kids play outside the Hull's house. Sasha, as usual, is in her garden, where I reckon she spends all her time trying to grow food to feed all those kids. From under her wide straw gardening hat, Sasha calls out hello, and I return her greeting. I do love riding past my neighbors. The bicycle takes me at just the right speed, slow enough to take a good look at things, but fast enough to get me there. I can stop and say hello to neighbors with less formality than if I had driven up in a car, or I can just wave and ride on by. I miss this ritual in the winter when the snow covers the road.

A rattler suns itself in the road. I take my gun out of my holster, pull back the hammer, aim, and press the trigger. The recoil makes my bike swerve dramatically, but I don't crash. I get closer to the snake, now dead, and stop. I walk to the side of the road without getting off my bike, pick up a stick, go back to the snake, and poke it. It doesn't move, so I pick it up and put it in the flower basket on my handlebars so I can skin it later.

I continue on until I reach the edge of town, then pass a row of houses, the feed store, the general store, and arrive at last at my destination, the post office. I park my cruiser, walk inside, and unlock my box. A letter from an old friend who moved to Kansas, a catalog full of stupid gadgets and useless junk I don't need, a subscription renewal notice for Beatrice from Prevention Magazine, and a yellow USPS card that lets me know I have a package too large to fit in my box. I present the card to Andrew Mabey, the postmaster, such a nice boy.

"Why hello, Mrs. Huffman, I hear we're supposed to get more rain today," he tells me.

"Couldn't come at a better time," I reply. My smile thanks him for the good news.

Andrew walks into the back and finds my package. It's my long-awaited box of Fort Laramie strawberry plants—two hundred of them. "My strawberries," I tell Andrew.

"Well, now I know where to be at the end of August!" he teases me. Secretly though, I know he does hope I bring him another strawberry pie like last year.

"I'd better hurry home and get as many of these in the soil as I can before the rain," I explain. I say goodbye, walk outside to my bike, take two bungee cords from under the dead snake in my basket and strap the box of strawberry plants to the rack over my back tire. I take the dead snake from my basket and carefully tuck it under the bungee cords to make room in my flower basket for my other mail. Then I pedal with more vigor on my way home, past my friendly neighbors, to beat the rain.

Anna On Being Territorial

I WEAR A black tank top while I paint today, even though I've become self-conscious of my arms. Hot flashes. I woke up last night drenched in sweat. I got out of bed, found some clean, dry sheets and took them outside to the reclining lawn chair where I spent the rest of the night.

Instead of my favorite jasmine tea, I drink some worthless herbal menopause tea and sit by the window in the breakfast nook, painting a black and white raisin with a bright orange, red, and yellow flame around it. I'll call it "Crone with Hot Flash."

Phil comes into the kitchen and begins to look through the cupboards. He takes all the small appliances out, neatly folds each one's cord, takes a twisty-tie from the plastic bag and foil drawer, and wraps each folded cord. I burn with irritation. Get out of *my* kitchen. I know, of course, that in truth, it is *our* kitchen. We have, after all, shared this house for fourteen years. But in those fourteen years, he has regarded this as my domain. It's the only place in the whole house where I care to spend any time. Now, here he is in my domain, thinking he can do everything better. What an insult.

Phil has moved on to the spice cupboard. He has taken all the spices out and arranged them alphabetically, as if the way they were was chaos. It wasn't chaos. I had grouped them according to ethnicity, purposely keeping the ones that crossed over in the middle.

Do you know he rearranged my garden tools, too? I had them arranged according to season. Metal rake and spade for spring. Hoe and trowels for summer. Bamboo rake and pitchfork for fall. His compulsive tendencies and boredom not only insult me, but mess up my systems as well. One could argue that the garden tools were his, too. Sure—the garage was his as well . . . but when, when had he *ever* done anything in the garden? Never. He never used to be around. Now he's around all the time—and at a time when I've never needed solitude more.

I paint more yellow into the tips of the flames around the raisin and bristle as I watch Phil take bags of food out of the cupboards and trim them down with scissors. Phil apparently doesn't like to reach down into bags. He trims the bag of corn chips, the bag of sugar, and the bag of flour, for starters. I wonder when he has ever reached down into a bag of flour. I like the long bags. I like having lots of bag to roll up several times so that they don't come open in between uses. So help me God if he starts implementing the use of those annoying clips. I don't want to mess with clips. I don't want to keep track of clips. I don't want clips. Period. I want my kitchen the way it's been for fourteen years, functioning just fine.

"Don't you have anything else to do?" I ask with my hackles up. I'm trying to be compassionate. I really am. I know this is the sum total of his entertainment these days.

His silence is all I need to know that he is crushed by what I just said. He puts the bags back in the cupboard and walks out of the kitchen.

I exhale. I blew it. I resent the fact that if no one had been around, I wouldn't have blown it. His mere presence set me up for a failure I really didn't need. I read somewhere that in some Asian country, when women turn sixty, they go live in a convent. Oh, that would be Heaven. I would have only six more years to tolerate, and then—finally—I would be no one's mother and no one's wife. As it is, there is no end in sight. There is no retirement for women who have taken care of others their whole life.

Phil on Finding a New Pastime

WHAT? DON'T I have anything else to do? No. No, I don't. I was just trying to make things nicer for her. I don't know how Anna ever found the spice she wanted, and the bags were out of control—before I took care of it for her, she probably got flour all over her arm when she reached down into that bag.

I retreat to the den and begin reading the phone book in hopes of finding something worthwhile of my time. Aircraft, no. Ballet, no. Boats, no. I never admired people who threw their money away on expensive toys like aircraft or boats. They were people who worked for the good life, instead of working because they loved work and success. There is a difference. I continue to finger through the yellow pages. Books, no. That's what libraries are for. Churches, no. Coffee, no. Cruises, not a permanent solution. Dance Schools, sure can't picture that. Dog Training, no dog. Embroidery, now that would be sad. Fishing. Hm, fishing, maybe. I hate to go there, though. Fishing and golf, what every man in America is reduced to every Father's Day. When I pass that fishing and golf crap in shop windows every June, I always think I'm either the only man in America who does neither, or there are a lot of people out there who don't have a clue who their father really is.

Do *my* kids have a clue who I really am? I'm not even sure *I* do. I used to know. I used to work all the time. I guess my kids knew I worked all the time, so maybe they did know all there really was to know about me. What is there to know about a person anyway? What they desire? What they enjoy? I enjoyed success. I desire more success. Yes, that's probably evident. They probably do know me.

Fishing and golf. Well, with fishing, once you have your equipment, it's free. Golf, on the other hand, continues to waste your money. I can't think of why wasting money would be fun. Between the two, I'd have to go with fishing. Though, with catch and release, what exactly is the point? How exactly is that productive? If you actually kept the fish you caught, well then, over time you could recover the cost of your fishing equipment and actually come out ahead.

I keep flipping through the yellow pages. Garden, probably not. Golf, went over that. Gymnastics, God, no. Horseback Riding, no. Ice Hockey, too old. Investment Advisors. I ache. Karaoke, no. Kayaks, no. Libraries, already doing that. Lingerie, hee hee. Massage, hey there's Jade's ad. Meditation, don't think so. Motorcycle, worthless suicide toys. Music, Music Instruction listed alphabetically according to the instructor's name. Guitar, guitar (different instructor), piano, flute, bagpipes—Bagpipes! Now that's interesting. I pick up the phone.

Forrest on Footwear and Cribbage

JADE GAVE ME a tent, but it was too hot to sleep in, and besides, I figured I'd better save it for the times when I really needed it. I slept in the open on the ground near some aspens and cottonwoods that grew near a spring. In the morning, I stared up at the beautiful branches of an old ponderosa pine and wanted to be held within them. I crawled out of my sleeping bag, took my jeans in my hand and wrapped a leg around each side of her trunk. With one leg in each hand, I took a couple steps up the trunk and shifted my jeans higher. I took a few more steps and shifted the jeans again. Before long, I was in the crook of her first large branch. I felt at home. That's how my idea for a tree house began.

The night the first phase of my tree house was done, a huge thunderstorm set in. I knew a tree was not a safe place to be in a storm like that, so I stayed. I stayed and hoped I would be struck dead. I wasn't.

The next day, I thought I would check on Lightning Bob.

I don't know how many hours it took me to walk to his tower. When I arrived, he walked out onto his deck and waved at me. His dog, Flash, ran down to greet me and herd me up the stairs.

"Good to see you! Good to see you!" Lightning Bob called out to me. I figured Lightning Bob probably thought it was good to see anyone.

I waved as I walked up the stairs.

"Cribbage?" Lightning Bob proposed.

I nodded. This time I made an earnest attempt to learn the game. Since I wouldn't talk, Lightning Bob had to read my cards or points for me after each hand.

"Fifteen-one, fifteen-two! You're catching up!"

I looked at his calendar. Seven tally marks from the night before for a grand total of five hundred forty-four. I held up seven fingers and gave him an astounded look. "Yes, seven," he said. "I wrote a poem about it." He didn't ask if I wanted to hear it. He simply dug out the notebook from under his cot, opened to the last page with ink on it and read "The Big Storm":

My hair stands up
My heart beats fast
When I see the flash
When I hear the crash

I scream, I jump
I dance around

When I hear that scary
Thundering sound.

When he was done, I slipped him the piece of paper I had in my pocket and bolted before he could read mine.

It is God's big chance
To strike me down
For the sins I have committed.
The bolts, like bullets
In Russian roulette,
Or from an executioner's gun
Miss me tonight
For reasons I don't understand.

Now, I come down out of the tree for thunderstorms.

I work leather with a bone awl and needle. I tanned the leather myself and made my own tools. I'm going to make Jade a pair of moccasins for her birthday this year. It doesn't feel too early to get started. She hardly ever wears shoes. I like that about her. Sometimes, though, you have to wear shoes, and if you have to wear shoes, at least wear ones where you can feel the earth (or grocery store floor) under your feet. I love her birthday. It's the one time of year I go into town and stay for a couple weeks. I have two tree houses there. My favorite one is right by the base of the chair lifts. Every year on or around Jade's birthday, there's always an outdoor concert going on out there. We have the best seat in the house. Last year, Los Lobos played, and the year before, Buddy Guy. I don't know who's playing this year.

I take a porcupine quill off my windowsill and bead it onto the top of the moccasin. I got these quills by throwing my coat on top of a porcupine and then just pulling the coat off him. Many people think porcupines shoot their quills, but they don't. The quills, like cacti, have barbs that get stuck in anything that touches them. I made this big score yesterday. I thanked the porcupine and offered it some cornmeal as payment, just like Grandma's friend, Hazel, would have. The porcupine waddled away from me, mumbling, leaving the cornmeal. Still, the cornmeal was a gesture, and I like to think intention counts.

Just like it was never my intention to kill anyone except a chicken house full of hens.

My moccasins are elk. I like to climb trees barefoot, but down there, these moccasins ease my mind with rattlesnakes and all. You have to really watch for babies in the spring because when a baby bites you, it releases all its venom, whereas an adult does not; adults budget theirs. Babies haven't developed rattles yet either, so they're easier to step on. So, I made these moccasins out of elk because elk hide is so much thicker than deer. It offers more protection.

Now, climbing the trees in the winter when the bark is frosty is a tricky proposition. For this, I go ahead and use old spikes. I ripped off the leather strap and the spiked boots from a logger's pickup down south of here quite a ways. I left him a pair of moccasins though. Technically, I think it's still stealing because he didn't agree to the bargain, but I like to think it helped karmically. Sure, on one hand, it could be argued I really didn't owe him anything. After all, he takes and never leaves any offering. Ultimately though, it's not my job to make judgments about his karma—only mine. Justifying wrong actions just gets a person in greater trouble. I wouldn't have done it at all, but I just can't afford an accident this far away from civilization.

I put Jade's moccasin project down and take a small pan off the shelf. I pour some instant rice out of one of the numerous glass jars I have stored food in ever since that unfortunate squirrel infestation. I pour water from another jar into the pan with the instant rice and put it on the little camping stove. I turn the knob, strike a match, and wait. I go outside and climb to a storage shack I built just a little higher than my house, where I store any meat I may have gotten my hands on. Today, grouse. Grouse and rice. Yum.

My house is a luxurious four by six structure built about fifty feet up in an old ponderosa pine. Over the years, I brought up a lot of newspaper to staple to the walls for insulation. Below zero temps in the Idaho Rockies are brutal. In addition, the newspaper doubles for interesting wallpaper I can read in my spare time.

I hear the screech of a hawk and peer out my window to watch a pair circle. Hawks mate for life, you know.

I don't suppose I'll ever mate for life. Well, that's what you get when you kill someone, even if you really didn't mean to. I could be in prison right now married to some guy named Rocko or something like that. Somehow this seems to have more integrity. If I were in prison, I'd have to get meaner just to survive, and I don't see how that serves society. I don't see how contributing to the dark energy out there helps anyone. Out here, I live in peace. I feed myself. I'm not a burden on taxpayers. I go to town now and then, and I go visit Lightning Bob occasionally, but I don't talk to him. Jade is the only one I let myself talk to. I don't know if that's cheating on my punishment or not, but I figure even inmates are allowed visitors.

My third tree house is in my parents' yard about five stories up in that ancient fir. I watch them sometimes, just to check up on them, but I never make contact. I never make contact with Olive either. We've never really been close. I don't know why. Maybe our age difference. Maybe just who we are. She's always been the good one, the one with perfect grades, the Junior Nationals ski race champion, the one who could do no wrong, definitely Dad's favorite. Unlike Olive, I never liked math much. I think I was a big disappointment to Dad. I'm pretty sure he hoped his only son would follow in his footsteps. I suppose I should have gotten over that by now, but I don't know—Olive is still perfect and I'm a bigger disappointment than anyone ever imagined. It's not Olive's fault. I know that.

I decide to go to town early this year. I don't know why. It just feels like it's time. I can swing by Lightning Bob's, play a little cribbage, and swap poems on the way.

Anna on Forrest

ON MY WAY from the back porch to the bathroom every morning, I stop and look at our family portrait, the one taken the Christmas before Forrest left us. I study his face and remember his letter to me. He told me he had done something really bad, but promised me he was okay. I look at his eyes and wonder what he could have done that was so bad, so bad he'd never contact us again. In the beginning, Phil and I speculated about many things, not trusting the perspective of a fourteen-year-old. Teenagers are dramatic. We figured surely he would come around and know that our relief would overshadow our condemnation. He never did though. Thirteen years.

Shortly after he disappeared, I remember receiving a letter from Mom telling me Willa Meyer had been killed, blown up in her chicken coop. I wondered. Phil assured me there was no way a fourteen-year-old boy could have gotten back to Summerville. I wanted to believe Phil. If Forrest *was* responsible for her death, I know he wouldn't have done it on purpose. Murder is the only thing I can think of bad enough to keep him away for thirteen years.

Not a day goes by where I don't wonder if he's all right, if he's still alive, and where he is. Not a day goes by where I don't want to take him in my arms and tell him everything will be all right.

He would be twenty-seven now. Twenty-seven. Not just a young man, but a man. I wonder what he looks like now that he's a man. I wonder what he looked like as he turned from a boy to a man. I wonder if I'd recognize him now. I look at those eyes in the photo. Yes, I'd recognize those eyes.

I collect my box of photos of Forrest that I keep under my bed and take them to Otto's Office Supply Store where I photocopy them.

At home, I cut maybe a hundred black and white pictures of people out of the stack of newspapers in our garage, then put Forrest's eyes everywhere. This is my life, looking for those eyes in crowds, looking for Forrest everywhere.

Jade on the Complications of Past Life Memory

ARETHA LOVES TO go for bike rides. I equipped my mountain bike with this little trailer she can hop on. Sometimes she prefers to run beside me, and that's okay if we're not in traffic. I glance back at her. She's smiling big. Aretha has the best smile.

I like to wear a metallic gold superhero cape with a dark green J on it when I mountain bike or do anything else involving speed for that matter. People here take themselves so seriously. I see it as my civic duty to help them lighten up.

We swing by the post office. I pick up my mail and ride down toward the lifts to my condo. I reflect on the benefits of my self-imposed nunnery. It's my last life. I can't have any dead weight. Technically I'm enlightened, so who, really, is going to be any kind of match for me? This is okay. I accept this. There's still so much to enjoy about planet Earth. Telemark skiing, for instance. I do have to give white people credit for telemark skiing. I love carving sweet tele turns.

I turn off before I reach the lifts into the parking lot for my condo complex. Aretha jumps off the trailer and runs over to a stunning man who walks out of the condo next to ours, the condo that has been for rent. His head is shaved and his skin is darker than Grace's. His arms are as wide as his head. I look at those juicy arms and think *He is my Mount Everest.* His eyes look familiar to me. Aretha seems to recognize him, too.

"Friendly?" he calls to me as Aretha closes in on him.

"Very!" I answer. "And so is my dog." Shit. I finally meet a hunky guy and I'm wearing a superhero cape.

"That's a nice cape." *Ohhh, and those are some nice lips.*

I model it for him, strutting three steps forward, putting my hand on my hip, pivoting, and strutting back. "Thanks, it makes me go faster."

"Really?" Clearly, he's a disbeliever.

"Really." Duh, people are always faster if they're happier.

Mount Everest walks toward a maroon Pathfinder, but stops to introduce himself. "I'm Josh," he says, but when I look in his eyes, I recognize him.

No you're not! I think. *You're Nisa! I remember you! Nisa!* "Nice to meet you, Josh. I'm Jade." *Nisa, you're a man! You're even a hunky man! Oh, my God, you really did mean what you said!*

"I'm your new neighbor," he states.

No you're not! You're my old best friend! "Oh, welcome." I try to sound casual.

"I just moved in yesterday."

"Nice." I look at his eyes for any sign that he remembers

me, even on a subconscious level. I think I see a glint. *Don't you remember me? Don't you remember me?* I want to shout jubilantly and hug him. I know better.

"Well, see you around," he says and gets into his Pathfinder.

"See you around," I reply, as if nothing huge just happened, as if I hadn't just been reunited with one of my favorite souls in the universe.

Wow, Nisa. How nice to see you again. I let myself inside my condo and remember the last time I saw her. I remember we were sitting under a tree on a hill overlooking thatched huts in our village below. We were wearing layers of beads around our necks and not much else.

"I'm getting married," she broke the news to me in Swahili, and began to cry. "My father picked him. He lives to the south."

"I'm so sorry," I replied, also in Swahili, and began to cry myself. I knew what this meant. She would be moving away. She was the closest thing I had to a sister in that life, and the severing I felt at her news was gut-wrenching. She rested her head on my shoulder and cried awhile, and I tried to comfort her, but really, there's no way to ease that kind of pain.

"I wish one of us was a man so we could marry each other and never be torn apart like this," she said earnestly.

This made me giggle through my tears. "Which one of us would have to be the man?" I asked.

Her offer was more than generous: "You can be the woman. You're prettier."

Well, Nisa, here you are to heal old wounds. I sure wish I could ask Josh how the rest of that life turned out, but I know he won't remember and will only think I'm more nuts than he already must, thanks to the superhero cape.

Phil on Lesson One

"GOOD TO MAKE your acquaintance, Phil," Al says to me in a heavy Southern accent. He looks like Colonel Sanders in a skirt and sips scotch. He points me to a seat in his bare living room. "I am sorry to hear that your marriage is in the toilet." What? How did he know? Before I can ask, he adds, "No one learns to play the pipes unless their marriage is already in the toilet, Phil. Okay now, hold this." He hands me a long singular pipe. "This here is a chanter. First you play the chanter. In a few months, we add the bag, but cork the drones and you practice blowing your arm off the bag. That, Phil, is called 'playing the goose.' Although you are clearly experiencing marital problems, do not confuse playing the goose with choking your chicken. True, pants are worn for neither, but other than that, they are entirely different. Now, when you find you are able to play the goose, keep your tone even, and march simultaneously. Yes, Phil, when you can do that and not pass out, you are ready to uncork one drone at a time. This is no overnight process, Phil. This requires patience,

Phil. You do not look like a patient man."

I'm at a loss. What do you say to that?

"At one time, I was not a patient man either, and then I discovered scotch. Okay now, place your fingers over the holes. You will play notes by removing one finger at a time. Try not to cover the holes with the pads of your fingers. Keep your fingers flat. Yeah, like that. Good. Now blow."

I blow. It squeaks. It's the worst noise I've ever heard. Still, I can hear potential and am encouraged. I keep trying. I'm finally able to hold a note. After a little time, it begins to sound pretty good!

"Now uncover this hole here. Blow." I blow again. Wow! I love this!

"Phil, it would appear as though you are a natural. Let us begin learning the fingering for 'Amazing Grace,' the greatest song ever written."

I have always dreamed of playing "Amazing Grace" on the bagpipes! This is great! I concentrate hard on keeping my fingers flat. I am determined to be the best student Al has ever had. He thinks it takes patience; I think it takes commitment and determination.

At the end of the lesson, I pay him sixty dollars for the chanter and book, plus thirty dollars for the lesson. That was ninety dollars well spent. Ninety dollars would buy a halfway decent putter had I chosen to pursue golf. No, ninety dollars wouldn't have even gotten me to the first green. Bagpipe lessons are a screaming good deal.

Olive on Choices

IF I COULD have taken any road instead of the one I took and ended up in a different place or position than I am now, I would have chosen something different—I'm just not sure what. I look around and wonder who I would swap lives with. Is anyone out there experiencing contentment? I look around the bank where I work and don't see any content-looking people here.

On the drive home, I look for contented people. No contended people today. No contented people yesterday. Maybe I'm just seeing the world through my own experience. Maybe I wouldn't recognize contentment in someone even if I was staring right at it.

I pull into my parking place, get out, and walk toward my apartment. The afternoon breezes blow distinctive smoke down to the courtyard. I look up to see Todd, Dave, and Chad pass a fattie on the deck above my door. I watch as they take turns inhaling deeply. They look temporarily content, but I don't think that's the answer for me.

As soon as I'm inside my apartment, I begin taking things down off my walls. Since I can't afford this place on my own, I gave my thirty days notice. I take down the painting of sunflowers I've always loved. It reminds me of being in South Dakota, stillness and warm wind. I take down the peach blossom painting Mom did when she was pregnant with me. I look in the kitchen. The only thing on the walls in the kitchen is my calendar. I look at my calendar and try to remember when my last period started. Let's see, it was St. Patrick's Day. Yes, that's right. I remember it distinctly now because my period always begins on major holidays, giving me cramps and wrecking all special occasions. When it missed Easter, I thought it was weird. That's one, two, three, (flip the page), four, five six, seven, (flip another page), eight, nine weeks ago. Five weeks late? Oh-oh. Let it just be stress. Let it just be stress.

I get back into my Honda sedan and drive to the drug store. I pick up a plastic shopping basket and toss in a package of Thank You cards first so I'll have something to cover up the EPT with. If I am pregnant, I'll need post-shower Thank You cards, and if I'm not, well a person can always use more Thank You cards. I walk down the girl aisle, pluck an EPT off the shelf without stopping and bury it under the cards. Why is it that I've never seen a handsome guy in this store, but the moment I have a pregnancy test in my basket, they're everywhere? I get in line. One of the handsome guys gets in line behind me. I pretend I forgot something and go off to look at toothbrushes while I wait for the coast to clear.

I get in line again. The checker is young; she's wearing a gold cross around her neck. I wonder if she practices abstinence. Power to her if she does. I look at my left hand—no ring. I take my little cardigan sweater off and hold it in my left hand to hide my ring finger. I thought I was too old and too educated to ever be in this situation. I thought I was mature, confident, and capable enough not to feel self-conscious about this. I'm not, though. I feel totally exposed, totally vulnerable. Everywhere I look, I see judgment. I'm sure it's simply my own judgment mirrored back to me, but it makes my heart race just the same. The checker remains expressionless and slips my merchandise into a white plastic bag. The bag isn't completely opaque, and I can see the letters EPT right through it. I'm quite sure everyone else in the whole world has nothing better to do than to try and see through my bag and figure out its contents.

I put my purchases in my car and walk next door to the grocery store for a bottle of water so I can prepare to pee. I see babies everywhere. How is it I never noticed all these babies before? I study the mothers. Do they look happy? Yes . . . a little tired, but pretty happy. All but one wear rings and look economically comfortable. In fact, they look content. They are the content people I've been looking for. What is contentment anyway? It has to be more than just economic comfort. The one mother without the ring looks hardened. In her eyes, I can tell she too sees judgment everywhere. She even sees it from me, which is ridiculous given my circumstances.

"What a beautiful baby," I tell her.

She looks down at the baby with a reluctant and heart-broken smile, then up at me for a quick second. "Thanks," she says and quickly rolls her cart away.

My heart aches as I realize I may be looking at my future.

Forrest on the Forest as a Tree Farm

"NICE TO SEE you! Nice to see you!" Lightning Bob calls to me. Flash runs down and herds me up the stairs as usual. When I reach the top, Lightning Bob pats me on the back and guides me into the tower with a fatherly hand on my shoulder.

I sit at my usual place and study the calendar. It's been an unusually dry May. No storms. No lightning.

"Going to be a bad year for fires," he says when he sees me studying the calendar. "Only May and already everything is as dry as bone." He pauses and looks out toward the south. "Back before fire suppression, there used to be about twenty trees per acre out here. Fire would rip through and thin the weak ones out pretty regularly. Those fires didn't burn hot, so the strong trees survived just fine. Now there's two hundred trees per acre out here. That's a lot of fuel, my friend. That's an uncontrollable inferno waiting to happen. We see firestorms now like we've never seen before—fire moving at fifty miles per hour—sometimes faster." He puts the kettle on and strikes a match as he turns on the propane, then opens a window. "I look out there and feel this love for this land; it's been my home for so many years. I'm the fourth generation in this tower. I know it's only a matter of time though. Each year that it doesn't burn, the stakes get higher. It's only a matter of time."

The look on my face must have revealed my feelings of horror about the fire. The idea of these hills burning turns my stomach.

Lightning Bob studies me carefully. "Tough one, isn't it? Fire is natural, but fires of the magnitude they become now aren't. Some burn so hot, they sterilize the soil."

I show Lightning Bob my cards. "Fifteen-one, fifteen-two," he counts aloud for me. He pauses for a moment and adds, "Someone once said to me, 'Water cleanses, but only fire purifies.' I'm not sure I have much need for purification. I feel pure enough already."

I look out the window and see the sheep coming. I say a prayer that the wolves will stay away from them and that the shepherds will stay away from the wolves.

"Fifteen-one, and a pair is two," Lightning Bob counts.

In my pocket, I play with a folded-up poem which I brought to share with Lightning Bob. When he gets up to go to the outhouse, I take it out and reread it:

Your branches, like arms
Hold me like the mother you are to me now

Free of the judgment
And knowledge of my unworthiness
In the wind you rock me
And sing me lullabies with your leaves
Because you are not human
You do not push me away
And I do not resist you
Because you are a tree
You can connect me to
All the life that surrounds us.

I decide not to share this one and go on my way.

Olive on Blue

OH MY GOD. It's blue. It turned blue. I put the stick down on top of the toilet and walk into the living room. Maybe when I walk back in later, it will have changed back to pink. I water my plants and put them all in a box. I turn on the TV. I turn it off. I turn it on again and flip through the channels without pausing long enough on any station to really judge any program as worthwhile or not. I walk into the kitchen, open the refrigerator, then shut it. I walk back into the bathroom and stare at the stick. It's still blue. I shake my head and then let it drop like my dad does when he's disappointed, disgusted, or in a state of disbelief about something stupid I've done. I feel all three. I raise my head and look at myself in the mirror. Instead of seeing my own eyes, I see my father's, so deeply disappointed in me. Oh, oh! Pow! The nausea hits me just like that and I spew a small amount of watery puke in the sink. I stand a little longer, struggling with the dry heaves, then lean back against the bathroom wall and slide down, out of sight of my own reflection, out of view of my father's judging eyes, down until I find relief by lying on the bathroom floor. My eyes fill with tears, and in doing so, they feel like *my* eyes again. Lord knows, I never saw Dad cry. I start to shiver, so I reach up and pull a bath towel off the rack to cover myself. How am I ever going to get through this alone?

Anna on Phil's Problem-solving Strategies

TODAY PHIL ASKED me if I wanted to go on a cruise. Inspired, I take a pencil and outline a few things in what will be the background to this raisin painting. Behind the raisin is a beach, filled with young beautiful girls in bikinis. Should I paint a bathing suit on the raisin? Maybe one of those with the little skirt attached? I have observed enough women older than I am to know that I will reach a place where I won't care, where I'll accept this new era of my life and wear a bathing suit to the beach without being critical of myself. There comes a time where you are simply happy for good health, and not worried about packaging so much. But I'm not there yet. Call it vanity if you want, but it's deeper than that. It's grief for a woman I'll never be again.

It's easier to be considered good-looking if you are an older man than if you are an older woman. This is compounded by the fact that women are valued for their appearance, whereas men are valued for their intellect, strength, or income. It's sad, but undeniable. You know, men don't get dimples all over their legs. Look at an old man's legs. Can you really tell he's old just by his legs? Not really. Okay, there is the hair loss thing, but frankly, I don't think hair loss makes a man any less sexy. Now, trying to cover up hair loss with a bad comb-over makes a man less sexy, but hair loss by itself does not. It's masculine, in fact. Now, how many men out there are thinking the same things about women's dimply legs—that they don't make a woman any less sexy—on the contrary, because they are feminine? Not many.

The other factor I struggle with at this time in my life is that Phil is retired. He had a clear job description, and now he has a clear retirement. I never had a clear job description, and now it's obvious I'll never have a clear retirement. Phil will never hand me a plaque thanking me for decades of good service and wishing me a great rest of my life. I have a life sentence where I will never come first.

The phone rings. I answer, "Hello?"

"Mom?" It's Olive. "Can I come over and talk to you about something?"

Crap. I know that tone of voice and it fills me with dread. I want to run to my car and drive far, far away. Any place will do. "Sure," I say instead. "Now?"

"If that's okay," Olive answers.

"Sure."

I hang up the phone and grab another canvas. I sketch out another raisin, this time sitting at a family dinner.

Within fifteen minutes, Olive lets herself in and finds me

in the kitchen, where I steep a pot of jasmine tea.

"Hi," she says, and hugs me.

"Hi." I hug her back. "Nice to see you. What's on your mind?" Better to just get it over with than wait any longer for the bad news.

"Matt moved out ten days ago," Olive announces. She's always stoic when she's really upset about something.

"Oh?"

"We had a big fight about how to go from being renters to being owners."

"You know, it sounds like your father would be a good person to talk to about this. I'm sure he could help you both come up with a plan."

"Hey, maybe you're right. I don't know why I never think of talking to Dad."

"He really needs something to do these days. You'd be doing him a favor," I tell her, happy that my plan to deflect someone else's problem is working. "He's in his office," I add, driving my suggestion home. She starts to go, but turns back and looks at me for a long minute. Her mouth opens like she is about to say something, but she changes her mind and shuts it. "What?" I ask her.

"Nothing," she replies. Her eyes gloss over as she goes to that place in herself where I've never been able to reach her.

After an hour, Phil and Olive emerge from the office and enter the kitchen with Phil's twenty-four by thirty-six inch tablet. I cringe. I hate that tablet. The tablet generally means one thing and one thing only: graphs. He never makes his case without graphs.

"Hey, Anna," he says, "As you may know, Olive has been struggling with how to become a homeowner instead of continually throwing her money away on rent. Now that Matt's left her apartment, she'd be lucky to break even every month and doesn't stand a chance of accumulating a down payment."

I look at him with dread. I suspect that he has become so focused on the bottom line, once again, that he has failed to truly examine the consequences of whatever decision he's about to promote.

He flips his tablet open to show a bar graph in alternating blue and red bars. "Here we have Olive's income in blue, compared to her expenses in red. You can see that there wasn't much of a buffer before, but this month, without Matt's financial contribution to their household, her expenses exceeded her income. You can see she's headed toward a financial crisis. Now look at this one." He turns the page. "Here we have her income, minus some minimal expenses, in savings over the next six months. You can see that if she finds a home loan where five percent is required down, she could afford to get into a nice home in five to six months and have some money left over for unexpected expenses associated with purchasing a new home."

Olive looks down at the floor, distracted, as if she's still trying to think of other solutions.

Phil flips the page. "Now we all know, there is no such thing as a free lunch, so here is a list of jobs Olive is willing to commit to in payment for renting her old room."

His choice in words rubs me the wrong way.

Olive nods and glances up distantly. I see my solitude slipping even more, but still, there's nothing I wouldn't do for my children, nothing I wouldn't give them if they needed it. I just wish that Olive didn't need it. Maybe I'm looking at it the wrong way. At least I still have Olive, which is more than I can say about my youngest.

"Olive, home is your soft place to fall. I don't like the idea of you 'renting' your old room back. That's not what home is to me. I prefer the idea of everyone contributing to the household."

Olive gives me a little smile. In it, I see gratitude, but I can tell she's still upset. "Good job on the graphs, Dad," she says. Phil beams. He doesn't seem to notice she's still upset. I wonder if referring Olive to Phil was really the right thing to do.

"Okay, I need to go pack." Olive's attempt to smile and sound excited about the plan doesn't fool me.

"It's going to work out, Olive," Phil says as he walks her to the door. Olive bites her lip and slips out the door.

Phil on Communication

"PHIL, MAYBE YOU didn't notice, but Olive was still upset when she left. Why didn't you just give her the money for the down payment? At this point in my life, I would like to not worry about everyone else. If Olive is here, I'm going to stew over her problems. That's what mothers do. It's like there's always this psychic umbilical cord that connects mothers to children. We're not happy if they're not happy. If she's not right in front of me, I can forget about her frustrations sometimes, but having her here will mean having her frustrations in my face all the time. Do you know how exhausting that will be for me? Lately, I feel the need for a lot of solitude to figure out this new era of my life," Anna tries to explain.

"A) Cut that umbilical cord. The kids are grown-ups. Just because one resumes living here doesn't mean you have to resume being a mother. B) What are you talking about—this new era of your life? Your life is a continuum." I have just shown her the illusionary nature to her problems.

"A)," she mocks me, "My motherhood is a continuum. I

wish it weren't. I wish it was something I could retire from. You wouldn't know anything about this kind of parenthood because you spent about a total of twenty minutes with the kids the entire time they were growing up." She is too angry to regret this comment yet. "B) You also don't know anything about menopause, or womanhood in general, so don't presume you do. Don't patronize me with your male approach to life. It doesn't work for me."

I stare at her angry face and listen to the clock tick fifteen times. Fifteen seconds seem like fifteen hours. I'm shocked by her insults directed at my well-intended attempts at problem solving. She stares right back, cold. What did I do to deserve this kind of hatred? Will someone please tell me? It's got to be some misunderstanding that can surely be cleared up. I try to explain myself, "I wasn't patronizing you. I was just trying to show you the illusionary nature of your problems." Her eyes widen with disbelief and fury.

"Oh? Menopause is an illusion? I'm just dreaming this up? Go to hell, Phil."

She storms out the kitchen doorway, and in a couple seconds, the front door slams. What just happened? I cannot come up with an action plan until I truly understand what the problem is, and I *clearly* do not truly understand what the problem is. I do not know that my marriage would survive another mitigation of the problem. Maybe it would be better just to not say anything for a while so that I can evaluate without making things worse. Maybe it's just a phase that will pass on its own.

I take out my pocket calendar where I've been charting her menopausal symptoms. On today's date, I write "anger" and "unreasonableness." Yes, if I can only find the pattern, maybe I can predict the best times to talk to her. Yes, when I can organize her physiological chaos, I'll be able to cope with her much better. I study the calendar and examine the last three months. No pattern yet. Not encouraging.

Anna on Cottonwoods

SINCE I DON'T want to talk to Phil, I walk to the river with a bottle of Chardonnay and a glass. There, I find a place to sit, pour my wine and breathe. I am in the natural world now. In the natural world, everything gets old, and if you study it, you find beauty in it. Here, among the ancient cottonwood trees that line the river, I find some peace. The tree feels motherly to me, sheltering me from the sun and providing me with a strong trunk to lean against. The humus of last year's dead leaves creates a soft place for me to sit, like a grandmother's lap. I lean back against the cottonwood grandmother, and wish this culture had elders who would explain to me this new era of my life. I feel clueless in the chaos of it.

I study the trees of all ages from the painter's point of view. The young ones have little shape or form. They are not complex or particularly interesting. I would not choose to paint them. That one—that one over there is the one I would choose to paint. It has exquisite form. It's gnarled, with swollen, knobby joints in its branches. With leaves or without, it would be a captivating subject. Is it only painters, black and white photographers, and wine tasters who can appreciate the beautiful complexity of aged beings?

I start my second glass of wine and wait for it to take some effect.

Pearl on Life

MY BACK AND forearms ache from putting in all those strawberries, but I don't have time to indulge in the pain. I walk to my modest orchard to check on things. My honeybees are active; it appears they're pollinating clover today. I talk to them, asking them how they're doing and thanking them for all their hard work and all the ways they make my farm a nicer place. They are busy little OB-GYNs doing in-vitro fertilization everywhere.

I push my little mower through the first couple rows of trees, having figured out that if I mow two rows of the orchard every day, the grass never gets long enough to be difficult to mow, and by breaking up the task, it's never a large job.

I survey my trees for pests, but find none. I do find birds, and thank them for eating the bugs in my orchard. I carefully examine a few more trees, and when I see the trees have begun to set fruit, I feel the same anticipation I used to feel as a child.

On the walk back to the house, I hear a rattle. I take out

my Ruger and stop in my tracks. I can't see the snake through the grass, but I listen carefully, then aim and fire at what I hope is the source of the sound. The rattling stops. I wish I had a rifle so I could use the barrel for a stick. I slowly take a few steps forward and that's when I see it. I blow its head off just to be sure it's dead. Then I pick it up and carry it back home. What a beauty. At home, I skin it, stretch the skin out on the side of the barn and tack it up to dry. I figure if I present Wallace, the cobbler, with a lot of snake skins, maybe he'll trade me for some red cowboy boots.

Up on the hill, I see Dean burning a chunk of old carpet in his burn barrel. Amazingly, the breeze is blowing it west. I could have sworn he only burned on days when the wind blew the smell of burning plastic right into my house.

Beatrice walks by when I'm almost done. "God, Pearl, do you have to shoot everything? What did this one ever do to you?"

"We can eat it," I suggest.

"No. No more snake. My life is too short to eat any more snake. My meals are numbered and I'm not wasting any of them on snake. No more taking snake casseroles to church potlucks either. I think that's poor taste."

"Be a shame to waste it."

"Well, then, stop killing them."

"Okay," I say in an attempt to save our friendship, but what I really mean is that I'll skin them and tan them somewhere else.

"Don't you think this gun fetish of yours is kind of

Freudian?" Beatrice suggests.

"That was a low blow, Beatrice."

"If the shoe fits . . ." she replies as she turns and swishes off. I want to be mad, but I'm struck by her beauty and it softens me.

Forrest on the Walk Home

I MAKE MY way east up and down ridges and draws I have named. I climb "First Hill," then walk across "The Ridge with the Warm Wind." I continue up "The Hill Where I Fall" (I usually slip on the return trip down), and wind through "The Place Where the Spirits Live." I think I see them from time to time out of the corner of my eye, never directly, and always in this eighth of a mile stretch. I'm not sure what they are. When I spy them, I feel neither welcome nor unwelcome. Mostly I just feel them watching. After that, I climb up "The Wall," the steep hill where I usually begin to feel tired, until I reach "The Place With the Tree Where I Rest." Usually, I rest there on hot days, enjoying some shade offered by the ancient ponderosa, but not today. Today I start right up "The Hill that Never Ends."

I decide to walk into the night to finish the journey early. The moon is full, the wind is down, the rattlers are asleep in the ground, and the temperatures are bearable. My mind is full of clutter, and walking often clears it.

Part of the reason I chose to check out of society is because it lacks humanity. How exactly am I contributing to the solution? Given, just not being part of the problem is a huge accomplishment. Somehow, though, I'm left with the sense that I'm wasting my life. I don't know what to do about it, though; I've burned so many bridges.

These thoughts overwhelm me, so I do my best to replace them with disjointed lines of poetry, building blocks for a new poem to be written later.

From the top of "The Hill that Never Ends," I see a campfire below. I don't recall ever seeing a camp there before. I walk down a ridge in the general direction of the camp and find a somewhat clean-cut guy sitting on a log just staring at the fire. I'm worried about his fire, so although I normally don't talk to anyone but Jade, I decide to make another exception.

"Hey," I say, a little startled to hear my own voice after so many months. I wasn't half as startled as this guy, though. He jumped, and then tried to pretend he hadn't. "Got a water bucket?" I ask. With a puzzled expression, he shakes his head. "It's dry. Your fire may have already ignited roots in the ground. The fire travels along these roots and springs up all over the place. Root fires are almost impossible to fight. Do you have a shovel?" He shakes his head. His eyes are fearful. I take a minute and consider how I look. I reach up and touch a long lock of dreaded hair. Yeah, I bet I'm quite a sight. "From now on, use a camp stove so you don't burn down my home and the home of everything else that lives out here." He nods timidly.

I take a moment and survey his camp. A little truck is parked below on the other side of a stream that is nothing but mud now. He dug his pit toilet in the flood plain. Gross. He's been chopping at a large log, not even sawing first. What a moron, chopping at a big log instead of just collecting the right sized pieces. He has five gallons of store-bought water in a wheelbarrow that's stuck in the mud stream. A little tent sits right next to the mud stream where all the mosquitoes hatch out. He hasn't put his food up in a tree. It's clear he has been eating food too close to his tent. Even though he really should be selected out, I don't wish a bear attack on anyone, so I say, "Never eat by your tent. Never have food anywhere close to your tent. Get a rope, and hang all your food from a branch at night. Toothpaste, too. If you keep eating near your tent, you're going to wake up one night with a bear on top of you." His eyes widen with alarm.

"Are you living here?" I ask.

He nods. "I'm saving for a house. I'm Matt," he says and holds out his hand. I ignore it and choose not to introduce myself.

"Do you go to town every day?"

He nods again. "I have a job."

"Where do you shower?" I ask. I'm always looking for good shower spots so I can be presentable before I see Jade. My last annual shower coated Jade's tub with a film Comet couldn't remove.

"I just run through the sprinklers of that alfalfa field

down the road. Feels extra good after waking up in a hot tent. Once the sun hits it, whew, it's a sauna."

If he was smart, he'd ditch the tent and sleep up on that hill over there. Good breezes up there. The breezes would help keep the mosquitoes away. Slap, slap, slap. He keeps slapping at mosquitoes. I can smell him from here. I don't know if it's deodorant or cologne or what, but it burns my nose, and I have no doubt that it's attracting the mosquitoes.

I start to walk away. "Where do you live?" he calls after me. It's none of his business, so I just keep walking.

Olive on Packing

MICHELLE POURS HERSELF a cup of coffee in the employee lounge. "How was your weekend?" I ask as I pass by, find my coffee cup, remember I shouldn't drink coffee, and put my cup back. Michelle always has a funny story, and I could use one.

"Oh, you know, it was a Twin Falls weekend." Yes, I know. She's explained it to me before. Twice a month now, she has to drive her baby down to Twin Falls, give her baby to a neutral party, who then gives him to her baby's father for a few hours. Why the third party? Because she has a restraining order against him. After they broke up, he showed up at her house one night and tried to break in. I'd be damned if I'd hand my baby over to him. I'd leave the country first.

Somehow, Michelle's story isn't that funny this time. I try to distract myself with work, but the entire day, my mind keeps drifting back to Michelle and the position she's in now with her baby and the baby's father. By the end of the day, I have a splitting headache.

On my way out of the bank, I survey all the pictures of kids on people's desks again. Probably thirty kids in all—all those kids in daycare . . . all those kids being raised by someone else. What would it feel like to miss my child's first steps? The questions keep ricocheting through my mind, intensifying my headache.

I walk through the revolving doors, glance back, and wonder what I'm dedicating my life to. This is my only life. I'm about to be a mother. Is this really how I want to spend it?

On the drive home, I look at Cottonwood carefully. Where exactly do I fit in here? Not in the boutiques. Not in the five-star restaurants. Not in the numerous art galleries. Not at Edward Jones. I park my car and walk to my apartment. Jane and Shamiel, the neighbor kids who live on the other side of the couple that shouts obscenities at each other, run toward me and start barking at me. I bark back. They stop barking and start panting with their tongues out. Jane licks my arm.

"Ew! Dog germs!" I shriek, and this makes Jane laugh.

"I'm wearing a pink shirt and pink pants," Jane tells me.

Shamiel picks up where Jane left off. "Hey, guess what? Tomorrow I'm going to wear a black shirt and black pants! Hey, guess what? You should wear a green shirt and green pants tomorrow!"

"I'll work on that," I tell them.

Their little brother, Malcom, comes running out of his door toward us. He's wearing a blue shirt and no pants.

"Hey Malcom, how's the potty-training going?" I ask.

Malcom stops and looks at me thoughtfully. "I think there are little workers in my bottom . . . and when they look down and see the water, they pull a lever and let it all go."

Shamiel looks at Malcom like he's full of it, and Jane rolls her eyes.

"Wow, Malcom, how do you feel about that?"

"I feel . . . okay."

"Good news," I say.

Their mother comes running out of the house screaming for Malcom.

"Uh-oh," he says.

"Looks like you scared your mom," I tell him.

They all run to her. She looks so tired.

I'm seeing mirrors everywhere and I know it. I'm just getting it that Matt isn't coming back. Even if he did, I couldn't be sure that if I told him, he would abandon the tipi idea—I couldn't be sure that he wouldn't make things worse.

I let myself into my apartment and go to the half-empty bottle of Shiraz. I want to drink it, but I throw it out. I look around the kitchen, thinking about what to have instead. Garlic. I crave garlic. I love it. In fact, now that I'm single, I'm going to eat garlic every night. That's right, I'm going to wear cotton underwear and smell like garlic. I think garlic was rumored to keep evil away because really it kept potential mates away, and really, aren't all potential mates pretty much evil? Yep, they just devastate your life.

I order a garlic pizza and start packing what's left.

I pack my kitchenware. I feel sad, putting the hand-blown

Mexican glasses in boxes for hibernation, the hand-painted Italian pasta bowls, my wine glasses with the colorful stems.

I am not a failure, I repeat over and over. I say it, but really, I can't believe how badly I've messed up my life.

I pack my silverware, pans, muffin tins, glass casserole dishes and bread pan. I pick at the packing tape, unroll some, cut it, and seal the box. With a giant black permanent marker, I label the box, "pans and silverware." I pack my fancy cookie sheets and my beloved pizza stone in the next box. I study the odds and ends in the kitchen. The terra cotta garlic cooker (which I will be using much more often now), the ceramic teapot, and the stainless steel teapot also fit into the box.

I'm doing this for my child, I remind myself.

I am going to be one more woman with a picture of her child on her desk at the bank. To what end? How, exactly, is my plan so great for my child? What is the point in having a child if I just have to turn around and farm the baby out? Are these really my only two choices? Make my child live in poverty, or hardly see my baby at all?

I sit on a box of books and wonder if my thinking is too limited. Do I have choices I just don't know about? What would my life look like if it could be anything I wanted? That's the million-dollar question.

Matt knocks and lets himself in, finding me there sitting on the box, looking tired, a handkerchief keeping my hair out of my face. I look up at him with great disdain.

"You're moving?"

"Why does that surprise you?"

He doesn't answer my question. "Where are you going?"

"I'm sure not going to a tipi." We stare each other down for a moment. As strongly as I dislike him now, for the sake of my baby, I need a moment of truth. I say a silent prayer: *Please God, if Matt is capable and willing to be a father to this baby, please give me a sign so I don't needlessly rob my child of a father. If he shows me he's willing and capable, I'll make every effort to let go of my anger, open my heart and create a new beginning.* And now, to ask for the truth, but not leave my interests unprotected, I pose these questions to him, "Matt, what if we were living in the tipi and I got unexpectedly pregnant? Would you really expect me to raise children out there? Would you really think that was adequate shelter for a baby?"

"If you got 'unexpectedly pregnant,' I don't think the issue would be whether or not a tipi is adequate shelter for a baby."

"What's that supposed to mean?"

"The question would be: just how 'unexpected' was it? I mean, come on—if you don't want to get pregnant, then you *don't.* If we're living in our tipi and you're telling me all the time that you don't want to get pregnant, and then all of a sudden it just 'happens,' I'd have to wonder just how accidental it was."

"Are you saying I'd get pregnant on purpose!?" I feel like I'm going to throw up.

"I'm saying I'd have to wonder. People do it all the time—you know, find ways to manipulate their partner, force them into things when it's not what they want. I wouldn't fall for it, that's all I'm saying. I know you better than that. If you didn't want to get pregnant, you wouldn't."

"Are you serious?!? So if I did, it would be all my fault? I'd be trying to manipulate you!? You really believe that?"

"I already told you what I think, but fine, let's just say if we're living in a tipi and you 'accidentally' get pregnant, I don't know how that would really be *my* problem—adequate shelter and all those things. I'm pretty sure I'd be thinking more about why I'm living with someone I can't trust and seriously wondering if that's the type of person I really want to spend the rest of my life with."

Wow. Signs don't get much clearer than that. I swallow hard and thank God for a clear answer.

"So, where are you going anyway?" he asks again.

I look at him and shake my head, defeated. "Why do you care?" I didn't realize how much I hoped his answer would have been different. I feel like a punctured tire with all the energy draining out. "Look, Matt, I can't afford this place without you. Your decision has turned my life upside-down. Forgive me if I feel no need to tell you where I'm going."

"Oh, I see, you're punishing me."

"Of course you'd think that. Here's a news flash, Matt: I need to take care of myself now. I just want to get on with my life and know that you're not going to show up at my door unannounced after I've moved on."

"Right. You don't want me showing up when you're with a new boyfriend."

"Exactly," I respond, just to needle him. "Hey, you're the

one who left, not me. Did you think I was just going to wait around for you?" I get up and begin to pack plates, bowls, and coffee mugs. "Why did you come here anyway?"

Matt can't seem to remember. He stares at the floor.

"There's a box of your stuff over by the door." There's nothing else to say.

He picks up the box and leaves without saying another word.

Jade on Olive's Reality of Single Motherhood

"HEY, I'M READY. Are you?" I ask Olive. She opens the door to reveal a stack of neatly labeled cardboard boxes.

"I've packed everything except what I absolutely need in the next three days. I know it would be easier if I just moved into Mom and Dad's today, but I'm just not ready." Olive looks pale. Her eyes are sad.

"Are you all right?"

She looks at me long, takes a deep breath and says, "I'm pregnant."

"Oh." It's an important time for me to keep my mouth shut. "Do you have a plan?" That's neutral. I sit on a cardboard box labeled "Financial Records and Photo Albums."

"All I know right now is I'm not ready to tell anyone."

"Not even Matt? I mean, he's the father, right?" She won't look at me, just keeps focusing on the pile of boxes.

"I wouldn't call him 'the father.' He doesn't want anything to do with this."

"You told him?"

"Not exactly." She sits down on the box next to me, staring straight ahead. There's a heaviness in the air between us and I wish Grace was here to help me. "I asked him a hypothetical question about what would happen if I accidentally got pregnant."

"And?"

Olive puts her head in her hands and starts crying. I swallow hard.

"It's gonna be okay . . ." I whisper.

"No it's not, Jade." She gulps for air. "He honestly believes that if I got pregnant, I'd have done it on purpose as a way to manipulate him . . ."

"Oh, Jesus . . ." I wasn't prepared for that.

"He'd *'seriously have to wonder if he'd want to spend the rest of his life with someone who would do this to him.'* That's what he said. I mean, we're talking about a baby here and all he gives a shit about is himself!" She places her hand on the lower part of her belly. "I'm on my own, Jade."

I shake my head. "Man, Matt's really blown it."

"I can't believe I spent more than five minutes with him. You know, when I first fell in love with Matt, I really believed that he was in his guy chrysalis and that he'd emerge a man." She shakes her head. "Wrong. He's chosen to stay a guy. In fact, you could say he's adamantly chosen to remain in guydom."

"Well, I guess if this is who he truly is, it was nice of him to tell you now. You were smart to believe him."

"If I was smart, I would have made these discriminations before I ever slept with him. Maybe if all women refused to sleep with guys and only slept with men, maybe more guys would become men." She shrugs. "I gambled on Matt. I thought for sure he was in the final stage of becoming a man. I gambled and lost, and ultimately it's this baby who's going to pay for my error in judgment. All I can do is try to minimize that cost by not subjecting her to willful abandonment. It's always the children that pay. In retrospect, no sex is worth the debt I just imposed on this baby. I really screwed up. I'd give anything to be able to go back and do things differently."

"He flat out told you he'd want out?" I felt the need to clarify. "What were his exact words?"

"I asked him if I got accidentally pregnant if he would still expect me to live in a tipi, and whether he thought a tipi was adequate shelter for a baby. That's when he said the tipi issue was irrelevant and what was or wasn't adequate for the baby wouldn't really be *his problem*. The real issue for him would be whether he'd want to spend the rest of his life with someone he obviously couldn't trust."

"Olive, remember how when we were little, how obsessed we were with what we'd do if we ever saw a rattlesnake? And I showed you how I'd walk slowly away from it? Well, the first time I saw a rattler, pow! I was out of there! I didn't think at all. I just jumped. I didn't know I was capable of jumping so far. I just wonder . . . maybe it's just wishful thinking . . . but I just wonder if for Matt this might be one of those cases where you think you'd do one thing when it's just hypothetical, but when it's real, something else takes over and you discover strength you didn't know you had."

"What happens if I tell him and he decides to claim his custody rights? I'm then supposed to leave this baby in the hands—even for a minute—of a guy who thinks adequate shelter's not an issue?!?"

"If you tell him and I'm right, maybe you two can work things out where you raise this child together. That would be best for the child." Shit. Wrong thing to say.

I wait for her to explode, but she doesn't. "It's a long shot, Jade. I can't afford to gamble and lose. By telling him, I'd be handing this baby over to a really messed up legal system."

As I take in everything she's saying, I see Grace appear. *Finally.* Grace is smiling and nodding her head as she says, "Oh yeah, she's gettin' her mama bear mojo workin'!"

Olive's eyes are red and tired; this conversation has worn her out. "Trust me, Jade, no one wants a storybook ending more than me. It's just not going to happen."

I nod as I stand up and choose which box to carry out.

"Look at the bright side," she says. "At least I won't end up like Mom, sleeping on a lawn chair when I'm in my fifties in order to get away from a loveless marriage."

I pick up the box and carry it to my truck. She picks up another and follows me out.

"Did you pick a light one?" I ask. "Let me get the heavy ones."

"Blankets and towels," she replies.

"Good."

Jade on Checking In

AFTER TALKING WITH Olive, I figure it would be good to head over and check in on Mom. Aretha runs to the backyard while I search the house. I don't find her upstairs or downstairs, so I slip out the front door and walk around the house. I find her sitting on a bench under a blossoming cherry tree. Aretha sits upright on the bench beside her. Both Mom and Aretha watch as I approach and sit on the other side of Aretha.

"Are you doing okay, Mom?"

"Oh, you know, lots of changes."

"What's with sleeping outside?"

"Just feels good to be outside is all."

I realize Mom doesn't want to tell me anything. "Everything is temporary, Mom." I try to be reassuring.

"Everything is temporary," she repeats like a sigh.

I get up and kiss her forehead. "I love you, Mom."

"I love you, too."

I drive home and then skate through Cottonwood with

Aretha, repeating my daily affirmation, "I am asexual. I reproduce by budding. I am asexual. I reproduce by budding." I visualize strawberry plants that send out runners with new little strawberry plants on them to take root. I turn off the trail before reaching the lifts, into the parking lot for my condo complex.

When I see Nisa-Josh carrying his laundry to the laundry room, I no longer visualize strawberry plant runners. No, in my mind's eye, I see strawberry blossoms, and a very handsome bee. Aretha runs over to greet him. He puts down his basket and pets her with those delicious arms. Then he looks up at me. I can feel my face begin to burn.

"How's the superhero business today?" he asks.

"What? You think it's easy getting these Type A stockbrokers to lighten up? It's a *full-time job!*"

"Watch it," he says with mock warning. "I manage mutual funds."

"My sympathies. If it gets to be a little much, let me know and I'll make you your own superhero cape."

"That's really nice of you," he replies. God, he has a sexy voice.

"I'm a nice person," I tell him and continue on toward my home before I begin drooling.

He smiles. After I pass him, I turn back to watch him go. Okay, I turned back to check out his ass. And let me tell you, that was rewarding. Unfortunately, he caught me looking.

I unlock my door, skate through the threshold, close the door, take a deep breath, and begin to pant like a dog. I can't get the smile off my face. "Nisa is so hunky in this lifetime," I tell Aretha.

As I skate toward the answering machine, Grace appears. "Oh, yeah, girl, you're going to have good times with that one," she says. "Now, who are we working on this week?" I just smile and hit the play button.

"Hello, Jade? It's Garth." Alien Guy. "I'm in town for two weeks. I would like a massage every night at seven-thirty, except Friday. I have plans on Friday."

I nod, smile, and roll my eyes, but Grace looks suspicious and shakes her head. "I don't like that one," she says.

"Oh, he's harmless," I reply.

"Who's the guardian here?" Grace asks me. "You think I don't know some things you don't?" She keeps shaking her head as the next message begins.

"Um, hello. This is Peter Lemonjello, and I would like a four-hour butt massage." Brother Forrest. What a freak. I laugh. "Why don't you bring me breakfast tomorrow?"

"Been awhile since I got a call from Peter Lemonjello," I comment to Grace.

"He's ready for a new direction," she informs me.

"Jade. Thomas here." Rodeo Guy. "Got any time? Give me a call."

"He had a rough ride this weekend," Grace tells me.

"Um, hello. My trainer at the athletic club says you're good. I'd like a massage every Tuesday and Thursday following my workout, say three o'clock, from this Thursday until the end of the month. My name is Fannie," and Fannie leaves her phone number.

"Hey Jade." I recognize that voice. Barry White Guy. "If you've got time, the wife and I would like some of your brilliant work."

"It's nice to have fans," I tell Grace.

"He's in more pain than he's telling you," is all Grace says about that.

"Do you have any time today? It's Martin." Martin— whatever he wants, he wants *now*.

Grace disappears and I begin to return my long list of calls.

While I'm on the phone, Aretha brings me toy after toy, hoping one will be more interesting to me than talking on the phone. I look at her lovingly, and pat her head as I receive each gift.

Pearl on her Husband

HENRY JUST DIDN'T come home one night. I knew. I knew when he didn't come in by nine that something was wrong. I was smart enough to know that. I watched the clock with dread as it moved from 8:30 to 9:00. I promised myself that promptly at nine I would take action. I knew. I knew nothing was going to change between 8:30 and 9:00. Sure, I hoped, but deep in my heart I knew. I called Mike Halvorsen at the sheriff's department and told him I was going to search for my husband. I asked him to please check in on us in case I found something I wasn't prepared to handle. I hung up the phone and went to the shelf by the back door, found the big flashlight, put on my work boots, and started walking. I decided I'd best take the old Chevy pickup in case I had to transport Henry— in case he was still alive. I confess, I felt a little detached about what was going on. I knew what was going on, but it didn't seem quite real to me. It didn't and it did. I knew enough about what had probably happened to entertain the idea of what my life would look like if Henry was dead. I couldn't quite picture it, but it felt like something lifting from me.

As I drove the old road to the back forty, I remembered riding my horse out it as a girl to bring my daddy his lunch or some new water. This farm was so deeply in my blood, in my skin, and I recalled the sense of violation I had when Henry asked my father for my hand, married me, and then took over my home. He never acknowledged that this was my home. If I had been a man, it would have stayed my home. I thought about it a lot. It burned me. Marrying Henry seemed more like a business arrangement from the word go. His father owned the farm behind ours, and by marrying me, our farms would merge to become one of the largest in the county. It made good sense to him, and it made good sense to our families. No one really asked if it made good sense to me. I was coming of age and needed a place to go. My parents did not welcome the burden of a grown daughter living with them any longer, one who would bring them shame if I turned down a perfectly good suitor. I owed my parents more than that. They didn't deserve to be shamed or burdened. I married Henry. Henry must have known what I did not feel for him. I was more an observer and less a participant in our sex. Frankly, I never liked it. I found it quite repulsive actually. I did not like his corn in my field and I did not like his semen in my body. His presence polluted my home and my body. I tried to like him. I really did. I tried to think about the nice things he did—how he would chop wood for my parents, or occasionally treat me to a new dress. Little things mean a lot.

That's how I made it so long—thinking about those little things. Dutiful . . . Henry was dutiful. He knew his duties as a man, and he did them well, and for that, I could not complain. He protected, he provided, he was good to my parents. Being on the receiving end of a man's duties always has a price though. Some women don't mind paying it. Some women enjoy paying it. I did not. After a few years, I wised up and lied. I told him he snored so loudly I couldn't sleep and I went off to sleep in another room—in the room that was mine as a child. He didn't question it. Maybe he was just as relieved. I don't know.

First, I saw his tractor upside down. They are so easy to roll. Hit a bump, jerk the wheel, and it's all over. It happens every day in these parts. I stopped the truck and walked over to it. I dreaded what I would be confronted with the entire walk over to the tractor. I dreaded reaching in and seeing if I could feel a pulse. I shined my flashlight on the ground. "Henry? Henry?" I called, but not very loudly because I knew there would be no answer. I noticed the swerve of tractor tracks in the soil before me. I followed them with the flashlight, noticed where the tires had really trenched in, and then I saw it . . . his hand. At first, I didn't know what it was, but then the flash of his wedding ring gave it away. As soon as I recognized what it was, I moved the light of the flashlight, paused, turned and went back to the truck. Sure, if his hand had just been cut off, it might not have been hopeless, but I figured he had been there for a fair bit, long enough to have bled to death, and I didn't want to see it.

I drove away. It was a long, quiet, creepy ride back. I shook, but I did not cry. I didn't know what to think. I knew I should cry. I tried to cry. I just couldn't. When I finally reached the house, Mike was waiting for me. I stopped by the side of his car. He looked at me questioningly. I slowly shook my head. My eyes must have told him a lot. He got on his radio and called for backup. I drove on into the driveway, parked and went into the house.

I couldn't stop thinking about his hand. It struck me that he no longer had a hold of me, and that I no longer had his hand in marriage. I thought about his hand, how it had never been particularly tender, particularly loving. I thought about how I couldn't remember if we had ever held hands after our wedding ceremony. I don't think so. It was an interesting body part to find lying in the dirt. There is so much to a hand.

The house did feel strange without Henry for a while. That was about the extent of my grief though—uneasiness. Maybe because I didn't love him, or maybe because I just didn't have time, I never did grieve. I learned within two days that Henry had mortgaged the farm, and I was about to lose it.

Jade on Alien Guy, Part One

"YOU'RE DONE," I tell Alien Guy. Since his bathroom has no soap, I wash my hands in the kitchen. Aretha follows me there and sniffs his garbage. "Don't even think about it," I whisper to her. I eye the contents of his kitchen: two bags of Lays potato chips, a package of plastic disposable cups and a package of plastic disposable plates. Each night when I throw away my paper towel, I notice there are more disposable dishes in his garbage, but other than that, nothing changes.

I give all my massage clients my own names. Of course, I may call them by the names they call themselves to their faces, but when I think about them, I use the name I gave them. Alien Guy, for instance, got his name because the first time I saw him he had walked into the Cottonwood Massage Center in a big black cowboy hat, a long black duster, and moon boots. Remember moon boots? That's when I knew he was an alien. Yes, the moon boots gave him away. He talked to me in a monotone voice about explorations to the North and South Poles, supporting my theory by revealing his fascination with Planet Earth. The next time Alien Guy showed up, he was wearing the same hat, a wool sports coat with fringed leather sewn onto the shoulders—and again, moon boots. That time he told me how he had built a place up here inspired by the Ponderosa on "Bonanza," and he described his extensive art collection. The fumes from the beauty parlor across from the massage center irritated his asthma, so he asked me if I would make house calls, and as a result, I got to see his extensive art collection. It went something like this: painting of a mountain man, painting of a naked lady, painting of Native Americans camped near a river, painting of a naked lady, painting of the Grand Tetons, painting of a naked lady, painting of pioneers coming West, painting of a naked lady . . . you get the idea. I wondered when the last time was that I was in a room with this many naked women . . . high school P.E.? Alien Guy being an alien didn't bother me. I felt compassion for him. Clearly he is very lonely on this planet. I get that. It didn't even really bother me that I suspected his massages were less about relieving sore muscles after a day of skiing than about getting a woman to talk to him for an hour every night for the duration of his vacation. Another rich banker from New York coming out to what he believed to be the Wild West. It was cute, really. I just picture all these lonely guys as children who really wanted to be cowboys.

I pack my table and take my seventy-five bucks plus good tip. Aretha follows me to the door. I say goodnight, load up my table, and drive home.

Anna on Cold Cars

I LIE WRAPPED in two blankets on the patio lounger, looking at stars and contemplating how I got here.

What men don't realize is that women are kind of like cold cars. You can't just hop in and drive. Starting them can be tricky, and then you need to give them time to idle. You can try to drive a cold car, but it will lurch and sputter. It might even die at the first stop light. It's not good to drive your car before it's warmed up; it takes life off the car. Women are the same.

If you leave a car sitting in the driveway too long in the middle of winter, it won't start when you want it to. The battery will be dead. You need to take your car for a little drive every couple days to let the alternator charge up the battery.

For so many years, all Phil could think about was work, leaving me in the driveway for weeks at a time in the winter, so to speak. And then he would just hop in and expect me to run smoothly. I always felt like he had just penciled me in for a half hour at the beginning of a random day, at an hour in which I didn't really want to be awake. I imagined one of his daily goals lists I used to pull out of his shirt pockets before I threw them into the washing machine, with the first entry being "Make love to wife." Make love—what a funny expression for my experiences of the last twenty-five years or so. Sex had, in fact, done the opposite. Every time I felt like just a vagina lying in bed next to him instead of a whole woman, I loved him less. Each time I felt like he was just relieving himself, like sex wasn't so different for him than having a bowel movement—just something his body needed to do, I loved him less. And every time I felt like nothing more than another duty on his daily goals list, I loved him less. We weren't making love at all; we were destroying it.

Can I put all the responsibility on him? I have, after all, only tried once to talk to him about it. That was such a disaster, though—can you blame me for not trying again? I might as well have been speaking Portuguese.

I think back to when we were newlyweds. I had thought he would be my shelter, and I would be his sanctuary. I put so much effort into making our home beautiful and clean. I worked hard to make his meals delicious and ready at just the right time. I went out of my way to be welcoming when he came home, to offer him a different world than the world of bonds and futures, to offer him a world where it was safe to let his guard down and relax. He didn't seem to notice. I offered him this sanctuary, but he didn't take it. He didn't treat me like his sanctuary; he treated me like his employee.

After the kids were born, he had a daily goals list for me,

too. That was insulting. Here I was raising three kids right in front of him and he still had no clue what it took to do that. He had no idea what it was like to go seven years without sleeping through the night once. No idea how much energy it took just to make sure all three kids were alive at the end of the day. That I accomplished keeping the kids alive *and* cooked, cleaned, did laundry, ironed, mowed the lawn, shopped, and made sure everyone was where they were supposed to be on schedule was something for which I would have liked a little recognition.

I remember a night when we actually hired a babysitter and went to a movie. I don't remember the movie now, only that when it was over and everyone was filtering out of the theater, Phil bumped into a business associate and his wife. Phil made introductions, and after saying how it was nice to meet me, the business associate asked me if I worked. Before I could answer that yes, I worked very hard raising three kids and keeping a household running smoothly, Phil answered for me: "No, she doesn't." He might as well have slapped me across the face. I remember covering up my devastation with a smile and excusing myself. For a few minutes, I felt like the dam was about to burst, unleashing a flood of frustrations and tears I had been holding back for a long time. Then, something in me snapped. Instead of getting depressed, I got angry. I left a note on his car that said, "Since you don't think what I do is work, I'm sure you won't mind covering for me for the weekend." Then I ran. I ran as far as I could and then called Fiona from a payphone and asked her to pick me up at a nearby school. On my way, I plowed through the autumn leaves on the sidewalk, exhausted and heartbroken. I entered the schoolyard and sat on a swing. Angry tears fell. I laughed bitterly at myself for all my childhood idealism. I was so wrong about how wonderful it would be to be a mother and homemaker. After a while, Fiona came to pick me up. She took me to her house back in Rapid City, about a fifty-minute drive from our home in Summerville. At Fiona's, I slept for two days. She woke me from time to time to feed me, and then left me to resume my sleep marathon. On the drive back to Summerville, she gave me the name of a divorce lawyer.

"What was that all about?" Phil asked when I opened the door.

"The next time you tell anyone I don't work, I'm leaving you for good," I said, looking him squarely in the eye. If he had chosen to apologize and acknowledge my work, I might still love him today, but he didn't. As I watched his unapologetic expression, it hit me. I realized what I had committed my life to. It was in that exact moment I stopped loving him and began to find him utterly repulsive.

Now I sleep under the stars. I wish I had begun to do this a long time ago. I could have avoided feeling like there was something wrong with me for rejecting Phil's insensitive advances. There is nothing wrong with me. That I can't remember the last time I enjoyed sex with my cold husband isn't proof of any fault of mine. I sleep out here because I should have told him to "make love" to himself a long time ago.

Phil on Lesson Two

"GOOD MORNING, PHIL," Al says. "How's the marriage?" He takes a sip of scotch.

I sort of laugh, look at the floor and rub my brow.

"That good, huh? Phil, I must warn you, learning to play the pipes is the kiss of death for your relations. It is an appropriate instrument for hermits. If you have relations you value, learning to play the bagpipes is akin to suicide. Okay now, assemble your chanter. Let's see if you've practiced this week."

I assemble my chanter, placing the reed between the two parts of the pipe—carefully but firmly. He assembles his as well.

"If you have practiced well, today you will experience the euphoric power of playing with a fellow piper." He takes another sip of scotch and opens my book to page four. "You may begin."

I hold my chanter with perfect form and blow. My fingers are flat. My fingering is perfect. Al approves and joins me. He is correct. There's nothing I've ever experienced like playing with a fellow piper. Thirty dollars very well spent. Thirty dollars is less than the cost of one of Anna's haircuts.

Anna . . . I'd really rather not see Anna right now. I mean, I'm actually happy—happy for the first time since my heart attack. I'd like it to last longer than an hour and a quarter. I consider how to avoid Anna and decide to drive downtown in order to look at the possibilities for prolonging this rare happiness I'm feeling. The bookstore, no, been over that; the bar, no. If I wanted to drink, I could have just stayed and drank with Al; Juan's Burritos, only if I want another heart attack; the thrift store, no; the hair salon, definitely not; the grocery store, don't need anything; the hot dog stand, that would be suicide; the art gallery, no. That's hardly my domain.

I look up, above the town skyline to the giant ridge behind. I wonder what it would be like to play my chanter on a mountaintop? I turn right and drive toward the chair lift. I park, get out with my chanter and start to walk straight up under the chair lift. Jesus, I'm out of breath already. To my left, I notice a cat track. That's a better plan. Give me never-ending but gradual switchbacks over a short, steep incline any day. After all, it's a well-known fact that if you're above your target rate, you're not burning fat.

I almost catch my breath as I slowly walk. I imagine I'm marching with other pipers. I try out my march to see how it would feel. I lose my breath; it feels tiring. I go back to walking.

Finally, I reach the top. I'd give anything for some water right now. Wow . . . what a view . . . my house looks small from here. That means Anna's even smaller. For some reason, that comforts me. Yes, all my problems seem very small from up here.

Well, all except one: my missing, runaway, fugitive son. Still haven't made peace with that one yet. How do you make peace with something like that? I hired detectives to try to find him, you know. Five. I gave up after the fifth. These weren't some yellow pages shlubs; these guys came highly recommended by my colleagues back at the Chicago Mercantile Exchange. Maybe he's dead, I don't even know. It's not right. I'd like to know what happened to my son.

I take the chanter out of my mouth. My heart's not in it. Instead of playing "Amazing Grace," I try to play something close to taps, but it's not working. Ah, screw it. With my chanter in hand, I start down. I try to focus on the two daughters I still have. That usually makes me feel a little better.

Jade on her Reunion with Forrest and Massaging Businessmen

ARETHA AND I approach Forrest's tree. Barefoot, I carry a canvas bag filled with a bag of carrot-raisin muffins, a couple nectarines, and the flip-flops I always bring to wear in the store so I don't get kicked out. I only have one skirt long enough to hide my feet. When I wear anything else, I have to comply and wear shoes. Forrest lowers his "elevator," a rope and harness, so that he can spot me while I climb. I unclip the harness and clip the canvas bag handles to the carabineer, then give the rope two tugs. Forrest pulls the rope through the pulley above him and raises the bag to his tree house. I put the harness on. Forrest lowers the rope again, and I clip myself in and begin to climb. My aversion to shoes makes me a great climber. Aretha waits at the bottom of the tree, watching me climb, concerned, but when I reach the tree house, she turns three circles in the fir needles, and beds down for a short nap.

"Forrest!" I greet him, as I lift myself up onto the platform.

"Hey!" Forrest puts a hand on my shoulder, and we hug. He stinks. "Nice climbing."

"Thanks!" I take a moment to study him. He looks older and lonely.

"How's life?" he asks. "What's new?"

"Olive and Matt broke up. She discovered she's pregnant after they broke up. She's not going to tell Matt."

"What does Grace have to say about that?" he asks. He's the only person I can talk to about Grace. Since Grace helped me find him when he first ran away, he acknowledges her and respects what she has to say.

"Grace says it's going to be ok."

"Anything else?"

"Nah, she says it's not mine to know. She says *you're* starting to move in a different direction though."

"I wonder what that means," he says.

"I suppose it could mean anything. What do you *want* it to mean?"

"I don't know," he answers.

"Hm. Maybe it means it's time for you to leave your tree house."

"I haven't received a sign yet."

"Forrest, I keep telling you, it wasn't premeditated murder. Technically, it was manslaughter. Average sentence for that is four years."

"Hey, what's the sentence for arson?" he asks.

"I don't know."

"I bet it's longer than manslaughter."

"That I don't know," I answer.

"I really hate that word 'manslaughter.' It's a gross word. Makes it sound like I chopped somebody up."

"Yeah . . ." *What do I say to that?* "Hey, Dad's learning to play bagpipes."

"Bagpipes?"

"Bagpipes, my friend." I pause for a moment and study the view. "How about you, Forrest? What's new in your neck of the woods?"

"I've been eating lots of grouse. Saw a couple rattlers on my trip in. Sheep are making their way back up. Bad windstorm last week. I thought I was going to get bucked off my tree." Forrest sort of laughs.

"God, Forrest, doesn't that freak you?"

"Better than living on a boat."

"What if the top of your tree just snapped off?" I ask him. He shrugs.

"My old best friend, Nisa, moved in next door. She's a very hunky guy this time. I think she came back to marry me."

"Interested?" Forrest asks.

"Oh, you know. On one hand, I've never been so attracted to anyone in my life, and on the other hand, it's still hard to get past the part where I still think of him as a woman," I answer, like this is a problem everyone has.

Forrest imitates Billy Joel singing a couple bars of "She's Always a Woman to Me."

"You've got to stop it with that honky music," I tell him. "You know how I hate that crap."

"Poor you," he teases.

"Do you think it's easy having all this mojo trapped inside this white girl body? You wouldn't know anything about it, Whitey." I look at my watch. "I'm going to be late for work."

"I'll walk you home," he says, and belays me. I quickly rappel down the tree.

On the ground, I give the rope two tugs. Now Forrest weaves the rope around the figure eight attached to his harness, and clips the rope and the eight into the other harness. He gives the rope two tugs, so I know to hold it tight enough so that if he slips and starts to fall, I can take the slack out and stop him. He slides down without incident, as usual.

As he walks me home, I study Forrest through the eyes of someone other than his sister. "You know, Forrest, you're lookin' a little bit like the Unabomber. We may need to clean you up a little. Otherwise, you're going to attract too much attention."

He shrugs.

When we arrive at my place, I say "Feel free to take a shower. Lock up when you go. The key's under the white rock in the garden." He heads off to the shower as I grab my stuff and my dog and go. I get an ugly flashback of the last time he used my shower. "Clean the shower really well when you're done!"

He nods. "I'll probably go watch over the parents' place for a while today."

"All right. Later, gator."

"Later, gator."

I massage Martin for the second time in the workout room of his enormous house. The house has huge timbers in the corners, and in different places within the house to make it look like a post and beam house; but really, it's not. The timbers are purely for decorative purpose. In reality, the house is stick frame with OSB particle board covering the framing. The logs, once trees hundreds of years old, were sacrificed purely for decorative purposes. It's issues like these that make me feel very alone. I know I'm one of a handful of people in the world who truly understand that old trees are sentient beings. These decorative timbers are no different, really, than killing a cow for leather pants. Maybe the timbers are worse. It took hundreds of years for the tree to grow, but as little as one for the cow.

I can't imagine that he doesn't feel lonely in this house, dwarfed by it. There are no family photos in Martin's house, no ring on his finger, no toiletries in the bathroom to indicate the presence of another. His house lacks a woman's touch, having instead, the touch of an interior decorator I do not know, but whose work I recognize from other clients' houses: lasso on the fireplace mantel, saddle over the loft railing, pillows with southwest designs. I've seen it a hundred times—

decoration for the man who wishes he had been a cowboy instead of an investment banker.

"How's business?" he asks. Not *how are you,* or *isn't it beautiful outside,* no, just *how's business.* This one is in pretty deep.

"Grace!" I call in my head, and sure enough, Grace appears.

Grace struts around Martin who lies face down on the massage table, his face in the face cradle, which one of my clients thinks looks like a little toilet seat. "Mmm-mmm-mmm-MMM!" Grace hums. I know what that means: *Ohhh, we got trouble here!*

"Picking up again, now that people are back in town." I answer out of courtesy.

Grace rests her hands on Martin's head while I work his lower back. Grace, consumed by her own concentration, does not talk to me.

"I prefer a consistent business," Martin grumbles.

"I don't worry about it too much," I reply.

"What do you mean you don't worry about it too much?" Martin's disapproval is evident in his tone.

"Stress kills," I answer.

Martin doesn't respond.

I work the back of his legs and then tell him, "Flip over and scoot down so that your head is out of the face cradle." I work the front of his legs while Grace places her hands on his heart.

Although his eyes are closed, his face looks very sad.

I work his arms, and Grace moves to his abdomen. Martin remains quiet.

While I finish with his neck, Grace begins to sing African songs of prayer for healing. I close my eyes and drink up Grace's beautiful songs. At the end of the song, I place my hands on Martin's head and say, "Bless you."

Martin keeps his eyes closed. "Thank you."

Pearl on the Birth of the Thunderellas

IT WAS MY house, but it seemed temporarily foreign . . . my daughter gone, my husband dead, so few dirty dishes, so little laundry. Sometimes I felt like my husband was watching me when I was alone. It was creepy.

I never would have guessed it would be Miss Fern to turn my life around, Miss Fern who once whacked me with a ruler in her first-grade class. I was going a little nuts in the new emptiness, worrying about losing the farm. At night I would just walk laps around the house, pacing around. Miss Fern, my old teacher who lived up the street, stopped by after three days or so. It needs to be said Miss Fern was ancient. True, I was no spring chicken myself, but Miss Fern was truly ancient. We sat chit-chatting over a cup of tea at the small kitchen table the first night she came to check up on me, until she broke from the conversation and informed me, "Now, I will teach you a technique for getting through this time." She reached into her large wicker bag, pulled out two pairs of black tap shoes, and handed one pair to me. "These belonged to my friend, Elsie. She's dead now. She was a mammoth woman—Polish, you know. Those might be too big for you, but you can put some cotton balls in the toes and they'll be okay." I studied Miss Fern, half my height, grey hair in a short bob with lots of bobby pins. She looked delicate and bright. Maybe it was just her yellow floral dress that was bright, but I don't think so. I think it was her eyes. "Are you okay, honey?" I nodded and put on my shoes. "After my husband died, I was restless and crazy. Elsie taught me this. Shuffle-shuffle-shuffle-shuffle. Like that. Good. Move your ankle more. Yes, you'll use your ankles like you've never used them before. Okay, now try this: shuffle-ball-change, shuffle-ball-change." Miss Fern began to sing "Boogie Woogie Bugle Boy" slowly as I tried to follow along with her taps. "After my husband died, I started thinking about ghosts a lot. Ghosts hate tap dancing. It drives them away." She flashed me a winning smile. "And it keeps your legs looking great." She pulled her dress up high to show me her legs. Then she tucked the extra fabric into the top of her underwear to make her skirt shorter. "Look! I'm a flapper!"

I nodded approvingly and laughed, sure Miss Fern must be a little touched. She laughed with me. I realized it was the first time I laughed not only since Henry died, but since years before his death.

Miss Fern paid weekly visits to my house, except during harvest, to give me tap dancing lessons. When Beatrice moved in, Miss Fern taught her, too. Those were the days—

Miss Fern, Beatrice and I drinking wine in my kitchen, and Miss Fern warding off my husband's ghost with loud tapping.

We picked up Hazel a year and a half later, after her sister died. For a while, the three of us would make house calls to her place. Then Fiona returned to care for Trudy, her mother who had developed dementia, and we knew we better get her out of the house once a week to keep her sane. Tapping at her house seemed like a bad idea, because it might really frighten Trudy, so we began renting the grange hall. There was quite a group of us by then, and the wood floors at the grange hall are ideal for tapping. That's how the Thunderellas began.

Jade on Her Recurring Nightmare

IT'S THE SAME every time. You know why? It's not a dream; it's a memory. It's the late sixties. I'm him, the Reverend Byron James.

The black and tan mutt who slept on the steps when the church was empty mixed her way into the crowd to hear the congregation sing. Sometimes she would sing along as well. The choir began to sing "Sweet, Sweet Spirit." Their joyful voices lifted me up. I loved that congregation. How I loved those beautiful souls who came together every week to celebrate their blessings. Suddenly, the mutt ran to the back door and began to bark. The congregation stopped singing, turned their heads and watched the dog, concerned. A rock came through a window at the back of the church, then two bottle grenades. On the other side of the church, two rocks flew through two windows. One hit little Sally, only five years old, in the head. She fell limp as chaos erupted around her. Three torches and another bottle grenade flew through those two windows. I took a chair and knocked the rest of the broken window out, and put the chair in front of the window. Brother Nigel, Brother Samuel, and Brother LeRoy went through the window first to protect the children who came out next. Grace led the choir in singing "May the Circle Be Unbroken" while the congregation began to evacuate. It seemed to calm the church members somewhat. I tried to keep order and to get my beloved congregation out as fast as possible, and as I did, I was thinking, damn, I hoped Jesus would forgive me for the hatred I felt in my heart for white people right then.

All in all, sixty-one of the eighty-four who were in attendance that day made it out before the smoke filled the church and the fire consumed the Earthly bodies of the twenty-three remaining, including Grace who held little Sally in her arms, the mutt, and me.

I wake up sweating and unable to breathe. Grace touches my face, brushes back my red braids, and then places her hand on my hand. "There, there, sweet child. Now let me tell you the end of the story." Grace sits on the edge of my bed next to Aretha, who sleeps with her head on my chest. I sob for a minute, as I always do, saddened and shaken by this dream. Some acts of humankind are so much uglier than I like to believe my kind is capable of.

"Shh, now child, everything is all right. That was just a chapter in a book that has a very happy ending." Grace takes my other hand now, which rests on top of Aretha, and tells me the rest, as she always does. And thank God she does.

"As you, the Reverend Byron James, floated up, up out of his Earthly body, and up to the Kingdom of Heaven, you began to remember some things. Yes, you began to remember the last twenty times you made that journey. You began to remember the other names for the dimension you were going to. You began to remember a few of the numerous identities you had had."

I vaguely remembered this. As I went through the tunnel, I remembered walking on the bottom of the quarry where my brothers and I swam when we were little, and then floating back to the surface. Earth life—not so different from walking on the bottom of the quarry. On the bottom of the quarry, you could not see a clearer and more hospitable world above. No, you could only see some light filtering down. And just as my brothers and I couldn't wait to get to the surface of the water and finally take a good satisfying breath, so did I feel the same anticipation as I floated up, up to God's Kingdom, as I called it in that life.

Grace continues, "On the plane of bliss, the Kingdom of Heaven, whatever you wish to call it, you, the Reverend Byron James, saw the other twenty-two. 'Well, Hallelujah! We made it!' you called out to them. The black and tan mutt ran up to you, and changed forms into at least thirty other dogs—remember that? It triggered your memory of being with that dog in many lifetimes. You were filled with great love for this dog, and bent over to greet it properly. Who is that dog now, child?"

"Aretha," I answer like a little kid.

"That's right, child, see nothing is really permanent. Everything is always changing form, always evolving. Okay now, back to your story. Since your exit was rather traumatic, the Angels cocooned you and the others in green light for a time that cannot be measured, so that you could rest and heal. When the time came to leave the green light cocoons, a representative came to guide you and the black and tan mutt who always followed you, to the Council. 'You have broken out of the Samsara of the life and death cycle!' announced one member. Remember that? Oh! That was good news! 'Technically, you are enlightened!' he told you. 'Technically, you may go to the plane of enlightenment!' And you thought ah yes, yes, yes! Then that Council member said, 'But you do have a bonus lifetime option.'

"'Now why would I want that?' you thought. Remember that? Oh, you had so much dread just thinking of another birth!" Grace laughs.

"'Now, I know what you're thinking,' another member of the Council said to you. 'Why would you want to do that, right?' The Council member smiled knowingly. 'When one goes down the chute for a bonus life, he or she has unique opportunities. In addition to getting to tie up any loose ends that aren't really important enough to merit a whole 'nother life but are nice to have tied up nonetheless, one also has the opportunity to elevate countless others . . . to speed up their journeys . . . or sort of just grab onto them and bring them into enlightenment with you.'

"'Yes, think of it like running out of a burning building,

but then going back in to pull out others, and it's not like you have to do this all on your own. You'll have cream of the crop guides,' the first Council member added. Oh Lordy! Those Council members were campaigning hard!" Grace always laughs when she remembers this. "And that's when they told you about me, remember? 'The soul you most recently knew as Grace has offered to guide you through your bonus life, should you choose to take it.'

"And you thought, 'Hm! I do like that Grace! That Grace is one brave soul! That Grace is one good cook! Where would I be without the fine, fine cooking of my favorite soul in the whole Universe, Grace!'" Grace takes it a little far just to make me laugh. "Oh yeah! You didn't know I wouldn't be cooking for your sorry self in this lifetime! Ha! So the Council explained to you that guiding is what you do when you're not quite ready for the full force of another incarnation. You still experience enough of the heartache of human existence by virtue of the compassion you have, mind you, so it's by no means painless, but it's not as intense as another round of actual human existence either. Only the bravest souls go back down to Earth for another round. Oh yeah! You liked the sound of that. You liked bein' the brave one! And you felt plenty brave at that moment, didn't you? You were feelin' all good from your green cocoon rest, and of course, good in the way everyone does on the plane of bliss. Yes, you were feelin' that Superman kind of good, that invincible kind of good . . . that kind of good where you find yourself agreeing to all kinds of ideas . . . ideas that seem neutral on the plane of bliss, but not on Earth! Ha! Next thing you know, you're thinkin' 'Goddamn!' after you left your mamma's birth canal and saw your blueness turn to white. Oh yeah! Experts will tell you that babies don't recognize their hands as their own for some time, but Jade, honey, you had been through this routine thousands of times, enough times to know that you had indeed come into this life as a white girl! Ha! You looked around the room and saw me, all beautifully rich, coffee-colored, looking down at you and I said, 'Hot damn, Reverend! You're looking mighty peaked!' Ha!"

The end of the story, or the beginning, depending on how you look at it, always makes me laugh to hear Grace tell it.

"Yeah, I'm sure I didn't know bein' a white girl was part of the contract," I add.

"Yeah, God wanted to make sure you purified that hatred of white people that you exited that last life with!" Grace laughs some more at my journey. "Child, do you think you can get back to sleep now?" Grace asks me tenderly.

"Nah," I answer. I never can get back to sleep after these dreams.

"Well then, what do you say we put on a little Motown and dance these blues away?"

"How about a little Kirk Franklin?" I propose. "You know, I really miss listening to you all sing that glorious gospel choir music."

Grace makes my radio play some Kirk Franklin gospel choir music and I savor the sweet sounds of my favorite soul, Grace, singing along as we dance together in celebration of all that is light.

Forrest on Going Home

HOW SMALL MOM looks from up here.

People who stay on the ground never look down and get this perspective on their little world. I watch her in her fenced-in backyard, like a mouse in a maze. I wish I could reach down and lift her out. It's so easy to get trapped when two dimensions is all you know.

Mom, dressed in her usual black, looks sad, and I notice a degree of resignation in her movements.

I feel bad about the way I deserted them, the way I just dropped off the face of the earth. I know I contributed to the burden I see her carry now, and wish I could have done things differently, but I couldn't have.

I know it wasn't Mom's fault what happened to Moose. Moose chewed through ropes, broke chains, and dug his way out from under fences when he couldn't jump over them, and he could jump over most.

I remember getting off the bus just as the sheriff pulled up. As Moose ran to greet me, the sheriff shot him, dead in his tracks. "I had a report from one Willa Meyer regarding a vicious dog," was all the sheriff explained. I died just then.

That's what I remember—darkness, silence—a black hole into which my spirit was sucked. I watched in horror as my best friend tumbled, fell, and bled. I remember covering Moose, sheltering him with my own body, only too late, and I remember that hole in his chest, which I could not remove or undo. I remember mom squatting next to me, her arms around me, the weight of her head resting on my back. I remember a few of her words, ". . . killed another of her chickens . . . asked her to shoot him with rock salt instead . . . told her you would pay her with money or with work . . . wouldn't listen . . ." I remember her trying to lift me off Moose, but I wouldn't let go.

I didn't let go as dusk turned to night and my best friend grew very cold. I loosened my grip sometime in the middle of the night to pet his belly.

I didn't sleep. Moose was the only thing that kept my recurring fire nightmares away, the one where I'm burning, but can't move, the one where I can't do anything but burn.

I remember the next morning, digging a hole just as the sky became a little lighter. Digging, digging, digging—it seemed like forever. I dug so that my body would hurt, so that the pain in my heart might transform into a pain I could better deal with. The sun was partway up its arc by the time I finished.

The school bus had come and gone. I'm sure all the kids were staring, but I didn't look at them.

I brought the wheelbarrow over, but couldn't lift him up. Moose was at least twice my weight. Mom appeared out of nowhere and lifted most of Moose's body while I supported his head. I remember how the ground was saturated with blood. I wheeled Moose to the hole in the field. Mom walked next to me. She helped me lift the giant dog out of the wheelbarrow and gently place him in the hole.

"Go now," I told Mom. This funeral was private. I remember looking at my dog in the hole, wondering how you tell a dog what he meant to you when the language you share is unspoken. And then I remember how the dirt bounced and scattered as it hit his side, and how my dog, my friend, disappeared through this veil of dirt.

Then I just remember fire.

I didn't bomb Willa Meyer's chicken house right away. I had to study for quite a while to learn how to build the right bomb for the job. This took months of correspondence with Uncle Helmut, who had once blown up his college dormitory while doing a chemistry experiment under the influence of LSD. Helmut is the first person to tell you that dropping acid and chemistry experiments don't mix. He really is harmless, not the threat that Hamill County believes him to be. Anyway, it was this gap of time between Moose's murder and the murder of Willa Meyer, in combination with the fact that I was only thirteen and had moved to Idaho by then that led no one to suspect it was me. Truth be told, I didn't intend to murder Willa. She just walked into the coop after I had lit the fuse.

Jade says it's because I'm a Scorpio, and Scorpios made up that eye for an eye business. You know, I knew there was no way her chickens could mean to her what Moose had meant to me—she didn't sleep with her chickens—but blowing up her precious coop was a start. Still, I only meant to even the score, not end the game.

I watch Mom and wonder how it all shook down, wonder how long it took her to piece it all together, wonder if she ever confessed to anyone that she suspects her son is a killer. I wonder if she feels like she failed. Probably. What bigger failure is there as a parent than to raise a killer?

I hate that word—killer; it sounds like a jagged knife. I hate that it's a word that's attached to me, actually part of me like a tattoo. Murder is so permanent. You can't undo it.

I wonder sometimes if the world would be a better place if I were in jail. Prison, it's argued, serves one of three purposes: punishment, protecting the public, or rehabilitation. I consider punishment. Would conventional imprisonment be worse than the one I imposed on myself for all these years? I froze, sometimes I starved, I went for four and a half years without speaking to anyone, and even now live most of my life in solitary confinement. During storms, my house whips around like a carnival ride and I never know if it's going to hold. I don't believe society needs to be protected from me. I feel great remorse over what I did, and rest assured, I won't go blowing up anything again. As for rehabilitation—yes, I could use some rehabilitation, but who can heal their soul in prison? Perhaps a monastery would be an appropriate place for rehabilitation, a place where men who have dedicated their lives to the philosophies of life and death could counsel me on the best way to approach creating karmic balance, righting my wrongs. They could help me with the concepts of divine forgiveness and self-forgiveness, if there's any difference. So this is where I stand now. I suppose I could probably filter back into society somehow, put myself on parole, but do I deserve it? I've been waiting for a sign that my penance is over. I've been waiting for a sign that there is good I can do in this world. I've seen neither.

Mom's birthday is approaching. I wish that just for once, I could bring her happiness.

Olive on Maps

SOMETIMES LIFE JUST doesn't work out the way you planned. I know this. I also know I need to let go of it and keep moving forward.

But shouldn't I examine my failures so I can create a future different than my present?

I wonder how much of what happens to us is our own doing. There are those who believe that God has a plan for us and that we should surrender to it. There are those who believe in destiny or fate. Then, there are those who believe in karma, that we are living with the results of our past choices at present and creating new karma for later. Perhaps there is no divinity to what happens to us at all. Perhaps everything in our life is just luck of the draw and how we react to it.

I do know, without a doubt, that I will buckle over and puke if one more person tells me the answer is visualization. I've been visualizing the life I wanted for a couple decades now and what do I have to show for it? I've come to the conclusion that visualization is fine as far as determining where a person wants to end up, but it's just a step—it's no means to an end. For instance, you can sit in your house and visualize yourself swimming, and you can visualize until the cows come home, but the only way you're actually going to get to go swimming is if you get yourself out the door and to the lake.

I take a few deep breaths.

I visualized my life completely different than this.

I need an action plan. Yes, I'm essentially turning into my dad in this way. I need a map to show me where I am and how to get to where I want to be.

It's hard not to just react. It's hard not to simply say to yourself, *This really blows,* and just jump into any new situation. I know I need to think carefully, make careful choices, and execute my plan methodically. But do I really have a plan? Sort of. I have Dad's graph. That's something. But what if I buy the house only to find out that the rest of the dream isn't present? What if a person only has so much energy, like money, to spend on a dream, and what if the house takes all of mine, leaving none left for my child, who is the reason the house matters in the first place?

Jade interrupts my thought when she enters the house with Aretha. She takes one look at me and says, "You're in a funk."

"I suppose I am." I don't get off the edge of my bed. "Just trying to figure out where to go from here. The idiot siege has left me in an uncertain place."

"Hm," she says.

"I think about all the homes I've rented and how I planted a little garden in each of them. If I'd stayed in one house this whole time, imagine what my garden would look like. The men in my life have been like rental homes . . . dumpy places I could never own, places to which I had little commitment and no right to paint the walls."

Jade is quiet for a moment and I assume she's really thinking about what I said, but then she chimes in with, "Remember that one guy you liked so much who had pictures of men all over his walls—Elvis, Sylvester Stallone, and Randy Travis? Remember when he said that he wanted to wear a white Elvis sequined jumpsuit when he got married? How is it that you didn't get it he was gay?"

"He said the men on his walls were men he wished he could be like. He swore he liked women."

"The man had a pet bunny, Olive."

"Yeah, he was probably gay," I agree. My heart's not in this conversation. I have so many decisions to make and not enough choices.

"Probably? Man-posters plus Elvis jumpsuit plus pet bunny equals no probably about it. Man, we've dated our share of losers. I dated that one guy who asked me if both he and Aretha were in a burning building and I could only pull one out, who would I save—remember him? And I said, 'If you're in a burning building with my dog, how come you're not saving her? What, do you have jealousy issues or something?' Remember that? What a loser. Every guy since has been allergic to dogs. Gotta take it as a sign."

"Jade, just stop talking. Stop talking for a minute," I snap. "I'm pregnant. I'm supposed to move in with the parents. They don't know, but I won't be able to hide it forever. Am I going to live there forever? Am I going to raise my child there? Am I welcome to? Am I going to give my child time or money? Because I don't think I can give her both. I'm freaking out about the future, Jade, so you're just going to have to forgive me if I'm not up for a trip down memory lane."

Jade looks at me a little confused. "But it's going to be all right," she says. "We already know that. Grace told me it's going to be all right."

"*I* don't know that. Maybe your invisible friend knows that, but *I* don't know that." We lock eyes for a minute. "You know, it really drives me nuts the way you're so high and mighty . . ." I begin.

"—High and mighty?" Jade acts confused, like she doesn't understand what I'm talking about. That only infuriates me more.

"Like nothing can touch you, like you never feel any pain because your invisible friend tells you it's going to be okay or it's all for the best . . . like you're above it all. Well that's just great, Jade. I wish I was more like you. Really. And then another part of me wishes something would come along in your perfect life and knock you off your high horse."

Jade couldn't even get mad at me like a normal person. She looked at me like she felt sorry for me, turned, and left.

Phil on Lesson Three

FOR NEARLY THE last forty years, every morning I open my eyes, my first thought is, *What do I need to do today?* All those years of starting each morning hitting the ground running have deeply etched this pattern into my consciousness. Now, I wake up asking myself the same question, and the answer is usually, *Nothing.* Sometimes it's, *Go to the bathroom.* I haven't decided if I like bathroom mornings better than nothing mornings. Sure, it gives me a sense of purpose for all of two minutes, but after that, I'm left high and dry, back to nothing—only now I'm out of bed, wandering around.

Monday mornings are different though. On Monday mornings, I have a place to go. I go to one of the few remaining small houses left in Cottonwood, the red one with the plaid door, small porch and overgrown hedge. That red house is my salvation.

"Good morning, Phil. I trust the demise of your marriage has been expedited?"

I laugh, but don't reply.

"Are you still in the house, Phil?" he asks me directly.

"I am," I tell him. *But my wife is not,* I think.

"Your wife must be a saint," he replies, amazed. "It wasn't long before my wife banished Junior and myself to the garage." He motions to his bagpipes. "Junior here speculates that our friendship with one mister Jack Daniels may have contributed to our new residence as well. The missus was a God-fearing woman who did not approve of partaking in the spirits. Now Phil, an un-air-conditioned garage in Alabama is insipid—that's why Junior and I have relocated to Cottonwood. The climate is considerably more hospitable, which is why you will be pleasantly ambivalent when your wife invites you to live in the garage."

I laugh, though Al doesn't crack a smile. If he did, I'm not sure I'd see it behind his huge handlebar moustache.

"And now, we will play the greatest song ever written. Page seven."

I live for these Monday mornings. For a half-hour every week, there is understanding in my life. Another thirty dollars well spent. Thirty dollars wouldn't even get me dinner and a glass of wine at D'Angelo's. These lessons are truly an excellent value.

Afterwards, I go up the ridge again, this time with water. I think about Forrest again, rehash the same conversation I've had with myself for the last thirteen years, nothing new. I never reach any new conclusions, never get any new insights. It's a waste of energy. I know that. Still, I can't let it go. It's got to be my failure. If only I had been at home more, he would have known me better—enough to trust me with his secret, enough to have faith I could have offered a solution. If only I hadn't failed at being a good father . . . At the very least, if only I hadn't failed at finding him. Maybe it's time to bury it —I don't know. Even if it is, I don't know that I ever could.

At the top, after I've sat a spell and caught my breath, I play "Amazing Grace." If my son is alive, may he have the kind of awakening, the kind of new beginning or second chance sung about in this song. If he's dead, may he be forgiven for whatever he did and be given his second chance above.

I hate to admit this, but I really don't know whether I believe in God or not. I say a prayer now and then just in case. When I look for the evidence of God in my life though, I just don't see it. I've had my share of miracles, but I've always been the one to make those happen. When I really needed some divine intervention, I never did see it.

I play "Amazing Grace" and hope for an event so miraculous it would restore my faith, because I really would like to believe in something.

Jade on Alien Guy Again and her Specialty, Burnt Pan

ALIEN GUY PICKS out some of the weirdest music I've ever done massage to. The first night he played *Diana Ross's Greatest Hits,* but night two he played *K-Tel Hits of the 80's* featuring "Ghostbusters" and "We Built this City on Rock and Roll." Tonight he has chosen *Bob Seger's Greatest Hits.* As I work on his quads, he begins to sing "We've Got Tonight" along with Seger.

Grace appears. "Girl, you better change the subject! You talk to him about that nasty toenail fungus of his. That'll snap him out of that heinous serenade!" If I had a dollar for every time Grace saved my ass. I give Grace an appreciative look. "Man, and why can't he play that Diana Ross again? What do white people hear in this crap anyway?"

I finished his quad as quickly as the serenade began, spent about thirty seconds on tibialis anterior, and then went to his foot. "You know Garth, there are pills you can take that will keep this toenail fungus from breeding," I interrupt. "Left untreated, sometimes people have to have their toenail removed or their whole toe amputated."

"I'm not too worried about it. With my other health problems, I'll probably only live another ten years or so."

"Mmm! He is one foul creature! You watch yo'self here," Grace warns. Times like this, I am so glad to have Aretha at my feet.

"You've probably noticed that I don't have male massage therapists. I'm not really comfortable with that, plus I just kind of like having women touch me," says Alien Guy.

"Garth, I wish you hadn't said that." His comment makes me feel like a whore instead of someone who helps facilitate healing. "How's your injured knee, Garth?" I grab his medial collateral ligament on the inside of his left knee and roll it mercilessly between my fingers and thumb like a pencil. I feel scar tissue tearing like Velcro. He yelps. "Pretty gunky in there. Lots of connective tissue building up."

"Oh yeah, girl, he needed that," Grace says.

I finish his arms and neck, pronounce him done, and go to the kitchen to wash my hands. I pack up, take my seventy-five bucks plus tip and rush home with Aretha to shower his vibes off me as fast as I can.

Wrapped in a towel, wet cornrow braids whipping water everywhere, I jump up and after a few tries, knock the cover of the fire alarm off to stop that horrible screech. I open the door and let the smoke drift out. Once again, I forgot to put water in the pan of what was supposed to be steamed vegetables. I put the pan on the stove, turned it on high, and then stepped into the shower. Burnt pan, my specialty. When the fire alarm goes off and the pan is welded to the element, it's done.

Aretha runs outside when I open the door, hating the metallic smoke and fumes and the noise of this regular occurrence.

I put the bottomless pan on the doorstep. The phone rings, and I run to turn down the Geoffrey Oryema CD I was cranking while I was in the shower. Instead of picking up the phone, I stand there in my towel and wait to see whose voice I'll hear on the answering machine. A silly voice says, "Hello, this is Peter Lemonjello, and I would like a four-hour butt massage."

I pick up, "Ya, Peeta," I say in my fake Swedish accent, "Ya, dis is Helga and as you know da butt massage is my specialty."

"Knock, knock," I hear from my open door. Shit. Josh.

I hold up a finger to ask for a minute. "Forrest, I have to go. Tell me when and where . . . okay, bye."

"Hey, neighbor . . ." I'm clearly frazzled.

"So butt massages are your specialty?"

"That was my brother. Running joke. Sibling thing. You know."

He smiles. "So, am I too late for dinner?"

With a small chuckle, I close my eyes and drop my head.

"No, actually, you're right on time. I made my specialty, burnt pan. I put it on the doorstep because I had you pegged for a man who likes to dine al fresco."

Josh smiles and nods. "Yes, absolutely. Al fresco." He pauses for a minute. "Hey, if you like, I have spaghetti on the stove next door. You're welcome to join me. No need to dress up. Come as you are," he teases.

"Thanks." I accept.

"Come over whenever you're ready." He steps over where Aretha has fallen asleep on the sidewalk behind him, and walks back to his place.

I leave the stove and go to my bedroom to dress. I survey my clothes and decide this is a T-shirt and overalls kind of occasion. Then I walk out into the kitchen to find Grace looking at the element.

"Girl, when are you gonna learn to cook?" Grace badgers.

"Grace, when are you gonna let me know I've made this mistake before I wreck yet another pan?"

"Can't you do anything for yo'self?"

"I don't need this!" I sass.

"Well you sure needed my cornbread and collard greens an awful lot last time around, didn't you, Reverend? I made you Sunday dinner every week for ten years and this sassing is the thanks I get?"

I don't really remember this part of my Reverend Byron James life very well, but Grace likes to tell me all about the part where she played the organ and carried a secret torch for me, which I was apparently too focused on my work to notice. Once a week, though, she could hold my attention with Sunday dinner. Grace tells me that, in fact, we had been friends many times throughout our lives. We had even been married a time or two.

"Grace, I'm going over to Josh's now. Are you finished razzing me?"

"Lot of good razzing you does. One of these days you're gonna kill yourself in a fire if you're not careful," Grace cautions.

"I already died in a fire."

"Very funny." Grace is not laughing. "Well, you're just asking for that exit again."

"You mean if diabetes doesn't get me first." She's always razzing me about eating so much sugar.

"That's right. See now, I'm so glad to see that you're actually listening to me," Grace replies.

"Be a little hard not to, now, wouldn't it?"

"Well, after all the boring sermons I sat through during your last life, I think you can probably listen to a few things I say this time around. I think you owe me that." Oooh. Low blow.

"Okay, Grace, good talk. We're working on Alien Guy and Barry White Guy tomorrow. I'll see you then."

"Oh, yeah," Grace says, imitating the way Barry White coos throughout his whole massage.

Aretha follows me to Josh's house. I knock.

"It's open!" he calls.

We walk in.

"You changed!" He sounds disappointed.

"Well, you know, this time of day it begins to cool off rather quickly," I explain.

"I suppose." He concentrates on dicing the tomatoes for our salad and then says, "You know, I hope it's okay that I give you a bad time. Sometimes after I say something, I think, *Josh, I can't believe you just said that! You don't even know her!* But you know how there are some people you meet that seem so familiar? It's hard to remember you haven't known them your whole life?" He looks up to see if I get what he's trying to say.

Nisa, you little cutie.

"I do that all the time." I look around his living room for clues about what he's done in this life. "So where are you from?"

"Most recently, Denver. I spent the last eleven years there. The boss wanted to start a small office up here since this area has so many investors. I grew up in Philly. You?"

"I've been here since I was teenager. Before that, Summerville, South Dakota."

"Your family still here?" he asks.

"Oh, yeah . . ."

He laughs. "Sounds like there's quite a story there."

"My mom sleeps in the backyard on a lawn chair and paints raisins all day, my dad is learning to play bagpipes, my brother lives in a tree house a few miles out that way, and my oldest sister recently discovered she's pregnant right after she and her partner broke up. That pretty much sums it up."

"Is your sister going to raise her child on her own?" he asks.

"Yep," I answer.

"What about you?" he asks. "Do you want kids?"

"Not if I have to raise them by myself."

"What if you didn't have to raise them by yourself? What if you met the perfect guy—then would you want kids?"

"Ask me after I meet the perfect guy. What about you?"

"Yeah, I want kids."

"Do you think those things are up to us or up to destiny?" I ask.

"I don't know," he answers. "What do you think?"

I go out on a limb. "I think we make some agreements before we come here."

"Like with other people?"

I wish I could feel him out better on this before I say too much. "You know how when you meet someone you feel like you've known a long time . . . maybe you feel a sense of connection . . . I think those are the people with whom you share agreements." I wonder what he'll do with that.

"So you think you and I had an agreement?"

"You mean you don't remember?" I try turning the question into a joke.

"Refresh my memory." He sits back and smiles, waiting for the entertainment to begin.

"If you don't remember, I'm not going to tell you." I fake offense.

"So you don't remember, either." He thinks he's called my

bluff.

"Oh, I remember," I assure him. "Ultimately it doesn't matter if you remember or not. You'll still fulfill your part of the agreement." I take a couple sips of my wine. "So what's your family like?"

"My mom's family immigrated here from Sierra Leone in the sixties. She met my dad in college. He's a journalist. My sister is a chef and owns a Thai restaurant in Miami. That was a nice try at changing the subject." He carries the spaghetti and salad over to the table. "So what did we agree to do?"

I look him directly in the eye like I'm joking. "Get married," I answer honestly. "So your family—are you close to them?" I try to change the subject again before I freak him out. I'm not capable of lying. The best I can do if I can't dodge a question is to tell the truth and make it sound like a joke. If he keeps asking direct questions though, the conversation is going to get really weird, and then perhaps he'll use his free will to change his mind about our agreement. I don't know. I wonder about that a lot—how easy or hard it is to mess up destiny, and if I mess it up, whether it really is messed up, or if it just is what it is, and so I move on to plan B and it's really okay. I don't know. I really don't want to mess this up, though. We've waited hundreds of years to be together again. I roll some spaghetti onto my fork.

"Sort of. I don't get to see them much though. Work keeps me really busy. So we're getting married?" He takes a bite of spaghetti, wipes his mouth, and waits for my answer.

"I think our agreements are like signing up for college

classes—you can always choose to drop them later." Wasn't that an artful and honest way of dodging his question?

"So what are you saying, that you've already decided not to marry me?"

"No, I'll marry you," I say like I'm being silly, "but I don't recall you asking me yet. This wine is delicious." Please let my subject change work this time. I take another bite of spaghetti.

Josh's voice softens. "You'd marry me, huh?" He seems flattered.

I just roll my eyes, feel my cheeks burn once again, and continue eating.

Olive on Rediscovering Dirt

THE MAN SITTING across from me is saying, "We wanted to build this house without going into debt at all, but we figure we could build it faster if we just bit the bullet."

Build a house without going into debt? No one builds a house without going into debt.

"Here are our plans, and here are a couple articles, in case the loan officer is unfamiliar with this construction technique," he continues. "We decided against a load-bearing bale house given the snowfall up here. We're going to go ahead and build a stick frame, and just fill the walls with straw bales, so if you think about it, it's really not so different from a regular stick frame house—it just has a lot more insulation."

The woman with him says, "We read one article that encouraged us to tell you guys we were insulating with agricultural cellulose."

I smile, unsure how to respond. "Well, I don't know what to tell you. It's hard for the bank to evaluate something like this because the loan is based on resale value. If no houses like the one you're building have sold in the area in the last year, the bank may shy from it." I feel for them. These people deserve a chance. But that's not how the system works. It comes down to numbers and statistics, nothing else. "You should hear from us in six to ten working days."

"Well, if the bank doesn't come through, it'll just take us a little longer, that's all," says the man, and they stand up and leave.

"Good luck with everything," I call after them, truly meaning it.

After they go, I flip through the articles. One of the articles has information about straw bale building, and another, cob, which looks like a mix of mud, straw, and a little concrete. Dirt? Who would want to live in a dirt house? I examine the pictures. The dirt houses actually look nice—sort of like adobe. Well, hm . . . adobe is also dirt. As I glance through all the pictures, a world of possibilities opens up to me, and I imagine building a nice house like these without going into debt.

I go home and read everything I can on the Internet about straw bale and cob construction. I look at picture after picture. Some look not so different than conventional houses, and some are wildly artistic. Most are something in between. A lot of the houses seem curvy and soft. They seem kind of feminine in that way, and inviting, like a grandmother opening her arms and saying, "Come on home, child. Come on home."

I read a little about the people who built these houses. Even though they come from many different walks of life, they share a common vision, a simplicity in life that resonates with me.

Imagine, having a house you own free and clear. Imagine having a house no one can take from you. I realize I might have just found my escape route.

I order a couple books on each of the construction techniques and turn off my computer.

Jade on Visiting Peter Lemonjello

I LOOK AROUND to make sure no one else in the family is watching, put on my harness, clip into Forrest's rope and run up the old fir. I take a bag of dried mangos out of a pocket of my fishing vest and throw it at him, "Here."

"My favorite!" Forrest opens the bag, and his eyes widen. "So what's the emergency, Peter Lemonjello?"

"I need to have a block of time when the parental units are not going to be home. A whole day would be great."

"Forrest, I can't get everyone out of the house for an entire day. I don't know what to tell you," I say. "If you stick around for a couple weeks, maybe you'll find your window."

He eats another piece of mango. "You're smiling more than usual."

"I had dinner with Nisa-Josh."

"Yeah?"

"Oh, yeah."

"Tell all!"

"I made burnt pan, and he made spaghetti. He confessed that I felt familiar. On some level, he remembers me. Not the details, but still, a part of him remembers. I told him I'd marry him."

"Did you kiss him?" Forrest teases.

"God, no. I'm still having trouble adjusting to his new gender. I get all lusty and then I'm like—whoa, that's Nisa!" As I explain this, I have to laugh. It sure sounds strange when I say it out loud.

"What about you, Forrest? Do you think there's someone for you in this lifetime?"

"Does it matter what I think?"

"Maybe," I answer.

"I probably won't create a love with a woman if it's up to me, and if there is such thing as fate, I've probably messed it up and consequently there's a woman out there who's very lonely and disappointed, growing considerably more bitter with each passing year."

"Have you ever considered that perhaps it was predestined for Willa Meyer to walk into that chicken coop right when she did?"

"Of course I've considered that. It doesn't make me less responsible, though. That's my beef with destiny—that people use it to excuse themselves from their personal responsibility."

"I can see that." Neither of us says anything for a while. "So, what, Forrest, are you just going to punish yourself for the rest of your life?"

"Yeah, pretty much."

"That's a waste."

He looks away and doesn't say anything.

"Why don't you pay back your karmic debt instead of just depriving yourself?"

Since he doesn't answer, I guess our conversation is over. He does that. He just crawls into his little Scorpio shell. No use ever trying to force him out of it. Best just to get some space and come back later.

"Hey, I've got to go to work. I'll see you later, okay?" I say.

"Thanks for the mangos," he says.

My last appointment of the day is Barry White Guy, whom I just adore. As usual, the first twenty minutes, he talks like Barry White mixed with East Coast expressions like, "Oh, yeah, that's worth the price of admission right there." During the last forty minutes, the only noise he makes is extremely loud snoring.

After I finish, Barry White Guy's wife comes in to say hello. Often, I work on her after her husband; that's how I've come to think of her as Hip Problem Lady. She's obviously dressed for a night out, not a massage. "We're going to the Cromwells' tonight," she tells me. I'm surprised and sympathetic. Everyone knows the Cromwells haven't been getting along, to say the least. The look on my face must have revealed my thoughts.

"I know, everyone thought they were doomed. They went to this woman down valley named Martina who claims to 'know the ways of love.' She's from Brazil or somewhere. I don't know what she did, but it worked."

"Hm. I know a couple who could probably use her number if you have it."

Pearl on Beatrice and Saving the Farm

BEATRICE AND I had actually gone to school together; she was four years my junior though. I don't believe we ever conversed until Henry died.

Beatrice was a CPA who worked with Leanne, one of the first female lawyers in South Dakota. Together, they started a consulting business called "Bought the Farm" to help widows straighten out bookkeeping, tax, or legal problems that would otherwise cause women to lose their homes. It needs to be said that Beatrice was a true visionary.

Our farm was the worst bookkeeping case she had ever seen. She told me straight up I'd need to get a job—a good job—a job traditionally done by men so that it might actually pay a living wage, and then I'd have to come home at night and farm. Selling this crop wouldn't solve my problems alone, but if I didn't sell it, I'd surely lose the farm.

Then she asked me how I'd feel about taking in a boarder.

I was reluctant and told her I supposed it depended on who it was. She explained that both she and her younger brother had been living on their family farm since their parents retired and moved to a small house in town, but recently her brother had found a woman to marry. Beatrice was looking to move out so her brother and his soon-to-be wife could have a normal life on the farm together. She offered me $150 a month. I gratefully accepted.

I was almost unaware I was sharing my house since I was rarely home, but when I was aware of Beatrice's presence, I was infinitely thankful. It was about that time I went to work as sheriff, and harvest was approaching. Beatrice kept my garden alive, made soups out of what was in season, and left them on the stove for me. Each bowl of soup felt like a miracle to me. Yes, I was so exhausted and so hungry all the time that someone else making a bowl of soup for me was taken as a sign from God to carry on.

I brought in that corn crop by myself under the light of the moon and on my days off. Still needing money, I planted a winter crop, semolina. I didn't have the machinery to bring in the semolina, so I had to contract out that harvest. Still, I made a profit. It was little more than marginal, but every little bit helped. I sold the giant corn combine at the auction for less than what it was worth, but enough to pay off the balance on it plus a little to start my spring crop.

I consulted with Phil before starting my spring crop, knowing a good choice could help me save the farm, whereas a bad choice could cost me the farm. Phil approved of sunflowers, though he also liked wheat. I intended to plant half of each and play it safe, but I don't know. I just had a strong feeling about sunflowers, so I gambled everything on them. It was a good thing I did. Wheat plummeted that summer and sunflowers skyrocketed. I made $400,000 off that crop, enough to keep the bank off my back for the year, and just a little short of what I needed to pay off the mortgage. For the first time in a long time, I knew I was going to be okay.

Beatrice made Miss Fern and me a chocolate cake that night. It was utterly indulgent. Miss Fern brought a bottle of champagne. We ate and drank and tapped and drank and tapped and drank and tapped and drank. And we laughed.

Phil on Lesson Four

"GOOD MORNING, PHIL." Al sips his scotch.

I immediately assemble my chanter.

"In no time at all, you will be piping in the annual Trailing of the Sheep Parade with Junior and me. Of course, this involves buying a pair of shoes for this purpose and this purpose only. The parade officials have placed us behind the sheep because our placement in front of them inhibited their willingness to go forward two years ago. So we follow the sheep now. Heads up, Phil—once you step in sheep urine and feces, there is no restoring your shoes to their original odor. It is one distinct and tenacious aroma. One just keeps his parade shoes in the garage for the remainder of the year, unless he is living in the garage, in which case, one must find a home for them outside where rodents will not nest in them. Now last year, the parade officials, in their infinite wisdom, not only placed us behind the sheep, but behind the horses as well. It would seem the parade officials that year were not the sharpest tools in the shed. We began to blow, and a large black Morgan by the name of Dusty Joe began to look for weak spots in the crowd. He found one. Two people were hospitalized. Playing the pipes is a heavy cross to bear sometimes, Phil. And now, let us commence to play the greatest song ever written."

The fruits of my diligent practice impress Al. "Phil, I have never allowed a student to spend less than six months on the chanter alone, but I do believe that next week, you will be ready to play the goose. Exceptional, Phil."

Play the Goose? It is so sweet to taste success again. I cannot wait to feel the bag under my arm. I will not rest until all the drones are uncorked and the sound of the pipes reverberates through my every cell.

Before I start up the ridge today, I take out my mini-tablet, turn back the page where I log Anna's menopausal behaviors, and make a new chart. Two weeks ago, I took three hours and forty minutes for the hike up and back; last week, three hours and twenty minutes. I draw a neat bar graph, using the envelope from my bank statement to help me make straight lines with my mechanical pencil. Today, my goal is three hours and ten minutes or less.

I wish I could think of a way to quantify my success with the bagpipes so I could graph my progress. Evidence of progress is needed now more than ever.

Olive on Anxiety Attacks

TODAY'S THE DAY, the big move. Before work, I pack the very last of my belongings into my car. I stand in the doorway and look one last time into the place where Matt and I lived. It looks just as it did when we moved in. We were so full of hope and excitement then. We really thought we would stay together forever. I'm a totally different person now —so little hope. I shut the door and lock it behind me. That chapter is closed. My heart aches.

As I reach for the handle of the bank's front door, I stop. I hesitate. I reach again and hold the handle for a moment. My heart races. Is this pregnancy hormones or a panic attack? Can anyone tell me what a panic attack feels like? I pull the door open a little. The way it rotates on the hinge reminds me of a letter on "Wheel of Fortune" . . . a letter beginning to spell out an answer in my life I don't like. What would happen if Vanna just stopped turning the letters? What would happen if she just sat there and refused to do her job? Would the answer to the puzzle still reveal itself? I look at the bench next to the door and consider just sitting there all day instead of going inside. If I don't go in, I can't go home; Dad would never understand this.

What would happen if Vanna just walked right off "Wheel of Fortune" and onto "Jeopardy"? True, not really much for her to do on "Jeopardy." Is "The Price is Right" still on? What if Vanna just dropped out of the world of game shows altogether? What if she wanted to work outdoors for a while? What if she at least wanted a window? What if she wanted to trade in her gowns for overalls?

When the thought of overalls crosses my mind, I know. For the first time, I have a vision of my future that I like. My heart still races, and my breathing is still shallow and laborious, but I know. Just knowing is huge.

I slowly start walking back to my car, looking back several times at the building with almost no windows and all those pictures of children on the desks inside. I look at the building's institutional lines . . . structured, functional, confining brick.

James walks toward me from his car on his way to the glass entrance. I wonder what his puzzle begins to spell out every time he opens that door. "You're going the wrong way, Olive!" he jokes.

"Um . . . I forgot something," I stammer. Yeah, Chief, I forgot my life. I'm just going to go get it.

I get in my car and just start driving. I listen to the Indigo Girls because their strong voices strengthen me. I sing along.

The sound of my own strong voice makes me hopeful that somewhere in me is a well of strength yet untapped, but available when I need it. I definitely need it.

The road to South Dakota used to seem so long when I was a teenager. Down out of this valley, through the old lava fields, around the Palisades, over Teton Pass, through the endless dry mountain landscape of Wyoming, past some Badlands and into the Black Hills, which, though dry, always seemed so lush after hours in Wyoming. Yes, this trip used to seem like forever, but this time it's too short.

How am I ever going to tell my parents I'm having a baby? God, this is going to break their hearts. My stomach sinks. This isn't the life they wanted for me. I can't even imagine how disappointed in me Dad is going to be. I try to imagine holding my baby, holding my baby I love so much, and facing my parents' scorn. Will the baby pick up on their conflicted feelings? Will the baby pick up on my shame? Probably. Maybe it would be better if they never had to know. My baby and I could just live in our mud house and grow our own food without anyone judging us. Yeah, that's not very realistic. I wonder if my stress is harming my baby. Probably. Will telling my parents about the baby just create more stress, or will not telling them, but worrying about the day when I'll have to, actually create the most stress? It just kills me that I'm going to bring this innocent little person into the world, into our family, and my parents aren't going to be happy to meet her. I can picture myself having just survived labor and childbirth, holding my precious child, feeling scared but proud, maybe even momentarily hopeful, and then my parents walk into the room. I see my situation through their eyes and I wilt. I want to disappear.

What am I going to say to Grandma? How am I going to explain this? Will she be ashamed of me? Will she cry? I don't think I could handle it if she cried. Maybe she'll understand. Probably not. Things are so different than they were in her time. I don't even understand my own generation and this time in history, so really, how could I expect her to?

At times in my drive, I feel a sinking in my stomach as the permanency and magnitude of my situation hit me. Sometimes I'm slammed by grief for the experience I always hoped pregnancy and motherhood would be, but which it's not going to be. In my dream, I had a loving husband and a comfortable house. He likes to touch my belly and rest his ear to it to see if he can hear anything. In my dream, my husband holds my hand during labor and delivery. In my dream, the three of us snuggle in bed together. My husband and I stare at our baby in awe and amazement. What overwhelms me in real life now merely gives my husband and me a sense of wonder in my dream. But that's all it was—a dream. It's not going to be my life. It's hard to let it go. I liked it. I liked how it looked and how it felt. I visualized it, and it didn't materialize.

Pearl on Independence Day

I DON'T KNOW how Beatrice sleeps through Dean's fireworks. God damn that Dean. I can't sleep. I hope he runs out soon. I pace the house restlessly.

A light catches my eye. Has Dean lit his field on fire? I look out the window—headlights. Headlights in my driveway this time of night? I peek through a window and watch the car approach. Out of state plates. I see the silhouette of a slim woman with a ponytail getting out of the car as I step out on the front porch.

"Grandma Pearl?" she calls out.

"Olive!" I exclaim quietly enough not to wake Beatrice. "Come! Come sit a spell!"

Olive and I rock in chairs on the front porch, watching Dean's fireworks. "Happy Independence Day," I wish her. I watch the flag on my front porch wave. "I love this country. What do you love most about this country?" I ask.

"The land," she answers. "And you?"

"Guns." Yes, I really love guns. Guns made this country

great.

"Grandma, I drove out here to talk to you about something."

"Oh?" I act as if I hadn't considered this, when really, of course I had.

"I want to farm here with you," she blurts out, and looks at me the way a drowning person looks at a life raft, an odd mix of desperation and hope. I wonder what has put her in this state.

I study her hard. "Why?" I finally ask.

"I'm at the bank," she pauses, struggling for words, "and I'm looking around . . . and . . ." Her eyes begin to water some. "I'm going to have a baby . . ." She shakes her head and looks down, then exhales and begins again. "I realized I didn't have to participate in a system that keeps people in jobs they hate because they're entrapped by debt. I don't want to hand my child over to someone else to raise because I'm entrapped by debt and have to go to work. And I don't really want to work entrapping other people in debt." She waits just a few seconds for me to say something, but I don't, so she continues. "I don't want to spend my whole life running in circles. I want to live a good life. I want to raise my child." I want to ask about the father, but decide her presence here is really all I need to know.

I rest my head on the back of my rocker and look off into the sky. "What do you want to grow?" I ask. If she says corn, she's out.

"Minor oil seeds," she replies. "Demand is high for

minor oils. Canola, flax and safflower . . . right now safflower is bringing in the most."

"Yeah, lately sunflower is down around $4.90 per hundred weight, but since I can insure the crop with a loan covering $9.30 per hundred weight, I've been selling the crop and taking $4.40 loan deficiency payment. You're right. Safflower is up around $12.50 now. Canola is around $9.50. You've done your research." I take a moment and study her proudly. What a good girl. She might be one of the farmers who actually make it. "Okay," I say with a nod and a smile. Oh, there goes Olive, crying like that, looking so relieved. What, did she think I was going to throw her to the dogs? Must be those pregnant hormones making her emotional.

Pregnant. It needs to be said I hated being pregnant. It was this time of year when I was almost nine months pregnant. God, I hated that, all hot, sitting right here and really sweating where my pregnant belly rested on my legs. Yes, I remember sitting here, shucking peas, and the smell of those peas nauseating me. I never knew peas had much of a smell until I was pregnant. Amazing what a woman can smell when she's pregnant. You know, I still can't eat peas to this day.

Wow, Olive is pregnant.

Yeah, when I think about being pregnant, I think about peas.

My God, I'm going to be a great-grandmother. I'll have to ask Beatrice if I look old enough to be a great-grandmother.

Olive on Fathers and the Power of Understanding

"Hey, Olive."

"Hey, Beatrice." Beatrice sits next to me on the porch, straightens out her knitting, and starts up. Her knitting needles click against each other in a soothing rhythm.

"Your grandma tells me you're going to be staying here." She smiles, and I feel welcomed.

"Yep," I nod. I don't know what else to say to that.

"And she tells me you're going to have a baby . . ."

I pause because it feels strange to hear it. I take a deep breath. "Yep," I say and nod. Not much else to say about that either.

"You know I'm the last person to insist that every woman needs a man, but I'm just curious—what about the father?"

"I don't think this baby has a father."

"Oh really? Immaculate conception?" I can't tell if she's joking or mocking.

"No. It boils down to how you define father," I explain.

Beatrice is quiet while she considers this. I continue to wait for her to say something, but she doesn't, so I continue. "To me, a father is a man in a child's life who's totally dedicated to that child. He's part of a *family*, and actively contributes to it. He's someone the child can count on. This kind of father is an amazing person—a true father. A true father deserves the rights he has by law, but the problem I see when I look around is that countless men are calling themselves fathers, when in truth, they're not, you know? They don't deserve the title of 'father' and they don't deserve the rights entitled to them by law."

"So what do you call the man that contributed to the creation of a child?" Beatrice asks, curious.

"I don't know . . . I haven't figured that one out yet . . . All I know right now is that the man who donated one cell to this child isn't someone I'd want to hand my child over to on weekends or holidays—it would kill me, Beatrice—I could never trust him to know or care about the baby's needs. He doesn't appear to be a stable force. Frankly, I don't see a lot of father potential. Am I supposed to ignore that and just hope he'll eventually come around? And in the meantime entrust my baby's life with him just because the law wants to give him those rights? I can't do that, Beatrice—I can't take that chance. How would that possibly be fair to the baby?"

Beatrice looks sadly at her knitting. "These are complicated times."

Beatrice's understanding means more to me than she'll ever know.

Forrest on Scavenging Materials and Café idiots

OH, WHAT A gold mine! The scrap pile at this building site is loaded! I look at one of the laborers and gesture to ask him if I can raid it. He lets me know it's there for the taking. I pick out the largest pieces first and put them in a neat pile. I make a second pile to pick up later. I notice some nails on the ground and put them in my pockets.

On my way home, I walk past The Daily Grind, the café where people prefer to eat outside. I survey the tables. I have no use for coffee, but the rest of that muffin looks good. I set down my pile of wood, and go scavenge. I put the muffin in my pocket with the nails. At another table is a half a bowl of soup and a couple bites of sandwich. I drink the rest of the soup and pop the sandwich in my mouth. All the while, I'm overhearing this conversation, half of which is in a familiar male voice.

"So I was like, screw the system, you know? But she was

so into that fear-based mentality that she couldn't even hear me. She just kept coming up with all these 'but what if' questions."

The woman's voice replied, "Right on. People don't get the power of visualization. Like if you picture bad things happening, you probably need insurance, but you don't need insurance if you just don't visualize bad things. I don't have insurance, because I don't need it. I just visualize myself healthy and safe. I don't use birth control either. I just don't picture myself pregnant, you know? I just don't give into the fear."

"Wow," the male voice responds. "You *totally* get where I'm coming from. I just don't want to participate in that fear-based system anymore."

I turn to go back to pick up my scrap lumber and look in the direction of the familiar voice. It's that guy who doesn't know how to camp. As I walk by them, I break my rule of silence again. "You guys are idiots. You're going to get eaten by a bear and you're going to be a welfare mom. Action is more powerful than thought." I pick up my pace again so I won't have to listen to any more of their painfully stupid ideas.

A half-block later, Jade pulls up next to me on her bike with Aretha in the cart. "Hey, Forrest, I saw you talking to that guy. Do you know who he is?"

"Some idiot who's been camping out in my direction. He says his name is Matt."

"That's Olive's Matt."

"He's an idiot," I tell her.

"I know. I hope Olive's kid is smarter than him."

"Lightning Bob told me intelligence is carried on the mitochondrial DNA, which is only inherited from your mother, so there's reason to hope. His new girlfriend's form of birth control is visualization though, so I don't have much hope for the child he's probably going to conceive with her before he gets eaten by a bear."

"He's going to be eaten by a bear?" she asks.

"Yeah, probably next spring."

"Well, Olive won't have to lie about her baby having no father then." She eyes my armload. "What are you up to?"

"Mom's birthday present."

"Oh?"

I smile and nod.

"All right. Later, gator," she says.

"Later, gator," I reply and watch her pedal away. Then I glance back at the idiots. On one hand, I'm the last person who should judge anyone, but on the other hand, ever since I had to ask myself what kind of person would shoot a kid's dog, I just see idiots everywhere.

Olive on the Thunderellas

GRANDMA PEARL, BEATRICE, and I were the last to arrive that night. The infamous Thunderellas had already begun to drink their wine. I hadn't seen these women in over fifteen years.

Hazel had not changed. One look took me back to sitting on her lap at Grandpa's funeral. I played with her long, black braids, tying them together four times under her chin, holding them over my own head to see what I would look like with her lovely braids. I wrapped them around my neck like a scarf. After the service, while people ate finger food and talked about Grandpa, she continued to hold me on her lap, telling me Lakota stories until I fell asleep. She is not technically my aunt, but I've always called her "Auntie." She's earned it, after all.

"Olive Oil!" She beams at me through her thick coke-bottle glasses. She's wearing a full denim skirt and a black T-shirt with a painting of a wolf on it.

"Auntie!" I call to her as I make my way over for a hug.

"Welcome home, Olive," Fiona, a generation younger than the others, greets me warmly. She is angular and earthy with small tortoise shell glasses and a long salt and pepper Spanish braid. She wears sweatpants and a T-shirt that reads, "Against abortion? Get a vasectomy." Mom always spoke of Fiona with great respect. She moved to Washington, D.C. in the late sixties and early seventies to march for peace and women's rights. Eventually she went to law school so she could start bailing herself out of jail. Yes, sometimes she did more than just march. She often handcuffed herself to things like doors of police cars. Mom always told us that we owed a lot of our freedoms and opportunities to women like her.

"Fiona. So good to see you." I hope she hears the respect in my voice.

"How was your drive?" Fiona asks.

"Good."

"I hate driving," Grandma Pearl interjects. "On our last car trip, I got that road rage so bad, I had to pull over and say, 'Beatrice, you drive!'"

I can picture that.

"Sparkling cider for you," Beatrice says and hands me a glass.

"Well, ladies, should we begin?" Grandma Pearl prompts. Beatrice and I scramble to change our shoes. "Let's warm up with eight shuffles to the front, eight to the side, six to the back and ball change, switch feet. Ready?" We warm up our ankles with this exercise. "Should we just get to it now?" Yes, yes, everyone agrees.

While Grandma Pearl puts on "Annie Get Your Gun" (that had to be her idea), Fiona asks me, "So Olive, what brings you back here?"

"Geez, Fiona, don't ask her that!" Grandma Pearl calls from the other corner of the grange hall. "She left her boyfriend, hates her old job and she's pregnant!" she explains as if I weren't there.

"Was your biological clock ticking?" asks Hazel.

"What's with this biological clock thing?" Fiona asks. "My generation didn't have clocks. We were so grateful for contraception and how it made motherhood a choice. I didn't know anyone with a clock. Now, suddenly everyone has a clock."

"You have *no* regrets?" Hazel asks her.

"Not that kind," Fiona tries to joke. "Seriously though, I remember helping a friend by watching her baby so she could take a shower in the middle of the day. A shower. *Aunt* Fiona has a great ring to it. That's enough for me."

"I had a clock," Beatrice announces. "I just kept hitting the snooze button until it finally stopped going off."

"But on the whole, don't you think there's something going on culturally? I mean it's sort of like there was no anorexia when there wasn't enough food. Now everyone's anorexic or into fad diets. Now women have reproductive choice and suddenly everyone has a biological clock. What's with that? I think the media is brainwashing women!" Fiona proclaims.

"Hundredth Monkey kind of thing?" Grandma Pearl asks.

"Exactly," Fiona answers.

"Interesting," Grandma Pearl replies.

I don't say anything.

"Okay, remember, flap-heel-heel, flap-heel-heel, eight times, then scuff-heel-toe-heel, scuff-heel-toe-heel, kick-ball-change, stomp-toe-hop-turn, stomp-toe-hop-turn. Let's try it that far," Grandma Pearl says. She puts the music on and I can't help thinking about Jade and how she'd cringe hearing these show tunes. I'm with her on that. I really do hate them.

When the music stops, Hazel gently says, "It's okay to want a baby."

"I wasn't saying it wasn't okay," Fiona says. "I was suggesting every woman should be clear about what her true desires are and what is the collective hysteria."

I look at my shoes and experiment with making different noises with the toe and heel taps. "I didn't do this on purpose," I say quietly. Is this a discussion we can really have or are all our worlds so different we can't even begin to understand one another's perspective?

"You know, Olive, one day when you're in your fifties, you'll just make peace with whatever you did or didn't do. You'll just make peace with it. I don't know if it helps for me to say that now or not," Beatrice says.

"Nothing helps when you're her age!" Grandma Pearl shouts. "Okay, now, anyone need a refill?" Yes, yes, everyone says and refills their glasses. "Next part: time step, stop, stomp-shuffle-ball-change, shuffle-ball-change."

I hope that someone will bring up some gossip or

someone else's issues, but I know better; nothing is ever as interesting as a single pregnant woman.

"So why'd you leave your boyfriend?" Fiona asks.

"Fiona!" Grandma Pearl scolds. "Give her a break! I'd have left too if my partner wanted me to live in a tipi!"

"Living in a tipi is no fun in the winter," Hazel says. "Especially if you're pregnant. You spend a lot of time throwing up in the snow. You get cold. You come inside, burn a fire to warm up and it's smoky even with the smoke hole open. I don't like tipis anymore. They're pretty to look at, but I like my house."

"What kind of man in this day and age would drag a pregnant partner into that?" Grandma Pearl scoffs.

"Careful," Fiona says. Grandma Pearl is infamous for saying things that come out wrong.

"Okay, from the beginning," Grandma Pearl instructs with her glass of wine. "Flap-heel-heel, flap-heel-heel . . ."

When I tap, I only think about my feet, and it's a relief to redirect my mind to a task other than figuring out my future. It's a relief to turn off that analytical part of my mind and just focus on the motor skills part.

Jade on the Entity of Marriage

AFTER I RUN into Forrest, I ride five blocks out of my way and stop by the parental units' house. Instead of going in the door, Aretha and I walk around to the backyard. I find Mom lying on her back in the grass, wearing black sweatpants with three small white stripes up the sides, and a black short sleeved T-shirt. I take a moment to assess whether Mom is unconscious or dozing, but figure the position she's in indicates she did not fall, rather planted herself there on purpose.

I lie down next to her, while Aretha sniffs her, then lies down between Mom and me.

Mom opens one eye, and looks over. "Hi, Sweet Pea."

"Hi, Mom. Hey, I know what goes on between you and Dad is none of my business. I just want to offer this. One of my clients says there's a woman down valley named Martina who has helped several couples in the valley."

"Jade, dear, I don't think counseling is going to solve our problems."

"She helped the Cromwells, Mom. You know we were all

sure their marriage was doomed."

"The *Cromwells?*"

"The Cromwells," I affirm.

"What does this woman down valley do?" Mom asks.

"I don't know, Mom. All my client told me is that she knows the ways of love." Then I dig into my pocket. "She gave me her phone number." I reach over and set the crumpled piece of paper on Mom's belly.

Mom does nothing with the paper. "Every time I hear someone use the phrase 'save my marriage,' I always picture a sinking ship," she states. "S.O.S.! Save our ship!"

"Yeah, that phrase makes me think that person is much more in love with the idea of being married than with their spouse." I study the aspen and cottonwood leaves shimmering in the breeze above us. "And there's something about people talking about their marriage in that way that I find creepy, like their marriage is a third entity. I guess it is. I always picture this big ugly ghost standing between them, only it's a ghost they created, if that makes sense."

"I picture bars, like a self-imposed imprisonment," Mom blurts out. "I probably shouldn't have said that. Is it appropriate to share this kind of thing with a daughter?" She tries to make a joke out of it. "You know, like if I was just dating your dad, I would go home when he started in with the graphs."

I give a courtesy laugh, but I know Mom was serious about feeling trapped.

"If I ever get married, I just hope that it can always be about me and him. I hope that I always care about whether he's happy instead of caring about whether my marriage is good. Likewise, I hope he offers me the same courtesy. I wonder if two people can have a marriage without creating the big ugly ghost. I mean, sure, the ghost is euphoric in the beginning, so the couple keeps feeding it and feeding it. But like everything, it has a light side and a dark side. One day it rears its ugly head and by then it's bigger than the both of them. I wonder if a couple can kill the ghost after they've created it? Energetically, can you starve it and still be nice to the other person?" *Because, you see, I already have enough entities following me around,* I want to continue, but I don't.

"Years of calling someone 'my husband' or 'my wife' . . . interesting to ponder how calling someone 'my' anything affects your sense of entitlement. Frankly, I don't want to be anyone's anything anymore. I want to be my own whatever-I-am."

"I think about it, about how marriage was originally a contract that helped each person survive better than when they were on their own, but now survival is easier, at least here, and I wonder what the purpose is. In this time and space, is there a more appropriate way to live with one you love?"

"I was thinking about the part where your father and I said, ''til death do us part.' You know, life expectancy was about half of what it is today when that ceremony was invented."

"True. People's teeth would wear out, or they would get a bad infection, maybe have a little childbirth trouble, and like that, check out time is thirty-five, forty years," I say.

"We have three, four more decades added to our contract than the ones who came before us."

"Yeah, you guys got the shaft."

"I heard that in some Eastern culture, that when women hit sixty, they leave their homes and go off to be nuns. That sounds really good to me," says Mom.

"Well, you know Mom, no one is stopping you from becoming a nun. We'd come and visit you from time to time if you wanted us to."

"Thanks honey, I'll consider that," she says, but she won't. For starters, she's not Catholic. "Good talk, Jade," Mom says to close the topic.

"Good talk, Mom," I say as I stand up.

Aretha sniffs Mom's ear, which makes Mom laugh. Mom pets her and pushes her head away at the same time. Then Aretha turns and trots to catch up with me.

When I arrive home to get ready for work, there's a note on my door: "Movie Friday? —Josh." I take the note inside and do a little dance. I write a note to leave on his door since I'll be working when he comes home: "You bet. —Jade."

Anna on Olive's Call Home

"MOM? I'M AT Grandma's."

"Grandma's?" I didn't see that coming.

"I just sort of freaked out going to work yesterday. I got back in my car and kept driving. I realized I wanted to be a farmer."

"A farmer?" I *really* didn't see this coming.

"Yes, I'm going to grow minor seed oil like safflower."

"Safflower?"

"And I'm going to build a cob house on Grandma's land. Cob is clay, sand, concrete, and straw. Mud."

"Mud?" Fascinating. One day she leaves for work in a suit, and the next day, she's building a house of mud. Forgive me for not seeing that one coming either.

"I wanted to thank you and Dad for offering to take me in and keep me from slipping through the cracks."

"Of course . . ."

"Grandma wants to talk to you," Olive tells me.

My mother never talks on the phone. She still thinks

long-distance is the equivalent of five dollars a minute instead of five cents. This must be important.

"Anna?"

"Yes."

"Anna? I can't talk long. I think you should come out here for your birthday." Something in her voice tells me there's more to it than that. Her suggestion sounds like an order.

South Dakota . . . "I suppose I could go." Really, what am I going to miss here? Receiving a Shop Vac from Phil? "Okay," I agree.

"Bring your tap shoes."

My tap shoes. I had forgotten about them. The Thunderellas might be more than I can take right now, but maybe returning to the place where it all began will be helpful somehow. "Okay. I'll see you tomorrow. I love you, Mom."

I pack my canvases and paint. My conversation with Jade inspired me to paint a raisin in prison. Maybe I'll even collage some bar graphs in there. Maybe the bars in the graph will be my prison bars.

I also pack a few clothes. I really don't have any good South Dakota clothes. I throw some toiletries into a bag, jot a note for Phil and go.

Driving out of the mountains and through the lava fields, I get it why Olive did this. It feels good. Wide open spaces. I've been needing some wide open spaces. Freedom. If you think about it, a valley is just a giant rut. I've been stuck in a giant rut.

I start to wonder what my mother isn't telling me about what is going on in South Dakota, but I stop myself. Why, really? It doesn't do any good.

Instead I just focus on the infinite possibilities of a big, blue sky and the open highway. I could skip going to Summerville where clearly some secret problem lurks, and just keep going. I could drive and never go home.

Phil on the Two Cardinal Rules of Gift Giving

I HIT THE button for the garage door opener and listen to the noise it makes. The garage door opener sounds a lot like the bagpipes. Actually, it sounds better than when I play the bagpipes. I sort of hum along with it. I get in my car and drive to Al's.

"Has your rehearsing put the final nail in the coffin of your marriage, Phil?" he asks.

I chuckle, but don't answer. "Her birthday is tomorrow," I say to divert the subject.

"Should you care to prolong your stay in the institution of marriage, Phil, you'll want to abide by the two cardinal rules of gift-giving. Are you familiar with these rules, Phil?"

"Regrettably not," I answer.

Al pours himself some scotch. "If you had, your marriage might not be in the toilet today."

I raise my eyebrows in lieu of a reply.

"Cardinal rule number one: No husband shall giveth his

wife any gift that has a power cord. Cardinal rule number two: No husband shall giveth his wife any gift associated directly or indirectly with cleaning in any way. Very important, Phil. Spread the word."

Al gives me the bag with the drones corked. This is a very big moment for me. I try to concentrate on his instruction, but my heart feels heavy. I'm remembering the vacuum I gave Anna our first Christmas. I didn't know what that look on her face meant then. It meant I broke her heart. Another year, I gave her a Dust-Buster. Stupid. Al's right.

"Phil, your heart isn't in it today. I can tell you are not fully concentrating. Are you still thinking about the countless small appliances you gave your wife over the years?"

"Vacuums," I answer.

"Dear Jesus," he mutters. "Not many gifts violate both cardinal rules simultaneously, Phil. How is it you are still married at all?"

"I don't know," I reply. I really don't.

"Well, you've got about six hours to research what your wife truly desires and take action, barring any mandatory special orders, in which case you may have dropped the ball for the last time, given the bagpipe factor."

"I think I better go," I tell Al, working up to a panic. I give him thirty bucks, still money well-spent, and drive off.

I start to the library to research potential gifts in *Consumer Reports,* but have no idea what I would research, so I change my course. I turn left instead of right at the light and go to Jade's condominium.

"Hey, Dad, come in," she says and offers to make me some wacky juice with seaweed in it. No thanks. Her dog sniffs me and then, satisfied, lies down. I look for a place to sit. Her house is a pigsty. I opt to stand.

"Jade, I'm in a bit of a hurry," I explain. "Your mother's birthday is tomorrow and I don't know what to get her. What do women really want?"

"That's easy," she says, and I feel relief already with my solution so close at hand. "A case of Annie's Tuscany Italian salad dressing, a skateboard, a drum set, and a deluxe plastic Viking hat with fake fur around the horns. Oh, wait, maybe that's just me."

Crap. She's going to be no help at all. I'm wasting precious time listening to bogus advice.

"Okay, hang in there, Dad, we'll think this through. We could make a rubric listing her interests down the side and potential gifts across the top and then assign points to potential gifts based on how well they accommodate her interests," she suggests. I can't tell if she's making fun of me.

"All she does is paint," I say.

"Then go home, look at the brand and type of paint she uses and go get her more of it. Maybe some canvases too."

"She can get that for herself. I want to get her something only I can get her."

"Okay . . ." I keep waiting for her to continue, but she doesn't. There is a really long pause. Finally she says, "Think back a long, long time ago, back before we were born, back when you were still in love. Wait, were you ever in love?"

she asks.

What? "Yes," I reply, somewhat insulted.

"Try to remember some detail about those good times . . . an activity, a place, even a smell, and figure out a gift that will recapture that."

"Okay." Surely I can do that. Problem solved.

"Good luck, Dad," Jade says as she sees me out the door. "Just don't get her anything practical!" she shouts as I'm halfway to the car.

Not practical and related to the era when we were still in love. That narrows it down. I drive toward the house, not knowing where else to go, and hoping something in the house will trigger my memory. On the way though, I pass a schoolyard and . . . Bingo! I detour to the hardware store.

When I arrived home to an empty house, I was at first relieved. Coast was clear to assemble the gift. Then I saw it. The note. "Phil, I've gone away probably just for a few days, but I don't know for sure when I'll be back." What if she doesn't come back?

I decide to act as if she is coming back. I take the materials from the hardware store out of the trunk and go into the backyard. I study the old cottonwood. There's a tree house there. I wonder how long that's been there? Did the girls build that? Where was I? Who knows. I make the ends of slip knots and throw them over a good branch of the old cottonwood. I slide the ends of the ropes through loops, reinforced with pieces of old garden hose, and pull the ends so that the loops ascend to the branch. I realize I'm going to need to drill holes in the board. I go into the garage, though I know I never purchased a drill. I was hoping maybe someone else had over the years. No such luck.

I pick up the phone and dial. "Jade, do you have a drill?" I ask when she answers.

"Dad, you do realize you have no margin of error here, right? The clock is ticking."

"Not so. I came home to an empty house and a note from your mother telling me she's not sure when she'll be back. I'm not sure if my marriage is over or not. If it's not, I'm hoping this gift will save it." I mean for this to be a joke, but the instant I hear myself say it, I realize there's too much truth in it for it to be funny.

"You know, Dad, I think it's really interesting to listen to you talk about your marriage like it's a possession, like it's bologna finally rotting in the fridge. You seem so much more concerned with not losing this possession than you are about Mom and her happiness. If I were you, I would be concerned that Mom is hurting. She's hurting so much, she's been sleeping on a lawn chair. She's hurting so much, she left. She's hurting so much she can't even talk to you about it. Are you even aware of this? Because you don't acknowledge it if you are. She's hurting, Dad. If you're concerned about her, instead of about saving *your marriage,* the marriage would take care of itself. A marriage is between two *people,* Dad. Are you married to her or are you married to your marriage? Because you sound married to your marriage."

"Jesus, Jade, I just asked you for a damn drill." Clearly, all women are psycho, even my daughter. Who is she to spout off unsolicited advice about marriage when she's not even married and knows nothing about it?

"I have no drill, Dad. Sorry."

"Thank you. That's all I needed to know."

"No, you also needed to know that wives and marriages aren't possessions; they're miracles." Then she hung up. What is it with women that they always need to have the last word?

I return to the backyard, grab my board, get back into the car, and drive around while I consider my options. I might just have to buy a drill. I go to Sears where I can get a Craftsman drill, which, like all Craftsman tools, has a lifetime guarantee.

After I make my major purchase, I return home and use my new tool. Sure enough, it's everything Craftsman said it would be. What a good purchase! I slip the ends of the ropes through holes in a small plank, then knot them securely. Next, I tie a piece of twine to the rope, disassemble a bouquet of carnations, and wrap the string around and around and around each rope, holding the carnations in place. Carnations last a long time you know. They're the best flower value for your dollar.

Before Anna and I part ways, I want to tell her something—something for which there are no words—something that can only be said with a swing. After attaching a birthday card, which contains a gift certificate for unlimited pushing, I pull back the empty swing and let it go.

jade on What Happens When You ignore the Signs

ON NIGHT FOUR, Alien Guy plays some Cher album from the late eighties—the one with "If I Could Turn Back Time" on it. It physically hurts me to listen to it. Grace hates it, too.

Aretha and I wait in the kitchen while Alien Guy gets on the table. I take a mental inventory of the contents of his kitchen. More plastic plates in the garbage. "So Garth, what's with all the disposable dishes?" I had to ask finally.

"I don't like to do dishes," Alien Guy responds.

"I can relate to that, but can't you at least use paper?"

"Um, no. I have to eat steak every night because I don't have the enzymes to digest vegetables, and steak knives cut through paper plates."

It was in that moment that I could no longer tolerate him. I could no longer see him as a child and feel maternal toward him as I did with my other clients. My maternal vibe is the key to feeling disgust for no one and no one's body. His unapologetic confession to disposable plate abuse broke my good vibe, and for the third time in my eight years of practice, a client disgusted me. I'd had it. I'd had it with his painful music, I'd had it with his serenades, I'd had it with his naked lady paintings, I'd had it with his toenail fungus, and I'd had it with the smell like something was rotting in his colon. I could take no more.

"I'm sorry. You'll have to find someone else to work on you tomorrow," I announce.

I watch the clock throughout the whole massage. I figure I make a dollar twenty-five a minute before tip, so every time the minute hand moves, I think, *That's another dollar twenty-five,* and it makes me feel better. When my hour with Alien Guy is up, I rejoice.

In the truck, I put on Sly and The Family Stone so Grace will come back. "Grace, what happened in there? I mean he's just a pathetic guy."

"Mmm, girl, you don't go falling into that trap. You pity him and he slimes you. He was tryin' to steal some of your core energy, girl. He even told you that. He told you he has you over because he likes women touching him and you went back. Ick, girl. You may have given him a legitimate professional massage in the physical realm, but in the psychic realm, he treated you like a whore, and you didn't even know what hit you. Now you sing with me and let's forget that rotten-ass man."

Pearl on Dean's Cows and Big Announcements

THERE THEY ARE again, trampling my young sunflowers—Dean's cows. That ignorant, no-good tapeworm. I know he's trying to push my buttons. Well, push this, Dean.

Beatrice, Olive and I solemnly march to the field like special agents. Rule number one: When your neighbor's cattle keep appearing in your field, do not, under any circumstances, correct the mistake for him. Correct it only for you.

As the sun sets, I open the other gate, the one to the neighboring Hildebrand pasture, and then Olive, Beatrice and I herd the cows through and shut the gate. We quietly give each other high fives. Dean can deal with Rod now. Rod's a good man and all, but I wouldn't want to cross him. Mark my words—just the first or second time Dean's cattle get into Rod's pasture, Dean will fix his fences and make sure it doesn't happen again. I know this is wrong, but I do secretly hope Dean gets an ass-kicking for this, or at the very least some kind of emasculating public humiliation.

The girls and I walk back, then sit on the back porch to enjoy the rest of the sunset. Olive brings us lemonade. We are quiet and pleased with ourselves.

"It must be Anna," I say as we hear the crackle of tires on gravel. We all get up to go greet her.

Olive takes a deep breath.

Beatrice takes Olive's hand and gives it a reassuring squeeze. "No matter what happens, you're going to be okay," Beatrice whispers to her. I love Beatrice for that.

"Hey, everybody!" Anna half-heartedly exclaims as she gets out of her car. Maybe she's tired from the drive or maybe she's trying to convince herself she's happy to be here. It needs to be said, she always was a difficult one to read.

"Come here and give your mother a hug."

"Hey, Mom," Olive greets her. They hug.

"Olive, it's been such a long time!" Anna jokes dryly.

"Anna, we were just having some lemonade on the back porch. Are you hungry? Can we make you something to eat? We have some leftover meatloaf we could heat up," Beatrice offers.

"Thanks . . . no . . . I already ate, but some lemonade sounds great." Anna pops her trunk and I grab her suitcase. "Mom, no, really, I can handle it." She snatches it from me.

"Suit yourself," I tell her. "Make yourself at home."

Anna goes inside to drop her bag, then comes back out to the porch. I get up and pour her a drink, then sit back down next to Beatrice. We look at Olive, waiting for her to tell Anna. She doesn't. Anna eyes Beatrice and me, clearly wondering what's going on. I raise my eyebrows at Olive, directing Anna to look over there.

Finally, Olive breaks the awkward silence. "Happy birthday, Mom—you're going to be a grandmother." Her forced smile goes unreturned.

We all wait for Anna to respond. We wait and wait and wait. Finally Anna says, "So let me get this straight. At a time when you've never needed security more, you leave the father of this child, quit your steady job with good benefits, and come here, where you are uninsured, single, and about to embark on a risky new career. Do you know how many farmers go under each year? Jesus, Olive, you've always been my smart one. I don't understand."

Olive is stunned and speechless, but finally utters, "I expected that from Dad, but I didn't expect that from you." She pulls her knees up to her chest and wraps her arms around her legs.

"Why? Why does that surprise you? I didn't raise you by myself. I didn't stick you in daycare. I made sure you had a mother at home with you and how did I do that? By making sure you had a caring father. He may not always have been there for you in some ways, but he was always there for you in others. You always had food, shelter, medical care, and me. You always knew you had a father who loved you. Will your child have that?"

"No."

Anna stands up and begins pacing. "I bet you can still get your job back at the bank."

"I don't *want* my job back," Olive says quietly, successfully avoiding eye contact.

"Damn it, Olive. You can't afford to leave that job now. And what about Matt? Have you told him?"

"Why would I tell him? Matt is not this child's father." Now Olive looks directly at Anna.

"Is that why you broke up? You were out whoring around?"

"I was *never* unfaithful to Matt."

"Well then, who is this child's father?"

"This child has no father." Olive's voice is surprisingly steady.

"Oh really. Second coming of Christ?" Anna gets sarcastic and mean as her anger grows, but you have to admit, to some degree Olive asked for it.

"No, this child has a sperm donor," Olive explains.

"What? You were artificially inseminated? You got pregnant on purpose?" Anna is really baffled now.

"No, I got pregnant the old fashioned way and no, I didn't plan this," Olive answers.

"How does anyone get pregnant accidentally anymore? Contraception has been invented!" Anna is almost yelling.

"It failed." Olive demystifies this for her.

"So you haven't told Matt."

"Matt isn't the father."

"I'm not stupid, Olive. I can put two and two together. I know Matt must be the father!" Oh, Anna is getting mad now.

"What is a father?" Olive asks her.

"What do you mean 'what is a father?' You know what a father is! You had one! Every child has a father and a mother! It takes two to make a baby!" Yes, I can't remember the last time I saw Anna this mad.

"Really, so that's all you have to do to be a father? Ejaculate? Pardon me, but that sounds more like a sperm donor, and I do not think the identity of a child's sperm donor is important," Olive argues. Oh, this is going to get ugly.

"Really? Is that what you're going to tell your child when he starts asking about his father? 'Sorry honey, you don't have a father; you have a sperm donor whose identity is unimportant'? Beautiful, Olive! That ought to sentence a kid to a lifetime of therapy."

"Well, a lifetime of therapy would be what she would need to begin to recover from being ripped from her mother when she's still on the breast so that her sperm donor could claim his visitation rights. Sorry, Mom, but I'm not going to let that happen. I'll never speak this baby's sperm donor's name again because I'm never letting anyone take her from me. She's mine."

"She's not just yours!" Anna yells.

"She *is.*"

"No, she's not! Matt has a right to know!"

"He doesn't." Olive apparently has had enough. She gets up and walks away, out the dirt road that leads to the fields and to the place where she plans to build her house.

Anna turns to me now, staring hard. "How could you? How could you support such a stupid choice of hers?"

"Maybe you should have asked some more questions before you decided this was stupid," I suggest.

"Maybe you should have considered that just because you don't need a man doesn't mean she doesn't," Anna spits back.

I give her the look, the one that used to stop her in her tracks. Tonight it has no effect.

"What happens when her crops fail and she drags you down with her?" Anna asks, still angry.

"She's done her research. I have full confidence and faith in her," I say.

"I don't need to tell you that farmers with a lot more experience than her are going under," Anna reminds me.

"She's a smart woman. She'll be fine."

"I fail to see that, Mom," Anna snaps and walks off in the opposite direction of Olive, toward the road.

Beatrice turns to me, putting her arm over my shoulders and says, "I think that went *really* well."

"Yeah, me too. I'm so glad we got that out in the open. The air is *so* much clearer now. And I think Anna is going to have her happiest birthday ever." We chuckle at our sarcasm.

"Think I should go after Olive?" she asks. Beatrice is so sweet.

"Nah, let's just give them time and space to cool off. Let's hit the hay," I answer. It's been a long day.

Anna on Swings

WAS MY MARRIAGE to Phil so bad that Olive wants no part of marriage? Is that it? When I thought I was holding it together so well, and I thought that was such an accomplishment, was it really a failure? I must have failed as a mother or Olive would have better sense. I must have failed as a wife or Olive would want what I had, right? Of course I failed. I'm sleeping on a damn lawn chair.

I'm the first to rise this morning. Can you say you've risen when you never really slept? It's my birthday. I think of other birthday mornings I've had in this house. On my ninth, I woke up to a bicycle in my room. That one was magical. I'll never forget the freedom of my first bike ride. I decide to indulge in the feeling of that memory. I slip outside, borrow Mom's bicycle, and sneak off in search of a place I hope will hold some answers for me.

I dig deep into my memory and try to remember how I felt in the beginning with Phil. I try to remember loving him.

I try to remember what attracted me to him in the first place. I remember being in high school. I had exactly two dresses to wear to school and another to wear to church. I hated that, hated being poor as church mice. Phil didn't have a dime, either, when we met, but something about him exuded capableness. I knew that this was a man who would never let his family go without. I didn't know then the extreme to which he would take this. In the beginning, he seemed so taken with me, and I never did know why, but whatever the reason, it seemed everything he did in his professional life, he did as an act of love for me. When did that change? When did he become consumed? In the beginning, I loved receiving his tokens of love. When did tokens of love turn into tokens of guilt—guilt for not being there when it counted? I hated his tokens of guilt. And when did my gratitude turn into resentment? I think about how men are often attracted to a spirited woman, but when they win her heart, the first thing they try to do is change the very thing they were attracted to in the first place—break her spirit and control her. Is my feeling toward my husband any different than that? I was attracted to his ambition in the beginning, only to grow to want to break it in the end. Is that fair? Is this really about fair?

I let my mind drift back, back to when I rode this path last. I used to sneak away on my Schwinn Cruiser to meet Phil when my father was focused on planting or harvesting and my mother was focused on cooking or something. Phil hung long ropes from a branch of the old cottonwood that stood alone in a field near a spring halfway between our houses, and made a swing for me. It would take five full seconds to complete swinging in each direction, the swing was so tall. He would push me, and I would lean way back and look at the leaves, the branches, the sky, and feel a freedom I didn't feel in the atmosphere of my home. The way the air filled my skirt made me feel like more than the dreary women of my hometown. I felt a little wild. Not wild like a woman without her own boundaries. No, I felt wild like a woman without the boundaries imposed on her by others. It was those sessions on the swing, oftentimes in silence, that I felt the sensation of being who I truly was, where I felt my spark, my spunk, my spirit. I loved Phil for that. He was my sanctuary from shame. Time with him strengthened me and revitalized me, so I could go back into my home without my spirit dying. Push, swing forward, swing back, push, swing forward, swing back. Just thinking about it puts me in a meditative state. Gosh, I haven't thought about that in a long time. The wind in my hair, the wind in my skirt, the wind on my feet after I kicked off my Keds, and his hands on my back every ten seconds. Push, swing forward, swing back. Push, swing forward, swing back. Nothing but Phil, the tree, and the sky. Freedom.

At last, I see the cottonwood. I anxiously search for the swing, but I only see a small bit of frayed rope hanging from the branch. I stop and study it. Then I notice the old seat, wood grayed with age on the ground. The only evidence of good times between us, pretty much gone.

Jade on Mud

THE RAIN CALLS out to me. *Come play,* it says.

It is my last life, and though I know I'll enjoy the next dimension, the one where everyone is enlightened—I mean, can you imagine living with only enlightened souls?—I still feel a severing in my heart for all the things I love about Earth. I want to see it all and smell it all, well no, actually only the pleasant smells, and I want to eat lots and lots of candy. Most of all, I want to feel it all one last time. This is why I haven't worn shoes for ten years. Sure, I wear flip-flops when I go into grocery stores, but that hardly counts. It's my last life to feel the Earth under my feet, and I intend to feel it.

When I walk with my bare feet on the earth, I imagine gripping Mother Earth like a baby gorilla clings to its mother, or sometimes I imagine massaging Mother Earth like Asian masseuses that walk on people's backs.

My feet have become tough, almost hoof-like. The soles of my feet, now thick, are much like the soles of other people's boots. Dirt is embedded in the cracks and doesn't come out no matter how long I scrub with a brush. This grosses out a lot of people, but I don't care. I have no time to waste.

I love silt and mud, sand and powdery snow. Slush is nice, too. Yes, I like slush a lot, but mud puddles are my favorite.

Aretha and I take off on foot out Rock Creek Road where the gravel ends and the dirt begins. It's our regular rainy day starting spot. We run and run through the silty clay-mud and splash through as many puddles as we can find. I wear next to nothing because I love rain, too. I want to feel the little air currents with their varying temperatures, and how the land holds pockets of cold air in lower places. I run and run as fast as I can with long, high strides. I run fast, but Aretha runs faster, so fast her own flesh seems to ripple behind her.

I feel the wind in my leg hair and thank God I'm enlightened enough to know beauty is a feeling, and not an appearance. Ah, yes, sometimes beauty is the wind blowing through your leg hair.

This afternoon, like I often do after a good mud run, I just lie down in the mud and merge with the beautiful Earth. For all its problems, its tragedies, its cruelty, and its suffering, Earth is still such a beautiful place. Aretha lies next to me and I think, *Life doesn't get better than this.* Good muddy planet and a good dog. What more could a woman want?

Anna on the Thunderellas

BEATRICE AND MOM made a cake while I was out looking for the swing. It sits on the table by the wine in the old Summerville Grange Hall. Not one of my better birthdays, despite their efforts. I stand on the other side of the hall from Olive. We have successfully avoided each other all day. I don't know where to go from here with her.

Naturally, tonight's topic is marriage.

"You need to love the way your man smells, and I'm not talking about his aftershave or deodorant. I'm talking about his smell. I could never leave John because I find his smell so sexy," Hazel tells me. "There's going to be times where you're not friends and it's just the sex that keeps you together." Amazing. Hazel. I can't picture it. I don't really want to. "Do you love Phil's smell?"

"I don't remember."

Hazel looks puzzled.

"She's been sleeping on a lawn chair on the back porch for a while now!" Mom blurts out. How does Mom know this? I look at Olive. Goddamn it. Now, the whole damn town of Summerville is not only going to know I have an illegitimate grandchild, but that I'm sleeping on a lawn chair as well. Perfect. Humiliation is just what I needed.

"Anna, nothing said here leaves here. Those are the rules. We all abide by the rules. So drink some wine and stop glaring at your family," Beatrice says.

"Whatever you do, don't go to counseling," Fiona advises adamantly. "I handle a lot of divorces. I don't know anyone whose marriage turned around because of counseling. If you need counseling, it's pretty much over. Save your money for court costs and a good lawyer."

Oh my God. Am I going to need a good lawyer? Is that where I'm headed?

"It must not be that bad," Beatrice speculates. "Or else Olive wouldn't want a husband and kids. See, now, Fiona's parents were bad, and that's why she's still single."

"Did you really just say that?" Fiona asks Beatrice. "Clearly, you're turning into Pearl! So there!"

"What does she mean by that?" Mom calls to Beatrice.

"She means you're tactless," Beatrice answers.

"You're just truthful," Hazel tries to soften the blow.

"And have we established that Olive wants to be married?" Fiona asks. "I mean, it looks to me like she doesn't. She's choosing not to." She turns to Olive, "Olive, do you want to be married?"

"I don't think that's the answer for me," she replies. Even though I feel angry with Olive for the choices she's making, there's something about the hopelessness in her expression that tugs at my heart.

"Olive wants to be married, but not to some poor excuse for a man. If a good man presented himself, I think she'd be interested," Hazel starts, eyes distorted through her colossal glasses. "Olive, I've been thinking about your predicament." I warm up my ankles with some shuffles and listen. "I was thinking about the Earth . . . Earth energy . . . how it transforms waste into something useful. I was thinking of the creative powers we have when we consciously join energies with her. I thought since your main motivation for being married would be to have support while you're in a state of creation, that perhaps you could marry the Earth and achieve the same results. See, like right now, your energies are everywhere. They're out there," Hazel raises her arms. "Like they're looking for that husband, but really they're just pushing away what you want. I can feel your energy from my house. It's strong. Nothing can get through it. Marry the Earth. Direct your energies down into her. She will be thankful. She will transform that chaos energy into something useful. It will allow that which you desire to get through your field." Hazel nods. "Have a ceremony and marry the Earth." She continues to nod and look Olive in the eye, and then reties the knot in her tap shoe and walks over to the wine table.

I wish just one of these women would tell Olive to try to make it work with Matt, that it's in her highest interest and that of her child. Really, I fail to see how marrying the Earth is going to offer any practical solutions. Oh my God, I'm turning into Phil. "I think she should marry Matt," I announce.

The room is now deathly quiet. All eyes are turned to me, except those of Olive, which merely look down. The silence hangs in the air until Olive gets up and walks out.

"Now that's what I call a pregnant pause!" Mom tries to break the tension.

Rather than laugh, Hazel approaches me and quietly says, "You're going to lose your daughter if you keep pushing for what you understand. She just took a step farther away. You have no idea what she's going through. None of us do. She needs people she can trust. She obviously can't trust this Matt fellow. You might want to ask her why she doesn't trust him before you insist she should marry him. You might find out that her choices are logical given her circumstances."

"It's a different game now," Fiona explains gently.

Hazel continues, "If you show her now in her time of greatest need that she can't trust you to make things better, not worse, she's going to cut off contact with you just like she did with Matt. She cannot afford to be drained by your judgment."

"She's making a *huge* mistake!" I know what I'm talking about. "It's not too late to change it yet, if she'd only listen. This is a crucial time. She can change the outcome if she acts now."

"You don't have all the facts . . ." Beatrice says. I bristle.

Hazel looks up through her thick lenses. Her eyes appear to bulge. "You can go out there now and listen to her, or you can dig in your heels and let this become such a big deal that you never get to meet your grandchild."

I reluctantly walk out the door of the hall. Olive sits on a bench to my left. I sit down next to her, but I can't bring myself to say I'm sorry. I'm not sorry.

"You really think I should marry Matt?" she asks.

"I really do."

"Really? That's what you'd really want for your grand-child? To live in a tipi through the cold winter because her father likes his $8 an hour job tuning snowboards and doesn't want to spend his money on rent anymore? You want your grandchild raised in daycare so no one in our family remembers her first steps or her first word? At least here, even if I have to get a job off the farm and leave her with someone else, her stories won't get lost. They'll stay in this town, which is like a big family. She'll be treated like family here. I know you wanted a perfect ending for me, Mom, but Matt isn't the man I thought he was. I'm not going to have the perfect ending. I'm just not." Her voice quivers as she fights to hold it together.

"I'm sorry," I say.

She looks at me and nods, but then takes off her tap shoes and socks, sets them on Beatrice's white Ford, and starts to walk home. I don't want to walk back, I don't want to go back inside, and I don't want to stay on this bench either. It is not a happy birthday.

Forrest on Phil's New Hobby

"FIFTEEN-ONE, FIFTEEN-two and a pair is three . . . God, what is that noise?" Lightning Bob moves the peg in the cribbage board, sets down his cards, gets up and looks around with his telescope. "There," he proclaims upon solving the mystery, and stands back so I can look. Wow . . . I close my eyes for a moment, then look again. I borrow a pen and scribble a poem on the back of a soup label.

> *That's my dad on the hill*
> *Playing bagpipes like*
> *The distress call of great apes*
> *Or maybe a car alarm*
> *Pushing people away.*
> *That's my dad on the hill*
> *Playing taps for all he's lost*
> *His son, his career,*
> *The love in his marriage,*
> *His identity.*

That's my dad on the hill
Unknowingly trying to resurrect
His power
Like a snake charmer
Only noisier
And significantly more abrasive.

"Really?" Lightning Bob asks. "That's your dad?"

I shrug apologetically. All of us up here hate the noise—the wolves, the antelope, the deer, the birds, Lightning Bob and me—we all hate it. How is it that someone with a fifty percent genetic likeness to me could be so . . . well, different?

Lightning Bob watches my Dad in his telescope for a minute and then sits down. "If unhappiness is the source of his music, maybe for the sake of all wildlife in a fifteen mile radius, you should go talk to him."

I get up and look through Lightning Bob's telescope. The music stops and I see Dad rest his head in his hands. For the first time ever, I catch a glimpse of his vulnerability.

Olive on What to Wear When You Marry the Earth

"SO, ARE YOU going to marry the Earth?" Mom asks me as we mix another batch of mud.

"I might," I answer. It's personal.

"I'd like to paint it," Mom announces.

"Paint what?"

"Paint you marrying the Earth."

"In a way, isn't that what this house is? I mean, how much more in partnership can I live with her than to live inside her? I'm already marrying her."

Mom stands up, looks around for a towel of some sort, and finally wipes her muddy hands on her black pants. "I just can't picture how this batch of mud is eventually going to make a suitable house for you and your baby. I don't understand why you're doing this, Olive."

"I know it's hard to picture, but it's going to be great, Mom. I'm not the first to do this, you know."

"Well, I do know that if you're serious about marrying

the Earth, we're going to do it right."

So I found myself, just beginning to show, in a sheer gold chiffon toga wearing a crown of wheat on my head while she painted me in a field of golden wheat. It didn't stop there. Next, I wore a short green chiffon toga with a crown of Russian olive leaves and willow leaves in a thicket near a creek. At first, I was peeking out around a tree, sort of hugging it, but then Mom decided I should be entwined in the branches of the tree, so she gave me a leg-up and I scratched myself all up finding a position aesthetically pleasing and interesting to paint. After that, she painted me in the green toga again in a field of Grandma's sunflowers, but this time I wore the gold chiffon on my head with a wreath of sunflowers over it. Last, she really pushed it by getting me to stand in the pond wrapped in blue chiffon with a crown of lily pads on my head. The lily pads were big and kept flopping in my face. I know there had to be snakes nearby, too. Still, Mom seemed genuinely happy for the first time I can remember, so I stood in the slime and did whatever she asked.

That night Jade called. "Hey Olive, Dad got a note from Mom—she's kind of AWOL. Any chance she's there?"

"Yeah, she's here."

"She okay?"

"I guess. She's not so thrilled with me, but she's making an effort. She seems sad." As I say that, it hits me how easily people you're close to one minute slip away the next.

"Okay, just checking in. And Olive? I don't like how we left things."

"I know." I don't know what to say. Once you say something, you can never unsay it. I lashed out at her and she'll always remember what I said, even if I do wish I could take it back—end of story. We endure a long pause on the phone. Neither of us knows how to make it okay.

Finally, Jade says, "Don't say mean things to me anymore, okay?"

"Okay." I'm relieved she made the first move. "Don't blow sunshine up my ass anymore when I'm scared and freaked, okay?" Did I just say that? Good God, I'm turning into Grandma Pearl! That was mean. I can't believe I said that. Was that my hormones speaking?

"I'll really try, Olive," she assures me. "Okay, love you, bye."

"Love you, bye."

Jade on Skunks and Pivotal Moments

I HEAR BARKING, and then yelping. I run out the door to see what's going on with Aretha and gather all the information I need with just one whiff.

Josh opens his door and calls out, "Everything okay? . . . Oh my God! . . ."

Aretha runs to me with her tongue hanging out. It's purple. She shakes. She's visibly in pain. It's clear she's been skunked at close range, likely a direct hit to the face.

Josh runs to his kitchen and comes out with a jar of Newman's Organic tomato and basil pasta sauce. "It's the closest thing I had to tomato juice," he explains as he hands it to me, his nose buried in his shirt.

I call Aretha to the garden hose. She tries to be cooperative despite her panic from her burning nose, mouth, and eyes. My voice comforts her some, and the cold water from the hose seems to feel good to her. Josh tries to comfort her with kind, encouraging words, too, and I don't know about

Aretha, but I find them very soothing. His voice is like warm, rich cocoa.

I don't know how to begin to wash Aretha's face, where the smell is most powerful. My own nose and eyes water from the fumes. I go inside to get a sponge, and that works a little, but I still can't figure out how to wash right around her eyes without hurting her.

"Whoever said that tomato juice takes away skunk smell was wrong," I say.

"I think it helped cut it some," Josh tries to be positive, "but it's definitely not finishing the job."

"There's no way Aretha can sleep in the house tonight." It will be hard enough to sleep just with the fumes lofting in through the windows.

"Going to tie her?" Josh asks.

"Nah, I can't see any reason. She's good at sticking around." I figure I can go to the vet tomorrow, pick up a better product and maybe get some tips about how to clean her face.

He nods. "Okay, then." He takes two steps to stand next to me, puts a hand on my lower back and kisses my cheek. Luckily, he walks back into his apartment before I can say anything stupid. I try to absorb what just happened and wonder if I'm reading too much into it.

Phil on the Business of Marriage

WITH ANNA GONE, I can openly go to the library and read *Forbes*. Oh, it feels good. An article on the dot-com industry. Oh yes, we all had such high hopes for them, but they just didn't grow . . . kind of like my marriage when I see it in hindsight.

My marriage is in a delicate state. It doesn't seem to matter anymore. Actually, my marriage is a terminal illness. I try, and she shoots me down. I try, and she shoots me down. Over and over. Thirty-five years now, and I still have no clue what it is that makes her so angry. I wonder if I strive to keep my marriage together because I truly love her still or do I do it out of sheer distaste for failure? Do I do it because it's simply easier to tolerate her unresponsiveness and unpredictable ways than it would be to explain to people that we're no longer married? It hits me that Jade is right: I do love my marriage more than I love my wife. They're not the same thing. I wonder when Anna stopped being my lover and started being my colleague. Colleague . . . Did I even treat her like a colleague or did I treat her like an employee? Did she choose this? Not likely. Anna isn't interested much in business. Perhaps it was my fault. Could this be? True, I am a man who values business more than romance. Ultimately, I guess I am a man who turned my love relationship into a business relationship. All evidence points to it. What was I thinking?

Almost forty years ago, I used to sit through seemingly endless sermons for no other reason except to admire her. Church was the one place I could just sit and stare at her for an entire hour. Usually, I would admire the back of her head; her dark hair was shiny and silky. On really hot summer days, oh yes, on those really hot summer days, she would wear her hair up, and I would get a good, long look at her beautiful neck. How sad that infatuation, like the beauty of youth, dies so early in one's life. How sad that these vital parts of a person die so long before his body.

I set down the magazine on the table before me. I don't know how long I've been holding it, appearing to be reading it, but really thinking about my wife, and I don't know how long the woman at the next table has been staring at me. She shyly looks back at her book when I notice her attention. She's smaller than Anna, with medium length blonde hair, and maybe ten years younger than us.

A little flustered, I get up to put the *Forbes* back on the rack. I set it down, turn around to see what the blonde woman is doing, and there she is, staring at me again. I give her an embarrassed smile, and she returns it. Oh my God, there's an opportunity here I never considered. I could have a second chance at love; I could have a whole new beginning. Yes, I could just cut my losses and start over. This time I could be the man I should have been with Anna.

I look toward the door, pause, and think, but before I can make a decision, I notice Jade come in and put something on the bulletin board. I quickly walk over to catch her before she leaves. "Hey . . ." I stop in my tracks. On the flyer is a picture of her dog. That dog is my daughter's whole world. "Oh, no," I murmur. She recognizes my voice, turns around, begins to sob, and clings to me. "Oh, no . . ."

Out of the corner of my eye, I see the blonde woman watching me. I don't look directly at her.

"Okay . . .okay, we need an action plan," I think aloud. "Have you checked the animal shelter?" She nods into my shoulder. "Have you reported this to the police?" She nods again. "Have you called all the veterinarians in the area?" She nods again. "Have you put ads in the newspaper?" She nods again. "Have you called the radio station?" She shakes her head. "Okay, I can do that, and I can offer a reward." She nods. "Okay, should we get back in the game here? Let's go to the phone outside and call the radio station, and then let's continue to put up flyers and look for her." She nods, lifts her blotchy face from my shoulder, pulls a tissue from one of the pockets on her cut-off army pants, and blows loudly. "Okay, we're going to get through this," I say like it's all under control.

Grace on the Veil

I STAND NEXT to Jade at the counter of *The Cottonwood Journal,* while she fills out a classified ad form. Sometime in the night, Aretha disappeared. She blames herself for not tying her up.

"Lost: Rottweiler-Husky female, 8 years old. Missing bottom front tooth. Just skunked. Last seen near lifts Friday night. Please return her. I need my dog girl back. I'm falling apart. 788-2174," she has written. "How much?" she asks the newspaper lady.

Newspaper Lady examines the ad and looks at Jade compassionately. "No charge for lost and found pets."

"That's really nice of you," Jade replies.

"I hope you get her back," Newspaper Lady says.

Jade nods and starts crying and turns to walk out the door.

"Are you okay?" asks Newspaper Lady.

Jade doesn't turn around. She shakes her head as she walks out the door. I put my arm around her and walk away with her. She cannot see me today. She is in Hell.

Jade takes her flyer to Otto's Office Supplies to xerox it two hundred times in black and white and six times in color. I stand next to her, unnoticed.

"Two hundred," Jade tells the clerk.

The clerk glances at the flyer as she rings Jade up. "Dog missing, huh? I'm sorry," she says.

Jade nods as her eyes well up with tears, and she bites her lip. She takes her change, her flyers, and gets out the door before she starts sobbing again.

She buys a staple gun and staples at the hardware store, and carries them with her flyers in her "Choose to Re-Use" canvas bag. She hits the grocery stores, then the library where she runs into her dad. This, of course, I orchestrated, knowing she needed some help and support. Together, they wander the streets of Cottonwood. She shuffles like a zombie, bursting into tears intermittently while posting flyers and looking in people's backyards for her dog.

At the end of the day, Jade goes home and checks her messages, hoping someone has called. Her message on the machine says, "I think my dog is dead. I don't feel like talking to anybody and I sure don't feel like massaging anybody."

Hip Problem Lady's voice comes on, "Oh, I'm sorry about your dog. Call me when you feel better." Then there are two hang-up messages.

I go next door and visit Josh. He's folding laundry. "You go next door and check on my girl," I tell him. He can't see me. Sometimes though, when I talk to people, they hear something and think it's their own thought. "I *said,*" knocking my voice up a couple notches, "you get yourself next door and check on my girl!" He pauses, looks out the window and puts his laundry down.

I return to Jade. There's a knock at the door. It's Josh. Good boy. "I haven't heard your fire alarm go off today. I was worried about you." He gives her his million-dollar smile.

"I think Aretha's dead," she spits out, and begins to fold over, crying.

"Oh . . ." he says tenderly. He catches her before she completely buckles over, puts his arms around her, and rocks her gently.

"That's right," I tell him. "You stay with her."

Over the following week, Jade's flyers soliciting the return of Aretha turned from simply stating the facts to featuring a picture of her hugging Aretha and shamelessly begging for the return of her dog, her family: *"I like to believe in divine order. I like to believe that somewhere out there a kid wanted a dog so bad that the universe/God had to put into motion a chain of events that would drop my awesome dog at her door to show her parents that 1) the kid needs a dog, and 2) dogs won't destroy your home or your life. Once that need is established and the fear's dispelled, please return my dog and go find a real stray. The animal shelter is full of animals that need nice humans like you. But as for Aretha, she and I belong together. She is my family. You've got to give her back."*

One caller told her he delivered something to a house on Ridge View and saw a dog that looked just like the one in the photo on the poster. Jade rushed out there, crying in the truck, so hopeful, wanting it so much, butterflies in her stomach as she rang the doorbell. A man who answered the door was on the phone and gave her a signal to wait. The dog was behind him. It wasn't her. It was a Rottweiler-Golden Retriever. It didn't look like Aretha at all to Jade. Her heart sank. It wasn't her.

Another caller was sure he saw her by a dumpster behind the Mini Mart. She ran a spiral around town beginning at the Mini Mart, hoping, hoping so much, but returned home more disheartened and in a deeper state of despair.

Yet another person called late at night because she had just seen the flyer. She was sure she and her mom saw Aretha at Frog Lake. Jade put on a coat over her pajamas, put on her hiking boots and sped out the West Road to Frog Lake. Frog Lake sits in a deep valley, where Jade felt dwarfed by the mountains, dwarfed by her helplessness. She parked, but remained sitting on her truck, and sang Aretha's name. She sang terms of endearment. "Where's my good dog?" Her voice bounced off all the mountains around her. She kept singing pleas for her dog to return, creating a chorus of echoes. It occurred to her that the mountains not only bounced her voice across the valley, but higher up each time too, up to the stars, up to the heavens, to where she imagined Aretha. In truth, Aretha was right next to her, just four feet off the ground. The geography of Heaven is a common misconception. In truth, it's just four feet off the surface of the Earth. That's why when you die and go through the tunnel, it's a horizontal tunnel and not an elevator. I put my arm around Jade. She seemed to sense me. "Girl, your dog has crossed over. She's right here. She's still with you even though you can't see her, just like me." Jade began that wailing again as her suspicion grew that Aretha had not been kidnapped— really, who would want a stinky dog in their house?

There was no moon that night, only the dark, dark Earth, and the bright, bright heavens.

Jade sang, "I love you sweet girl, I love you my sweet dog girl . . ." and let it fill the valley, and let the mountains bounce her message back and forth and lift it right up to Heaven.

I wish Jade could have seen me and known I was there with my arm around her, but she simply could not. Grief and fear are blinders. This is the root of Hell. Hell is the illusion of our separateness from God. Jade felt very separate. For the next month, in this way, Jade would stay in Hell. She could no longer see divinity in all the things she used to. She was blind.

Later, when the density of Jade's fear and grief lifted enough, I would talk to her about this night, about how Aretha heard her song from the other side, and how it was beautiful for her.

As Jade grew to accept Aretha was almost surely gone, she wanted to sleep outside where she could look up at the stars and see Aretha's new home. She imagined Aretha flying across the sky in a royal blue shiny cape, and in this dream Aretha had her tail back. Jade used to ache thinking about how someone cut it off before their lives came together. What kind of person chops off puppy tails? She loved the idea of her dog being back intact. But the peace Jade found for a few moments that night did not last. Like a patch of blue sky in a rainstorm, it, too, was only a sucker hole.

Anna on Coming Home

ON THE WAY home, I thought of paintings I'd like to do of Jade, mostly with her white body next to white Aspen tree trunks and her golden-orange hair with the golden-orange autumn leaves. In autumn, the leaves will be the same color as her hair. I suppose I mostly thought about art to keep myself from thinking about Phil and the decisions I should probably be making. Neither of us are getting much from this arrangement. He gets a housekeeper and a cook, and I get my expenses covered. I feel like I still need some time to develop a vision of what my new life could look like before I take any leaps.

When I finally reach Cottonwood, I notice pictures of Aretha on every telephone pole. Uh-oh. I stop by Jade's house on the way home. A handsome man answers her door.

"Hello," he whispers to me.

"I'm Jade's mother," I say.

"Josh." He shakes my hand. "Pleased to meet you. She's sleeping."

I step inside and go to her. I brush her braids away from her face. "Oh, little girl," I whisper to her. "Will you let her know I stopped by?" I ask Josh. "I just got back in town."

He nods. He looks friendly. I like him.

I continue home, drive into the garage, park, and wonder if I should even bother going into the house. Why? So I go directly to the backyard. First, I notice a swing with wilted carnations tied to the rope. There's a card tied to the rope as well. I read it. Wow. Not a Shop Vac. I look up into the tree at the branch where it hangs, and that is when I notice a tree house. I follow the ladder with my eyes, down from the tree house near the trunk of the tree. I climb the ladder, and sit on the deck at the top. I take a moment and look around before I go inside. Inside, another card. Phil, you have really outdone yourself. But wait, the card says, "Mom." Jade? I open it.

The kites we flew
Anchored to our hands
Could only soar because we held on
A kite that slipped from my little hand
Fell with no resistance
And tumbled along the ground
Aimlessly
How we loved to watch our kites
Sometimes still in steady wind
Sometimes struggling in wild currents
Sometimes so far away

They were just a speck
But we could always call them back home
And eventually they always returned
Now I am that kite
Thanks for holding the string.
Forrest

Forrest. Forrest is alive and nearby. I sob. *My little Forrest*
. . . My heart aches as the tears which I was so sure had run
out, spring up and flow again. *My precious Forrest . . .*

When I am finally able to compose myself, I descend the
ladder and sit on the swing. Though wilted, the carnations
still smell fragrant, like my Senior Prom corsage from Phil. I
kick off and swing. Forrest. Phil. Clearly things that appeared
dead are not.

Since it's obviously a time of unimaginable possibilities, I
go inside and call Martina.

Phil on Big News

JADE DIDN'T WANT to continue searching today. She wouldn't even look at me. She only wanted to lie in a little hole outside her condo.

"Here, I have a list of places we've called. Up on top are dates. I've put check marks in the corresponding boxes to show who we contacted on what day so it will be easy to see who we need to continue to follow-up with and when. Now, here is a map I copied from the phone book. Yellow represents the areas we plastered with flyers. Each little black X represents a reported sighting. A box around the X means it was a confirmed false alarm. Plain X's then, represent unconfirmed sightings." She still doesn't look at me. Her eyes drop big tears that moisten the gravel under her.

"We could go to these isolated neighborhoods today and put up flyers," I suggest, but she just lies there. She reminds me of Anna during the weeks after Forrest disappeared—devastated and inconsolable. Just as I didn't know what to do then, I don't know what to do now either. I rest my hand on her shoulder. "I'll tell you what. I'm going to go check the animal shelter today. They're very busy and might not identify Aretha right away if they did admit her. Then I'm going to go for a walk and keep an eye out. Call me if you want to join me."

She gives me a little tiny nod, as if to say thanks, and I head off to the animal shelter.

As I walk among the outdoor kennels, most dogs bark excitedly and some jump up on the fence. Some of the barks are ear-piercing. I check each and every kennel for Aretha, but she's not in any of them. My hopes drop. I would have loved to have brought Aretha back to Jade and to have made everything in my little girl's world okay again.

I return home, defeated, and decide to prepare a sandwich before my walk. I walk into the kitchen, but before I reach the fridge, movement outside the window catches my eye. It's Anna swinging.

I go outside and cautiously approach her. Her eyes are red and swollen like she's been crying. Great. I still decide to break my news. "Aretha's missing."

"Yes, I was just there. I saw the flyers as I rolled into town. I stopped by to check in. She was asleep. You know how she sleeps. She had a friend with her," Anna replies.

"Oh." I walk behind her and give her gentle pushes.

"Thank you for the swing," she says.

"You're welcome," I reply.

"I have some big news," she tells me. "Two pieces. I'm not sure which is bigger, or which to tell you first."

"Good, I hope?" What if she's about to break it to me she's leaving me for good? I can't see her expression from back here, so I can't begin to guess.

"Incredible." She takes a piece of paper from her shirt pocket and hands it back to me. I stop pushing her and unfold the paper. "It was up in that tree house. Our boy's alive, Phil. He's alive . . ."

I feel like the wind has just been knocked out of me. I read the poem. "Why won't he just come talk to us?"

"I don't know. I'm hoping this is a sign he's moving in that direction," she says.

"Maybe."

"Maybe this is stupid, but I feel like going for a walk and just looking for him. Would you be interested in that?" she asks.

"Sure," I answer. "We could look for Aretha, too."

"Before we go, are you ready for the other big news?"

"God, I don't know," I reply.

She turns the swing around so the ropes cross. She looks at my face as if she's looking for something . . . something she loves, something she recognizes, I don't know. "Olive's going to be a farmer, and we're going to be grandparents."

Huh?

Olive on Cob

G RANDMA P EARL PICKED this spot for me the morning after I arrived. After she showed me this spot, we took cuttings of a willow tree, a cottonwood tree, and some lilac bushes. They're soaking in a bucket now. Grandma Pearl says I'll want a good windbreak so I can grow a garden. I love this spot.

Grandma Pearl didn't flinch at the idea of a mud house. Her mother grew up in one in Nebraska, and that house is still in good shape.

I stir another batch of mud and clay, scoop it up in a bucket, and drop it in the form. I'm in the homestretch of my second six-inch layer. My house is only a foot tall at this point, but I'm happy. I'm on my way.

My house is not square, rectangular, or angular in any way. My cubicle days are over. I'm done being boxed in. A house for a woman should be all about curves, don't you think?

Truthfully, I had given up on the idea of true love when

Matt proposed living in a tipi. I mean, if Matt didn't think I was worth plumbing, why would anyone else? Matt and I were together for five years. He knew me well enough to see my worth, and yet, he didn't see my worth. It's hard not to take that personally. It feels *very* personal. Before Matt, there was a significant string of men who didn't see my worth either. I don't think any man ever will. Each disappointment, each failed love, is just one more ballot in the box regarding my worth. It's not that I think my worth is non-existent. I just think it must be invisible to men. The lonely South Dakota landscape comforts me. Maybe if I live in this abyss, I'll forget that I ever dared to wish for more. I'll forget companionship ever even seemed like an option. The traditional American Dream is not going to happen for me, and at some point, that just has to be okay. At some point, a woman just has to let it go and open her eyes to all the wonderful things in her life, even if they aren't what her dreams were made of. I am so fortunate to have the opportunity for a good life here.

I turn a bucket upside down and sit on it. Feed-store overalls do not need to be dry-cleaned, and I feel great liberation in being able to sit wherever I darn well please. Plus, they're roomy enough to allow for my growing baby. I take off my work glove to tuck a piece of hair that escaped from the scarf around my face, then place my hand on my belly to feel my baby. As I take a long drink of lemon water, I wonder if she can taste the sourness of the lemon. I wonder if she likes it. I don't know for sure that it's a girl, but one day, "she" just came out. Who knows if I'm right, but I decided to go with it. I take a moment to look around me at the blooming sunflowers, the summer sky with the cumulus clouds growing into thunderheads already.

The cumulus clouds first blossom into giant cauliflower shapes, and then begin to grow up, up, like white, segmented caterpillars crawling to the sky. At a certain height they stop and flatten out on top. This is the stage at which they turn black and spread out. In this way, all day, the tension builds. When it finally cuts loose and rains, usually around five, sometimes later, sometimes earlier, it's such a relief. Some energy in the atmosphere diffuses. Anyone can feel the change. Eventually the storm is over, and all that remains is freshness, drops hanging from the trees and grasses, and blue sky clear of the dust that often clouds it. I love the first few hours following a good storm. It's a time that feels so ripe with opportunity. It's a time of infinite possibilities and new beginnings. Life is like that—a series of thunderstorms, a never-ending cycle of tension-relief-renewal.

I have no misconceptions about the storms ahead of me. From what I observe, parenthood is equivalent to the Monsoon Season. No, I know more storms are coming; I'd just really like to finish my house before the next one if I can.

I feel at home. For the first time in my life, I really feel at home. I let myself fall back in the grass on my back, watch clouds, and just wait for my mud to dry.

Phil on His First March

"PHIL, THAT IS one shiny wedding ring still on your finger. Honestly, Phil, I think you have set a new record," Al says. "I trust things must be adequate?"

"Better than adequate—I'm going to be a grandfather!" I announce.

"Well that is cause for celebration. Phil, have a drink with me."

"Nine o'clock is a little early for me, but thank you very much for your offer."

"My pleasure." Al pours some scotch for himself. "Phil, listen closely and abide by this: Never, under any circumstances try to play a lullaby on the pipes to a small child. This is a recipe for disaster and inner ear damage. I rue the day I had a mind to try it." He glances at a picture of a child dressed in pink, presumably his daughter, on a shelf. "Well then, let us celebrate you marching into grandfatherhood by marching around the neighborhood. Let's keep your drones corked so you can keep your focus on your coordination. I believe that by parade time, you'll have your drones uncorked, but for now, we can't afford to lose you to hyperventilation. It's important to learn to breathe properly before you apply maximum pressure. I have an Uncle Bert who blew out his sinus playing the pipes. Poor guy. Had to take up the strings after that. The man plays a mean fiddle, Phil, but make no mistake. No fiddle holds up to the pipes, and Bert knows it. 'Amazing Grace' does not sound right on the fiddle. This was a tragic event to say the least." Al takes a generous gulp of scotch, stands, and leads the way to the front door. "I trust you have the fingering for 'Amazing Grace' memorized?" He raises one eyebrow at me.

"Yes, sir, I do."

"Then let us commence."

Al and I blow up our bags. He applies pressure to the bag with his arm, causing the drones to sing above his head. His face turns red. He looks at me and gives me a little nod, so I play the first note of the melody with him. He takes the first step, and I follow a fraction of a second behind until I am able to synchronize my steps with his and not mess up the melody. We play and march a total of four blocks, plenty for me, until at last we return to Al's living room, breathless.

"Phil, you did not pass out. It might surprise you to know most of my students do. Phil, we can begin to prepare for the parade."

"Great!" I'm going to be a grandfather and play the pipes in a parade; retirement is looking better all the time!

"Phil, at this time, I recommend ordering your traditional

dress." Al looks up a number in his Rolodex and scribbles it down. "Ian there is very helpful. You tell him what clan you're from and he will find your tartan. They even carry baby kilts, in the event you would like to pass this family pride onto your grandchild. Now, measure yourself metric before you call, Phil."

"Will do, Al. Here." I hand him his thirty bucks. "See you next week!"

"Sure thing. Tell Ian I say hi."

My own kilt. Maybe I'll get one for my grandchild . . . and my son . . . . For the first time, I truly feel rich.

Anna on a Home of Her Own

WHEN I WOKE and surveyed my surroundings, I smiled. At last, I was home. A place all my own, oh, what a delicious experience it was! I felt safe here—safe from ridicule, safe from invasion, safe from judgment, safe from displacement. There is nothing to make a woman feel more youthful than waking up in her very own tree house.

Light filtering in through the branches streamed through the east window and danced on the floor next to me as leaves quaked in the morning breeze. The patterns of light reminded me of water, and fireflies, and kaleidoscopes. Being inside the tree house while little branches blew around me reminded me of being in the safety of a mother's womb, in the womb of a dancing woman. The tree struck me as so feminine, the curves of her trunk, her delicate branches, and her leaves like a wild hat or a feather boa or precious jewels. Or maybe this beautiful woman tree was cradling me in her arms.

I saw myself in the woman tree. I saw within the tree, my family tree, each strong branch a child, and myself, the trunk, holding everyone up. In the youthful leaves that tremble with the slightest wind, I saw my children, vulnerable to the world and always reacting to it. In the leaves, I came to see the chaos of my children's lives as natural. I am the trunk, where people cut hearts, like the painful experiences of motherhood, that eventually come to appear as beautiful. I am what anchors her family in the wind, in the chaos. I cannot still my children, but I can anchor them.

The bark on the young branches is thin and vulnerable, whereas the bark on the trunk is strong. Deep cracks in the bark, the woman tree's stretch marks, give it texture and beauty. I feel the lines in my own face with my fingertips and think of that beautiful bark. Silvery lichen grows on the bark of the tree, like the silver that creeps into my hair.

I take out my sketchpad, but instead of raisins, I begin an intricate close-up of bark, and eat the raisins. I am no raisin. I am a beautiful, glorious tree.

Forrest on idiots

I KNEW DAD had been coming up here on Mondays, so I waited for him on top. I hid back in a grove of aspens in case I changed my mind and wanted to chicken out. I didn't know what I would say, how much or how little. I considered just visiting with him without telling him who I am. Wouldn't it be interesting to see if he'd recognize me? When I put my hand to my chin and felt the dreadlocks in my beard, I don't know—it seemed like a pretty safe bet he wouldn't. Of course, if he did, he'd be horrified. I guess I should have hacked back this beard when I was at Jade's. Maybe my hair, too. I don't know. They both keep me warm in winter. In the end, all my anxiety was for nothing; Dad didn't show.

I wondered if he was okay, so I made my way down to check in with Jade and get the news.

I alter my course just a little to see how Matt is coming along. As I near, I smell smoke. I walk a little faster through the beautiful grove of pine and aspen. Finally, I see his camp. That idiot has a campfire burning. He sits next to it, cooking something. His girlfriend sits next to him in a long Indian skirt. Her blonde hair is in two braids. She makes circles on his lower back with her hand, and from time to time, he leans over to kiss her.

"How funny," I say. "I was so sure you'd be eaten by a bear next spring, but it appears you're going to kill yourself and your girlfriend in a fire first. I can't believe you didn't listen to my warnings."

They jump.

I take off my moccasins and begin to walk around the fire in a spiral, taking smaller steps near two aspen trees. Fine, fine, fine, fine, warm, warmer. "Where's your shovel?" I ask sharply.

"Are you going to kill us?" the idiot girl asks.

I shake my head and let it drop with disgust.

"I don't have one," Matt answers.

I scratch my beard and look at him. He has no idea what he's done.

"Where's your axe?" I ask.

I hear the idiot girl whisper, "What if he kills us with it?"

I look around his wood pile and find it myself. I start chopping at the ground where my feet felt heat. Smoke begins to escape from the hole, and then a little flame. I stand back to let Matt see.

"Take a look at all of this." I raise my arm toward all the pine on one side of the valley, the golden, grassy hillsides on the other, the valley bottom, and the gold and green mountains behind these mountains. "Take a good look at all of it.

Take it in and remember it well, because in about two weeks, maybe less, thanks to you starting a root fire, it will all be black."

Matt and the idiot girl look scared. They should be. "If you had listened to me and got a camp stove, there would be no fire. If you had listened to me and got a shovel, you might have a chance at fighting this. Listen to me now. Pack your stuff. Be sure to take everything that would identify that it was you living here. Use your axe to bury your fire so it looks like you tried. Drive to town, call 911, report the fire, but don't give your name. Tell them you started it by accident, so that if they do catch you, they'll know you reported it. Campfires haven't been allowed for two months. You were incredibly negligent. If this fire blows up, you'll be serving time. If firefighters or anyone else dies in it, you could be serving life. Report it so hopefully it can be contained before it gets way, way out of control. Then, go south. Get out of the country. Don't ever talk to a soul about it. Wait to see if it blows over or blows up. If it blows over, you can come back to the States, but not here. If it blows up, stay in Mexico."

I leave them like that, stunned by their own stupidity, and start up to report this to Lightning Bob.

Phil on Holding On

I HAVE BEEN staring at the phone for a half-hour now. I know I want to say something, but I'm not sure what. My little girl is going to be a mother. Would I have chosen these circumstances for her? No, but still my heart overflows. I just want to give her my love. Does that sound sappy? God, I'm getting sappy. Actually, being sappy feels pretty good. I'm going to like being a grandpa.

I pick up the phone and slowly dial. My heart races as the phone rings. I can't stop smiling.

"Hello?" It's her. It's my girl.

"It's Dad," I say.

"Dad? Dad. Dad, I'm so sorry I let you down. I know this isn't what you wanted for me. I know you raised me to have more common sense than this . . ."

"Olive, stop." I take a deep breath. "I just called to tell you I love you. I can't wait to be a grandpa. You're a smart girl, and I know you'll take care of things just fine."

I hear muffled sobs on the other end. What do I say now?

"I've started graphing market trends in the minor oils for you. I'll email you weekly updates. As farmers go, you've got a lot going for you. You've got no debt, good water rights, good soil, and a good head for business. I don't see why you can't be one of the ones that make it."

"Thanks, Dad." I hear her blow her nose.

"You know, when my family lost the farm, I never really felt right after that. There is something about a farm."

"Yep." Sniff.

"I'm proud of you, Olive."

Oh, there goes the crying again. What is needed here is a strategic subject change.

"Now Olive? My sources say that flax is going to be hot this year. My two cents is to gamble on a little more flax than you otherwise might have."

"Thanks, Dad. Thank you so much."

"Okay, check your email now. I sent you this week's graph."

Grace on Jade's illusion of Separateness

JADE WAKES UP and immediately feels shattered. She cries and cries, barely able to get enough air. She buckles over, holding her gut, as if she's puking, puking grief. She bends down and brushes one of the holes Aretha dug next to the little privacy fence in the gravel next to the condo where she would lie, as if to touch any energy that might linger, as if to admire Aretha's work. Jade crawls in the hole, curling up in a tight ball on her side, and cries and cries. She picks through the gravel, picking out clumps of Aretha's fur. She strokes her face with Aretha's fuzz and smells the fibers, but does not smell Aretha.

Rationally, she knows better. She knows that this is just a blip in the continuum. She knows Aretha is always right next to her, like me, despite the fact we reside on a different dimension. She even knows that she will be with Aretha again. After all, she was with Aretha when Aretha was the dog that lingered around her church when she was the Reverend

Byron James. She has little snippets of past life memories of Aretha and herself all over the world, all throughout time. She knows, rationally, that she cannot be separated from Aretha. It never has been and it never will be.

But if knowing this helps, it doesn't help much. For even though she knows there is no such thing as separateness or permanence, these illusions seem so real here on Earth they bring her to her knees. This is the part of the human experience a soul forgets about when she agrees to come down for another Earth life. These illusions are so clearly illusions up there in Heaven, that a soul cannot imagine feeling this kind of pain over them. Even here on Earth, Jade usually recognizes illusions for what they are. But, no one on Earth can completely escape the experience of grief. It is not in the contract. It's in the contract to simply feel everything, including the polarity.

I sit next to Jade, stroking her hair and cooing comforting words she can't hear, but can sense a little. I sing Sly and The Family Stone songs to her quietly. She falls asleep like she did when she was a kid. Yes, after a good cry, this girl conks out—doesn't matter where, and there's no waking her up.

Josh makes his way to Jade's house with a pizza box.

He loved holding her last night. He hadn't intended to stay all night; he had intended just to help her to her bed. She sat on the bed, and he sat next to her. He put his arms around her and she cried into his chest, and just like that, fell deeply asleep, sitting up. He swiveled her awkwardly with one arm, while reaching down to pick up her legs with the other, so she could sleep lying down. But once he set down her head, his arm was still under her, and you know, it kind of felt good, so he left it there. He reached over her to grab the part of the quilt hanging off the side of the bed and folded that over her to keep her warm, and then he just held her all night. Holding her felt different than holding other women. He had this sense of connection with her that didn't really make sense to him.

Josh squats next to Jade fast asleep in Aretha's hole, moves a braid out of her face and tucks it behind her ear. He picks her up and moves her inside.

Pearl on Burning Garbage

I SMELL IT. Dammit, Dean. I warned you.

I pull my .22 off the wall and walk outside. Olive tags along several paces behind. "Stay here," I tell her. I walk toward the west edge of my property and fire two shots in the air. Then, when I have a clear shot, I fire at Dean's burn barrel. Ping. Dean hears it and jumps back.

"Goddammit Pearl!" he shouts at me, and throws a tire and a chunk of carpet on his fire. "It's a free country! I can do whatever I want on my land!"

"Your toxic fumes are filling up my house, Dean! We've talked about your illegal passion for burning plastic before, Dean. Now Dean, if you want to kill me with your fumes, that's one thing, but if you want to give my great-grandchild birth defects by subjecting my granddaughter to your air pollution, that's quite another. Now Dean, you can get that hose and put out your fire, or I can." Big black plumes of smoke rise up from the tire.

"Go home, you crazy old bat," he shouts. I shake my

head in utter amazement and disgust. He never learns. I approach him with the patience of a saint, grant him chance after chance, and still, he persists with name-calling.

I walk over and open the gate to his horse corral. I take a few more steps and open the pig pen. Dean's livestock makes a break for it. While he chases them, I get his hose and soak his burning barrel. I hang the hose over the edge of it, so it begins to fill up with water, then turn and walk home.

Mess with the bull, Dean, and you'll get the horns.

Grace on Jade's Closure

IT WAS BECAUSE she couldn't bring herself to call *The Cottonwood Journal* to cancel her ad after she had given up, that someone called Jade and said they saw a half-Rottweiler partway between Rock Creek and Copper Mountain. They said it was dragging a rope or something behind it. He had tried to catch the dog to take it to the shelter, but it wouldn't let him near it. Jade put posters out there, out in the middle of BLM land where there aren't many places to hang a poster. She put her dirty T-shirts out there, each with a card in a ziplock explaining what the shirt was for and what to do if they saw a dog lying on it. It was a tip from Ranger Guy who found many lost dogs for people that way. Lost dogs smell the shirt, lie on it, and wait. When Jade first got a call from the man who thought he saw Aretha, she cried. She cried the rest of the day. *Could it really be her?* she dared to wonder.

Another man called a couple days later to say he, too, saw a dog out there that looked just like the one on her poster. He described the spot. She went out there and searched, but all she found was a camp where two guys who looked like militia members, tattooed and missing teeth, lived with their dogs, one of which was half-Rottweiler and half Shar-Pei. It barked ferociously at her as she walked by, standing up and pulling on its rope. It looked nothing like Aretha to her, but she knew others had mistaken this dog for hers.

A week later, a woman called Jade and asked her if she had found her dog. Jade told her she hadn't. The woman said she didn't know how to tell her this, but there was a dead dog matching her dog's description at the high point between Rock Creek and Silver City, just off the West Road by the rocks. She explained that if it were her dog missing, and someone found a body, she would want to know. So although it was a hard call to make, she made it. Jade thanked her for calling, but inside, Jade really didn't think it would be Aretha. She had gone on so many wild goose chases.

Jade drove out the West Road, way out to the general vicinity the caller had described, and began walking. She no longer had faith any of these callers knew what they were talking about. Jade was so tired—tired and irritated. As she walked, she pondered how naïve she must have been to have ever thought the Universe compassionate. She walked and walked, but found nothing. Finally, she yelled at the sky, "Will you *please* help me find this dead dog?" I hovered above Aretha and blew her smell toward Jade. Two Angels came to help blow with me. It worked. Jade felt a gust of wind come out of the southwest, carrying on it the smell of death. Jade walked quickly, following it to the steepest side of the top of a little knob.

There, head downhill, and one back leg caught in a sagebrush, she found what remained of Aretha. Her skeleton was intact, and most of the fur on her legs, back, and head. Her guts had been eaten out, her eyes, too, and the inside of her mouth. Her tongue was gone. A few chunks of skin and fur other animals had ripped off of her were in the same bush as her leg.

"Oh . . ." The reality began to sink in. "Oh, sweet girl. Oh, my puppy girl. Oh, my baby dog," Jade cooed through her tears. I put my hand on Jade's shoulder.

Jade inspected the remains without touching them, studied her lower jaw to make sure the same bottom tooth was missing, studied the pads of her paws, and her toenails. Her nose looked shorter. Her face looked different, Jade guessed mostly because her mouth was open, but not smiling. When Aretha was alive and opened her mouth, the corners turned up and made dimples. Aretha had the best smile of any dog Jade had ever seen. Now there was bird shit on her head.

I told Jade, "Aretha's fine, honey. She says, 'Don't cry for me. Don't cry for me.'"

Jade studied the body more, looking for any clue about what had happened. Aretha had obviously been dumped. It clearly looked like someone backed up to the high point, a place where people parked and drank, and just dumped her over the edge. Jade wondered what Aretha experienced and examined what was left of her corpse to see if there was a bullet in her, to see if someone brought her out here and shot her for fun, but she found no bullet holes. Jade wanted to know if Aretha had experienced brutality. "Oh, sweet girl, what did they do to you?" she screamed through her tears.

"She says, 'I had no pain,'" I told her, but Jade couldn't hear me anymore. Jade wrapped her arms around herself and rocked back and forth. I sat behind Jade and held her, rocking back and forth with her.

Jade thought of how she'd longed to feel Aretha's velvety ears, her sweet, velvety ears just one more time, and so she reached out and stroked them, and then drew her hand away, spooked. They didn't feel the same. They were no longer silky; her fur felt stiff and starched. Jade extended her hand again and stroked the fur on Aretha's head, and on her back, and stuck her finger in the space between all the pads on the bottom of her paw. With one finger, she stroked the fur that went up the bridge of Aretha's nose.

At first, Jade contemplated what a miracle it was to just find her beloved dog after all these weeks. She thought about all the things that had to happen in order to lead her here. She was thankful for closure. And even though her dog was dead, she still felt like she had found her dog again. She still felt reunited. She sat on the hill next to the corpse, stroking it, looked across the valley and for one calm moment, felt Aretha's spirit sitting next to her, not in the corpse, but behind her, leaning on her. The moment passed, and she began to cry.

"I'm so sorry. I'm so sorry," she told Aretha through her streaming tears.

Her thoughts turned from gratitude to the fact that someone had killed her beloved dog and dumped her here as if she were trash instead of the love of her life. She began to feel crazy, angry and crazy. She shrieked up to the sky, "She was everything to me!" Then she just shrieked angry screams unlike any noises I'd ever heard her make before. She screamed and screamed, her screams echoing in the valley below. As unlikely it was anyone was out here, Jade hoped the person who left Aretha there could hear her, and she hoped it made him hurt. She sat surrounded by trash and empty beer cans in the stench near the bloodstains on the gravel and earth, just sat shrieking and screaming and stroking Aretha's stiff fur.

"Oh, child . . ." I felt for her.

Jade went to her truck and dug out a space blanket from the emergency box. She lifted Aretha and laid her on the space blanket. She noticed that there was nothing but ribs left on the side of Aretha that had been lying on the ground. The smell was unbearable and got in her mouth as she struggled to carry the heavy corpse down the steep talus slope, away from the Budweiser cans, down through the sage. Although Jade liked the idea that Aretha became part of all living things, coyotes, and crows, she carried her down to the aspens to bury her, to reclaim her. She carried her down, down, down to the aspen grove below, where the old aspens have died but new shoots promise the ever continuing cycle of life. Jade put the collar of her T-shirt over her nose to filter some of the stench of death, though it already seemed so embedded in her nose and mouth that she was sure she would taste it and smell it for days. Maybe the T-shirt filtered a little—she wasn't sure. Jade laughed as she remembered all the times Aretha had rolled in something dead, relishing the perfume, almost delirious with olfactory bliss, and how it brought Jade to new levels of fury each time. She'd angrily bathe Aretha with Suave green apple shampoo, the only thing she ever found to conquer that stench. Jade laughed at how it seemed Aretha got the last word in, and how if Aretha could smell herself now, she'd likely be quite pleased.

Jade dug through the layers of dirt in the aspen grove with a stick, not a great tool for the job. Looking out over the valley during breaks she took from digging, she considered how if Aretha was hit near their home, someone made an effort to bring her here to the highest, most scenic point. Although they dumped her among beer cans, maybe they, in their own way, tried to seek out a nice resting place.

Jade picked up Aretha and laid her in the hole. She cried while she picked flowers to fill up Aretha's chest cavity, to fill the place where her heart had been, to attempt to replace the beauty.

"Oh, she still has a beautiful heart, child. She loves you so much," I told her, hoping she could still hear me on some level.

Jade unbraided her cornrows and combed her kinky hair with her hands. She took handfuls of hair and put them in Aretha's grave.

"Oh, child, you want a part of you to merge with a part

of her? Honey, you don't have to do that. You two are so connected. You've already merged," but my words fell on deaf ears.

Even though it no longer felt soft like velvet, Jade touched the fur on Aretha's ears one last time, the last time ever, and sobbed while she covered her friend with dirt.

She cried so hard she couldn't see and stumbled up the hill with the space blanket, filled the space blanket with rocks and carried it to the grave below. Before leaving, Jade scattered wildflowers over the rock pile, hoping they would drop their seeds and grow through the rocks the following summer.

Forrest on Fire

I WALK AS fast as I can straight up the hillside, past two abandoned mines and around a talus slope. At the top of the ridge, I wave my arms toward the tower and point back at Matt's camp. It's well into twilight, so I doubt Lightning Bob can see me. I start running along the top of the ridge for several miles, over peaks and saddles. At times I land on a rock wrong, and it hurts my foot. Moccasins don't offer much protection. Still, I race the diminishing light since the moon is waning and won't be up for a while. When the light is gone, it'll be gone for several hours. I won't be able to see anything and will have to stop and wait, sweaty and cold, as the night drops into the forties. I push myself harder.

I run off the edge of this ridge, down halfway until I catch the saddle that leads up to Lightning Bob's ridge. I can barely see now and have to slow down to watch my step. Luckily, Lightning Bob has his light on and it guides me toward him even as the last of the light in the sky dwindles. I keep walking and walking toward that light.

Finally, Lightning Bob turns out his light. I'm stuck. I find a pine tree and dig a hole in the needles below. I curl up in it and wait for the moon, willing myself not to fall asleep. Every hour counts.

I wonder if Matt is just starting my journey. Nah, his only crime is negligence. My intention was vindictive. There's a big difference there.

I see a cloud. Not good. If a storm's coming, that means wind is coming, too. More clouds blow in as the moon begins to rise, interfering with the little light I have. I'm able to walk for a while, but then I have to wait for a cloud to pass.

When the moon is halfway up in the sky, I reach the tower. Flash hears me and barks. I climb up the tower stairs and wait on the deck. I look off toward Matt's camp and see orange.

Lightning Bob finally opens the door. "I thought I heard someone climb my stairs," he says sleepily. I rush past him to his table where the glass covers a topographic map. I find Matt's camp and point. "A camper started a root fire here around 7:00 p.m. I think it's grown." I point toward the glow.

Lightning Bob studies me, confused at first, having never heard me speak before, but looks at the glow and calls it in. Dispatch informs him they're sending a truck to check it out.

Confident I've done my job, I lie on the rug on Lightning Bob's floor and fall asleep. He puts a green wool blanket over me, and I appreciate the warmth.

The Moon on the Wonders of Ultrasound

THE MOON ABOVE sees it all. The moon sees Olive, Pearl and Beatrice watching Olive's ultrasound tape over and over. Beatrice watches the baby stretch on the TV screen, and cheers it on. "Yeah, stretch, little one . . . oh . . . good job. You are a good stretcher." They all chuckle.

Then the baby rolls partway over. "Ah yes, that's much more comfortable, isn't it?" Pearl asks the screen.

"Yeah, there's nothing like a good bladder to press your feet into," Olive answers for her baby.

The little legs on the screen begin to kick vigorously. Pearl, pleased, exclaims, "Oh! A Thunderella!"

Beatrice sits on one side of Olive, and Pearl sits on the other, their arms all woven around each other, wonder in all their smiles.

"You know," Olive tells them, "For the first time, I really feel like everything is going to be okay. I mean, I know it's not going to be perfect, but I know it's going to be okay."

"Oh, you bet," Pearl answers casually, "It's going to be more than okay."

"That's right. We're here for you," Beatrice adds.

The older women do their best to put Olive's mind at ease; inside, they privately feel the intensity of the journey she has begun. They give Olive a little extra squeeze and let her feel their strength.

"She really is quite a dancer, isn't she?" Olive says.

Beatrice sings a few bars of "Blue Suede Shoes" to the rhythm of the baby's kicking.

The moon knows that in reality, no phase is any better or any worse than any other phase. The moon knows everything is just one big divine cycle.

Jade on What She Misses and Potato Sack Races

"HEY, JADE, I heard. I'm so sorry." Olive. The last person I want to hear from right now.

"Yeah, thanks. Was this the knock off my high horse you wished for?"

"God no, Jade. You know I didn't mean that."

I do? "Yeah, well thanks, Olive."

"Okay, I just wanted to . . . I don't know. I'm just so sorry."

"Okay, thanks, bye."

"Bye," she says with uncertainty. Well she should. I know this is exactly what she wished for.

Yeah, this is it, Olive. I hope it was everything you waited for. I'm on my knees. I'm sure not above the human experience now. I'm sinking in it like quicksand.

Sure, I miss her spirit, but I miss her body, too. And knowing we'll have other lifetimes together or that maybe she'll even come back in this one doesn't change the fact that last month I had the perfect dog to pet and hug, and today I don't. I have nothing.

I miss her fur. Aretha had the best fur. On her head and ears it was like velvet, and everywhere else she had this hidden fuzzy fur under her silky fur. I loved that fuzzy fur. It was like a cashmere sweater. I miss her bigness, the way she took up my whole arm when I reached around her to rest my hand on her other shoulder. I miss her little dog lips, fuzzy on the outside, and like leather where the two met. I liked to play with her lips when she used to lie on her side and those lips would hang down. Aretha had the most gigantic tongue, and when she drank water, it sounded like music to me. I always thought it was the happiest sound I could think of. Her paws were huge, and I liked to stick my finger between all her pads and tickle her. I liked to tickle the fur there gently when she slept and watch her leg twitch. Everything about Aretha was meat and muscle, and when I gave her doggie massages, there was lots of tissue to work on. In Aretha's later years, when she finally figured out what I was doing to other people, she learned to beg for massages just like people do. She would sit right in front of me with her back to me, and that meant "massage me, please." I would give her doggie shiatsu. I also liked that she was so big because I didn't have to bend down to pet her head when we went for walks, and if we were waiting at a stoplight, I would pick up a velvety ear and play with it. Aretha seemed to like that.

But mostly what I loved is how Aretha felt like my partner. I think about Aretha's toys. What am I going to do with her toys? The squeaky squirrels I was so excited to find for her last Christmas . . . what am I going to do with the squeaky squirrels? Aretha had a squeaky squirrel that was her favorite toy. She disemboweled it, like she eventually did to all her toys in her youth, so then I just called it "squeaky squirrel bag." Then there's stinky toy. Stinky toy was one of those rope toys with two knots that are supposed to floss their teeth when they play with them. Aretha had shredded it until it was just the remnants of one knot, but all in all, it lasted so much longer than any toy she ever had. Aretha and I used to do stinky toy dances where she would tug on one end while I held onto the other. Somehow this all worked into a dance. Aretha liked to spin me around and around. I held onto stinky toy, my other hand extended like Ginger Rogers. We had good times with that toy.

I look at the inside of my truck window and notice Aretha's dried up slobber on it. What do you do with dead dog slobber on your windows? I can't bring myself to clean it off. I don't want to erase Aretha.

Everywhere I drive, I see the posters I put up. They're everywhere. Hundreds. Hundreds of xeroxed Arethas staring at me from every telephone pole, at the grocery store, and at the post office. I need to take them down, but I can't. What will I do with the posters I take down? Throw them away? I just can't throw Aretha away.

The fact of the matter is I'm very attached to the physical world and all signs of her in it. Some argue that attachment is a sign that a soul is far from enlightenment. That's not it. I think for most of us, attachment is part of the human limitations package we sign up for when we decide to come here. Earth life is like one giant field day where we willingly choose the limitation of racing with both feet in a potato sack, or sometimes we join up with another and agree to the limitation of racing as a team where each person has one leg tied to the leg of the other. Yes, whenever I go to a wedding, I picture two kids tying their legs together in preparation for a wicked three-legged race. Agreeing to run a race with limitations or live a life with limitations doesn't mean you're slow, clumsy or unenlightened. It just means you're showing up on field day, participating, and if you're really good, you try your best despite the obstacles.

Sometimes, when I'm tired, I really wish I could cheat at the field day of life. If everyone untied their legs or dropped their potato sacks, it wouldn't be a goofy field day anymore. It would be the Olympics, which is to field day what Heaven or Enlightenment is to Earth life, and there's time for that later.

For now, all I can do is wait for my clothes to dry after losing at the water-balloon toss of life. In the mean time, I have no comfort, no dignity, not enough warmth, and I've totally lost my field day spirit. In fact, I hate field day. I can't remember why I thought it would be so damn fun to show up.

Olive on the Genders Within and Annie Get Your Gun

"WITHIN EACH OF us is an inner-male and an inner-female. When you're in a relationship with a man, you not only need to have balance between you as a woman and him as a man, but your inner-male needs to have balance with his inner-female," Hazel says as we put on our tap shoes. "This is very complicated."

"Tell me about it," Beatrice mutters as she walks by us to get a glass of wine. Tonight she seems particularly sassy, her cropped hair fluffy from just being washed. She wears wine colored pedal pushers and a pink sleeveless shirt. Her cat glasses accentuate her wit.

"Okay ladies, did you bring your hats?" asks Grandma Pearl. We all put on our cowboy hats. "Guns?" We put on our holsters. "Here ladies, here are your cap guns." As per Grandma's suggestion, this number is going to include the discharge of firearms. She wanted to go with real guns and blanks, but decided that noise wouldn't be good for the baby.

"Flap-heel-heel, flap-heel-heel, eight times. Scuff-heel-toe-heel, scuff-heel-toe-heel," Grandma Pearl leads. "Now here we're going to do a little square dance kind of thing. Flap-ball-change, flap-ball-change, shuffle-shuffle, shuffle, shuffle, around each other like that."

Fiona takes a drink of her wine and says, "I would think a woman who has a highly developed inner-male would need a man with a highly developed outer-male so that her inner-male could finally rest."

"If he does not have a highly developed inner-female, her inner-male will have nothing to do and go to war with his outer-male out of boredom," Hazel says.

"Okay, I can see how that works in theory, but take me. I have a highly developed inner-male," Fiona begins.

"Clearly," Grandma Pearl says, eyeing the National Organization of Women T-shirt Fiona's wearing.

"You should talk," Beatrice says in Fiona's defense.

"As I was saying," Fiona continues, "I don't dream about having a man with a highly developed inner-female. I dream about meeting a man where just once I *don't* think, 'Yeah, Pal, I'm *twice* the man you'll ever be.'"

"Yeah, I gave up on that a long time ago," Grandma Pearl laughs. I think every single one of us has a wisecrack for Grandma Pearl, but none of us say anything. "Well, ladies, we could suck down more wine and gab all night about how manly we are, or we could just keep tapping and get to the place where we fire off our guns. I vote for guns!" Grandma exclaims. Of course she does. "Okay, ready? Flap-ball-change, flap-ball-change, shuffle, shuffle, shuffle, shuffle. Bang!"

"So Olive," Fiona says, "what's this we hear about you building a mud house?"

"Yes, my inner-male is building a small mud house. It's only two feet tall right now."

"What happens when it rains?" Hazel asks.

"Nothing," I answer. "It's waterproof. The mud is a mix of clay, sand, and concrete. When it's finished, I'll plaster the inside and outside. Similar building styles were used in Europe for hundreds of years and those structures are still standing."

"Are you going to have plumbing and electricity?" asks Hazel.

"Yes," I answer. "My inner-male is a good man who would never let a woman live in discomfort." Fiona hands me a glass of sparkling cider. "Eventually I'd like to get off the electrical grid and go solar, but that will take a considerable investment, so for now, I plan to just hook in."

"I would like to see what your inner-male is building," Hazel says.

"Anytime," I tell her.

Martina on Anna and Phil

I HEAR ANNA and Phil open the door next to the antique store and stomp up the narrow stairs of the old brick building. I can tell already, they do not move gracefully. I can hear the anger in their footsteps. Their footsteps stop in front of my door and pause. I assume they are reading the sign on my door: "Martina," it says, and under my name, "Wise to the ways of love." They knock. I crack the door and survey them. Anna is dressed only in black. This is not a good sign. They do not stand close to one another. Yes, these two will be work, but I will succeed, as I always do. I am Martina after all, wise to the ways of love.

"You will not talk," I state firmly. "The only words here will be mine. You will do exactly as I say."

Phil opens his mouth as if to argue. I can see it. His type is used to being in charge. Too bad. He holds his tongue. For this, I allow him to stay. I open my door, revealing to Phil and Anna a dance studio lit only by hundreds of red chili party lights stapled to the ceiling. Near the window, I grow hibiscus, gardenia, jasmine, tuberose and ginger. It is not what they expect. It never is. Phil and Anna stand awkwardly just inside the door as I walk over to the stereo and put on some Silvia Torres.

"Phil, you will put your hands on Anna like this." I put one of his hands on Anna's lower back and hold the other out. "Anna, take his hand. Put your other hand here."

Anna opens her mouth as if to protest, as if to begin to explain that they were here to work on their marriage, but I put one finger over her lips to remind her not to speak. "I am wise to the ways of love, not you. If you were wise to the ways of love, you wouldn't be here. Do not question me. Do not doubt. You are in good hands."

I break eye contact with Anna and focus on Phil. I stand at his side. "This is your job. One, two, cha-cha-cha, three, four, cha-cha-cha. Do it with me like this." He follows me, while Anna, in his limp arms, does nothing. "I see," I say. "Notice your wife did not follow you. There are no boundaries between you. You walk all over her and she just waits for it to be over. You do not dance together because your arms are weak. Hold your arms firm. This is the space your body needs. She has all this space to dance around it. You are not taking away from her to claim this space. You must claim it or she doesn't know where she belongs."

Anna thinks I am sexist. They always do. American women do not understand the nature of women and the nature of men. In a dance between two people, one person must lead, and the other person must follow.

Phil firmed up his arms, pushing Anna back and forth as he cha-cha-ed. Anna made no attempt to dance with him, only making a step forward and a step back when he pushed her or pulled her. The look on her face showed she hated it.

I now come to Anna's side. "Do you like being pushed around?" I ask. She shakes her head. "Then you must participate in the dance." I do the cha-cha steps for Anna to imitate. "You resent your husband's leadership because he has been a poor leader. He is becoming a capable leader. You will soon be in capable hands. Begin to relax into that. Begin to allow yourself to trust him again. There. Doesn't it feel good to not always have to run the show? He will take care of you."

I look at Phil quickly. "You will take care of her, right?" Phil looks like a deer in headlights. "She cannot be a woman if you are not a man." Phil opens his mouth, but before anything comes out, I stop him. "Say nothing. Look at her. Tell her with your eyes that you will take care of her. Tell her with your eyes: thank you, thank you for the children you gave me, thank you for giving me a family. Tell her with your eyes that you will always take care of her." I must say, I am not impressed with what I see in his eyes. "Look at her. She is small. She is delicate. She has become toughened because she did not think you would take care of her. Soften her. Soften her with your love. Melt her like butter with love in your eyes."

"Look at him," I tell Anna. Maybe if I can engage her, he will react to her. "Look in his eyes. He wants to love you. You must let him! Remember when you first met him. Remember him when he was a boy. He was crazy for you. He would have slayed dragons for you. You knew it. You loved it. You loved that he wanted to take care of you. Look at him. Look at what a good man he became. He has been a good father. Look at how his daughters made him tender." I can always tell a man with daughters. They have tenderness about them the others lack. All men should have daughters. "See his sweetness. He still wants to be your husband. He is dancing with you. He still wants to be your husband. He wants to know if you still want to be his wife. Remember how you felt during your first kiss, now look at him and tell him with your eyes that you still want to be his wife."

I see a hint of softening in each of their eyes and am encouraged. "Phil, tell her with your eyes that you are sorry for times when you were too insensitive and rigid and pushed her around. Tell her you are sorry for the other times she needed clear clues and your arms were limp. Anna, tell him with your eyes that you are sorry for dropping out of the dance. Tell each other you have many good times ahead. Do not look away from each other. Eyes are the windows to the soul. You must look in each other's eyes to find what you fell in love with in the beginning. Now we will just dance." I go to a corner of the room and cha-cha by myself, glancing at them occasionally, but knowing when to leave lovers alone.

Phil and Anna continue to cha-cha under the red party lights. They are not good at telling each other much with their eyes. They ask each other a lot of questions with their eyes instead. Do you still love me? Do you still think I'm beautiful? Can we recapture the feelings we once had? Do I even know who you are? Do you have any idea who I am? Is it possible to find our way back to each other? This is pretty normal. They continue to dance. They dance and do not talk. The questions in their eyes remain, but become more comfortable, less intense. How hard it is for them to look at each other for so long.

At eight o'clock exactly, I turn the music down a little. "You may not talk to each other. If you need to tell each other something, you will tell it to each other with your eyes, or with a gentle touch. You will come here again not tomorrow, but the day after at the same time. Is that a problem?" They shake their heads. "Here is a list of music. You may listen only to music on this list while you are learning the ways of love. Nothing else. You may only listen to these Brazilian artists. Brazilians know the ways of love. Brazilian music will help teach you the ways of love. You will go to the music store tomorrow and buy at least three CD's on the list. Raul will be expecting you and will call me if you do not follow through. You must not talk to each other. You will undo my work if you talk to each other. You must not do this. And you must not make love. There will be no lovemaking for a long time." Did I think they would make love if I didn't say this? Of course not. I could see it was a relief actually to be instructed not to do that which they desired not to do anyway. One wise in the ways of love must take the pressure off married couples so they can begin again. Anna and Phil shook my hand and walked out in silence. How businesslike.

Anna on The Drive Home

WE DRIVE TO the house in silence. Phil parks the car in the garage and holds up a finger for me to wait. So, I wait. He opens my door, and I look at him to ask what he's doing. He points to the house and then to the backyard. I motion toward the backyard. He gently touches my lower back, guiding me toward my tree house. I walk just ahead of him. At the base of the ladder, he takes a step back. I start up the ladder, but pause to look down at him. He gives me a look that thanks me for initiating some attempt to stay together, for reaching out to him. Then he turns and walks away. Since not talking takes away the pressure to fill space or leave it, I feel freer to watch him for a minute, to watch his walk, to remember rushing to the living room window after he dropped me off when I was a teenager so I could watch him walk back to his car, so I could look at him for a few seconds longer.

I finish climbing the ladder, crawl onto the futon I bought yesterday and light some candles.

I think about Martina's words, "Do you like to be pushed

around? Then you must participate in the dance." I think about how I felt in that moment, how much I've disassociated with my body, my husband, life.

When I think of my heart, I think of a nuclear fallout shelter. I remember considering nuclear fallout shelters when I was a kid, thinking there was no way I'd go into one because life inside a fallout shelter wasn't life at all. Now here I am. It's a different kind, but the result is the same.

I wonder what there is about me for Phil to even love. I have hardened so much. I've been a dutiful wife, but not a loving one.

"God, please soften my heart," I pray.

I remember a time when we were sixteen, sitting on top of the Ferris wheel at the county fair. When it stopped to load more people, Phil reached over and took my hand. He looked at me with a vulnerability I had never seen before or since. It appeared as if he wanted to tell me something, and indeed that look did tell me something, but it remains something for which there are no words. Nonetheless, the memory of that look softens my heart.

jade on invisible Dogs

I ROLLERBLADE DOWN the Rails to Trails going north out of Cottonwood. I don't feel like wearing a superhero cape today. It's my first time out in a long time. Even though I don't feel strong, I fall into the meditative rhythm. Then I notice Grace rollerblading next to me.

"Where have *you* been?" I ask her angrily.

"I've been here all along," Grace answers.

"Haven't seen you."

"You haven't seen anything but your low-vibration emotions."

"What's your point?"

"Remember when you were little and your folks started worrying about you, you know, having an invisible friend and all? They made you go to that psychiatrist? By the time they were done with you, you thought you were nuts. And you asked me, remember this? You asked me why you could see me and others couldn't."

"Yes, I remember."

"And what'd I tell you?"

"You told me that humans have to stay on the ground because they can't flap their arms fast enough, and that hummingbirds can fly because they can flap their arms a lot faster," I answer.

Grace is exasperated. "I said, 'Child, your spirit is like a hummingbird. Fast like that. And so it can be in the world, but float above it at the same time. That's what you normally do, float above your world, which is why you can see me.' But since Aretha crossed over, you haven't been floating, girl. You've slowed down."

Some people pass me on the trail. I try to look normal, not like I'm talking to someone they can't see.

Grace takes a good look at me. "You let your hair down. That's good. There's nothing cuter than a little white girl in braids, but as you were getting older, well, it wasn't such a good look for you."

"Have you been hanging out with my mother?"

"I'm just saying, you're a good-looking white girl. That's all."

"Grace, I want my dog back," I tell her.

"She hasn't left you," Grace says and points to a hologram of Aretha running ahead of us.

"Oh, no, Grace, did I not release her? I don't want her caught between two worlds or anything."

"Child, you released her fine. She made it. She just watches you from there and comes around for visits is all," Grace explains.

"That's nice and everything, but I really miss her in physical form."

"Ah, she'll be back with you in physical form again."

"You mean in this lifetime?" I ask.

"Yes, I believe so."

"When?"

"I'm not exactly sure. But I know this. You'll know her when you see her. You'll look into her eyes and just know."

"What if she reincarnates and I somehow mess things up and I'm not where I'm supposed to be at a certain time and we don't connect?"

"Doesn't work like that," Grace assures me. "Don't worry about it. Pets find you. They're really good at it."

"Grace?"

"Yeah."

"I'm sorry I got mad at you."

"Apology accepted."

Forrest on The Way Out

"FORREST, WE'VE GOT a problem. Wake up." I hear Lightning Bob throw a few items into his backpack before I open my eyes.

"Jesus Christ . . ." I can see the orange filling the valley and hillsides south of us, licking the night sky in flames higher than skyscrapers.

"Firestorm. My guess is it was traveling almost fifty miles per hour. It tripled in size in five minutes. No one has heard from the first fire truck to respond. We don't know if they got trapped."

I go to the topo map table. "Which way are you thinking of evacuating?"

"If we can go toward it just a little, we can catch Road 1103. Choppers will be able to see us, trucks will be able to access us, and we'll have a little buffer from the flames," Lightning Bob answers.

"What time is it now? Four? In less than an hour and a half, the morning wind shift is going to blow that fire back downhill. I predict it will go right there. You're gambling on rescuers finding us before we fry. If the fire heads back down, we could go into tonight's burn area where there's no fuel left, but the ground will probably still be hot enough to melt your boot soles and do serious damage to Flash's paws. I don't know. How long does it take for the ground to cool?"

"Depends on so many things," he answers. "We could always carry Flash at that point because there'll be no hurry."

"Okay, choice two: We could stay on the ridge top where we can watch the fire and choose to go off either side depending on conditions. We can be easily seen by choppers up there, too. Choice three, we could go off the other side now, hope the fire doesn't jump the ridge and rip through that dog hair down there. If that happens, we won't stand a chance. The forest will be slower to go through and we won't be able to see what's going on. If we make it to the river, we might not burn, but if the fire gets close and we breathe that superheated air, we'll die anyway. Our last option is to go back just a little, to the top of the draw to our north, so that we avoid the forest all together and go down on that side of the other ridge where hopefully the fire won't reach today, but if the wind changes and goes back there, there's really no place to go. We'd have to run uphill, and we know we can't outrun it uphill," I say.

"Storm's coming. They always come from the south. Winds are going to blow the fire over this ridge today. If we're down in there, in all that fuel, there's no doubt we'll die. In tonight's burn area, we may get burnt, but we won't die. I really think the road is the way to go. On the ridge, there's talus. The air under those rocks will fan the fire and create super-heated conditions. We're safer on a road," Lightning Bob argues.

"Keep your pack light; we're going to need to run fast."

He exhales. He knows I'm right. He packs three quarts of water, a first-aid kit, and his book of poetry, then clips his radio to his belt. He hands me a flashlight and takes one for himself.

"If we're on the road, I can let the base know our route so they can know right where we are and pick us up," Lightning Bob says.

"Winds like this flip choppers. They're not going to send a chopper out in this. They're not going to send a truck out either. If they send anyone out, they're going to look for the firefighters that haven't come back yet," I argue. I think it's stupid to go with a plan that's dependent on other people rescuing us. We can't afford the consequences if it doesn't happen.

"Maybe the firefighters are on the road. I still say the road."

"Okay, we'll stay on the switchback while it's still dark and take it down to the road. By then it should be light and we can really run. Is that the plan?"

"Yeah," he answers.

"Bob, I don't know. If we stay on top of the ridge, we can always run downhill to the road or over the other side. Ridge top is shortest and most direct. If we can get to there," I point to a place on the map, "we'll be safe. That's not that far. Please Bob, let's go ridge top."

Lightning Bob pauses and thinks. "Okay, we'll go ridge top." He radios our intended route, and we start down. We walk as fast as we can against the high wind. It would be useless to try to run against it. Flash stays close, but still out in front, checking back on us, occasionally running behind us as he would a herd of sheep. We walk too fast to talk, keeping our flashlights pointed in front of us, watching each step. As it grows lighter, the winds shift. They begin to blow the fire back east down the little valleys, back toward Cottonwood and us. The morning winds begin to blow more fiercely at our backs, and we begin to run.

I hear Lightning Bob breathing hard. "Here, let me take the pack for a while." I intend to take it for the duration of our escape, but I know if I offered that, he wouldn't give it to me. Pride. I take the pack, shout "Go!," put it on, clip the hip belt, tighten the straps and start off running again.

The morning winds blow all the smoke toward us, darkening the sky and turning the sun red. It looks like the end of the world.

The fire creeps into my peripheral vision to my right. It has indeed swept right down the road. I follow the road down a couple switchbacks with my eyes, down into yesterday's burn area and see a burnt truck. I hope only the truck was burnt and that the people made it out. Regardless, there's going to be a price on Matt's head for this. I hope he makes it to Mexico. Stupidity isn't the same thing as malice.

Whether stupidity should be a punishable offense is debatable.

I see fire out of my left eye now, too, and call to Lightning Bob to stop a minute. We turn to see a wall of flames at the top of the draw to the north of us, and scattered patches of fire on the next ridge north. Behind us, less than a half mile, the grass burns, spreading fast. "Morning winds should die down soon," I say.

"I wonder if the tower is gone by now."

"Water?" I ask. Flash is panting hard.

"We don't have time," he answers.

We start off at a jog again, negotiating a rocky outcrop. Where we find the top of the highest chair lift, the ridge begins to drop and descend toward Cottonwood.

We scramble over the loose rocks of a talus slope. The rolling rocks startle two deer below, who run off. Lightning Bob looks up at the deer instead of his next step and I watch him lose his balance and land on his left foot. It looked like a stellar recovery until his ankle rolled and he went down. He called out in agony.

"It's broken. I heard a snap. Get two sticks for a splint!" As I find two sticks, he takes off his shirt and rips up the lower part. I return with the sticks, hold one on either side of his leg, and he ties strips of his shirt around them tightly. Flash sniffs Lightning Bob's leg as I help him up. Above us, we see grass and small shrubs ignite. "If we don't make it out, it will be my fault," he says.

"We'll make it out. Just don't pass out." I get on his

injured side and put his left arm around my shoulder. The reality is if we don't make it out, it will be *my* fault; after all, it's my bad fire karma. We walk the rest of the talus slope and hear trees explode to the northwest. Once we get on regular dirt, I say, "Run this like a three-legged race. Our outside feet are one and our inside feet are two. Two is when you put all your weight on me. Ready? Start slow and get faster. One, two, one, two . . . !"

We run like that to the bottom of the chair lift. We continue down a ski run. The trail forks. A little sign with a black diamond points directly downhill, while a sign with a green circle points across the hill. "Which way?" I call out.

"Green circle. We'd never be able to keep footing like this on the black diamond." We follow that run as it winds its way down toward the base lodge. We slow down when the river's in sight and the fire's not. By now, the wind's died down—it must be early afternoon. Lightning Bob radios for a ride to the hospital and we watch a green Forest Service truck pull into the lodge parking lot as we descend down our final stretch.

The man gets out of the truck and runs up to meet us. Both of us supporting Lightning Bob, one on each side, we try to get him into the passenger side.

"I don't think that's going to work," Lightning Bob says. The man and I reach down with our outside hands behind Lightning Bob's knees creating a chair with our arms. We lift Lightning Bob into the back of the truck. He yelps. Flash jumps in.

"Can I give you a ride anywhere?" the man asks me.

"Nah, I'm good," I reply and watch them go.

"We made it! We made it!" Lightning Bob shouts as they drive away.

I smile and wave and start to make my way toward Jade's. On a pole though, I see a picture of Aretha. Not good.

The Moon on Germination

THE MOON ABOVE sees it all. She sees the thousands of acres of charred land and a pile of ashes that once was the home and prison of Forrest. The moon sees through the illusion of death, as though it were just another new moon, another time when what is truly there isn't visible. As she prepares to make herself full again, she knows the Earth is preparing, too. Underneath the veil of ashes, possibilities await divine timing. Forrest's old home and prison, now just elements in the soil, will nourish new life, a new beginning. It is true—water cleanses, but only fire purifies.

And the moon sees that Forrest, nourished by his own disaster for the last fifteen years, is ready. His divine timing has come. Like a pine seed, able to germinate only after fire, Forrest too, is ready to sprout.

Phil on Failure and Corsages

FROM THE TIME I was old enough to know what was going on, I knew the bank was one step away from foreclosing on our farm. I watched my father work himself into the ground, and during the harvest, I worked myself into the ground, too. In the end, it wasn't enough. When I was fifteen, the bank foreclosed.

Grandpa Fritz said it was all directly due to birth control. He said when there were ten kids to ride on five junky tractors, a farmer could come out ahead, but when a man didn't have all those kids, he had to buy a colossal, fast, and expensive combine to compensate. That specialized combine locked him into a crop that wasn't always in high demand, and locked him into more debt than he could usually pay off. Grandpa Fritz even drew me a timeline to show when birth control was invented and when the farm crisis began. He drew a bar graph showing the average number of kids a farm family had and the number of bank foreclosures on farms.

Sure enough, I did see the relationship.

Still, Grandpa Fritz's reasoning didn't help my devastation and sense of failure. When I heard my mother crying through her bedroom door, I felt so guilty. I should have worked harder; I should have worked as hard as five boys. I was ashamed when we moved to town, walking back and forth from the truck to the house with furniture and boxes. I was ashamed at the post office and at the store when people wouldn't make eye contact with me. Maybe it was easier to pretend not to have seen me than to acknowledge my family's loss, or maybe they blamed me for the foreclosure, too.

But the worst time, the worst time was when Anna invited me to the Sadie Hawkins dance. As soon as I got home from school, I put on my suit pants and discovered I had grown a good five inches since I last wore them. They still fit in the waist, though. I examined the inside of the pant leg to find two inches of hem I could take out. I didn't even consider wearing my dad's pants, for though he was a little taller than me, he was significantly wider. I took the hem out and tried to re-hem just the very bottom edge. Since my mother had taken to crying in her room all day when my father was gone, I didn't trouble her with my pants. I just took a needle and thread, and attempted to do it myself. My stitches looked awful. When I was done, the pant legs were better, but still high.

I looked in the mirror and fought the urge to cry. I didn't know what would be worse: If I cancelled with Anna, I'd save face, but it would probably hurt her feelings and she'd most likely end up going with someone else; if I showed up in these pants, she'd surely think I was a nerd and the other kids would ridicule me. I decided nothing would be worse than hurting her feelings. Yes, I'd rather humiliate myself and be rejected by her than hurt her feelings. I just hoped people wouldn't laugh at her because she was with me.

Panic hit me when I realized I didn't have a corsage for her. My heart broke. She, of all the girls, deserved the finest corsage, but I could not buy her even the least expensive one. Other boys would use those big stick pins with the fake pearl at the end to pin rose, gardenia, and carnation corsages, all backed with a dark, leathery fern leaf and finished with a satin ribbon. What would I do? I searched my mother's sewing basket. She had no big pins with the fake pearl. I took a regular one. I found no elegant satin or velvet ribbon either—just a piece of yellow yarn. I searched our new yard for flowers, but found none.

It was early spring and not much was in bloom, but I knew my mother's garden would have something. It took me a little more than an hour to walk back to our old farm, but I did it. I looked at my home and ached for it. Instead of indulging in sadness, I put my mind back on the task at hand and went to the garden. I found a few brilliant red tulips. I put a feathery yarrow leaf behind a couple tulips, and was reasonably pleased with myself. I sat on the steps of my old house for just a minute to contemplate how different my life would be if I still lived here. I felt such loss. I wanted to go through those doors and find my normal life again. I hurried away though before anyone saw me sitting there, grieving for my home. That would only be more embarrassing. As I walked home, I imagined pinning my homemade corsage to her in my high-water pants, and I tried to imagine it wouldn't be so bad. I took the yellow yarn from my pocket and tied it around the feathery yarrow leaf and the bright red tulips. It didn't look right. I doubled up the yarn and tried again. It was a little better.

My parents were angry with me when I came home: I was late for supper. I held up my homemade corsage. "Anna invited me to the Sadie Hawkins dance," I explained. Everything I had been feeling, my fear and shame, my worry and sorrow must have shown on my face, for my parents disarmed immediately. "I walked to Mom's old garden," I told them so they would know I didn't steal these tulips from neighbors. My mother looked away and fought back tears, and my father looked down, sorry he couldn't help me.

I wrapped my homemade corsage in waxed paper and folded the edges neatly, but when I went to the refrigerator the next morning, to my horror, the tulips had dropped their petals. I had nothing to give Anna. I remember lying awake the following night, the night before the dance, picturing all the ways I would surely bring Anna humiliation when the time arrived. It was the worst night of my life, far worse than the actual dance. That was the night I pledged that if Anna forgave me for my short pants and lack of a corsage the next day, that I would spend the rest of my life making it up to her. I'd make sure she never did without or had second best again.

I'd make her the luckiest woman alive.

I knew I couldn't accomplish this being a farmer. I'd have to be on the other end of the foreclosures. I'd have to be a banker.

If I succeeded in making her the luckiest woman alive, it doesn't show. Add that to my list of failures. But before we go to our second dance lesson, I go to the florist and order the corsage I couldn't give her when I was fifteen.

Martina on Phil and Anna's Second Dance Lesson

I GREET PHIL and Anna through a cracked door. "You have not talked?" I ask. They shake their heads. No, they had not talked. "You have listened to Brazilian music?" They nod. "You have not made love?" They laugh and shake their heads. I knew the answer to that question, but it's important to make lovemaking forbidden once again, as it had been when they were younger. That which is forbidden becomes irresistible.

"From now on, we will tango. Phil, you may not touch Anna yet. You may not touch her until I say. Phil, this is your job." I take large steps across the floor. Phil attempts. "No like this." Phil does better. "Do it with me now. Do it again. Your feet know what to do now. Now do the steps with gumption. You are a man. Move through space with force. You are a man. You are strong. You are a man. Be a presence. Again. Yes. Like a jaguar. Better. I want to see stealth. Do it again. Very nice.

"Anna, this is your job. Do it with me." Anna follows.

"Again, but this time lower. Knees bent." I show her with my movements what it looks like to be a succulent, seductive woman. American women have become so consumed with being powerful, they have lost the art of enticement. They are clumsy. We do the steps three more times. "Your feet know what to do now. Now you will think about doing the steps like a woman. Make a man want to come to you. You are irresistible. You are like chocolate sauce. Move like chocolate sauce. You are a woman. No man can resist you. You know their urges are almost more than they can bear, and you bring them to the brink of self-control. Yes! You are moving very nicely now.

"Now together. Hold her like this. Anna, let him lead you, but hold your space just enough to keep him from devouring you. He is a jaguar." Anna and Phil both laugh without making much of a sound. That is fine. Laughter is good. Laughter breaks tension. "You think that is funny now. You just wait," I laugh back at them. "Phil, move toward her. Move toward her with much desire. Desire, Phil. You have not made love in months, and although it's against the rules for now, you want to. You are a man. Men want only to make love. But they will settle for dancing. Move toward her in a way that tells her she looks delicious. Oh yes. Anna, look at him and move in a way that tells him you know he wants you and you know you are irresistible. Move away from him in a way that tells him he cannot have you . . . yet. You will make him work for it. You will make him beg for it. Lower. Stay closer to the floor. Bigger steps. You want your bodies to be closer, but they cannot be. It is forbidden. Move. Jaguar and chocolate sauce. Move together. Nice. More tension. Phil, you would take her now, but you cannot. Show her. Show her your desire. Show her your strong desire. Look at her. She is beautiful. She is elegant. She moves beautifully. She is a woman. Yes! I saw that, Phil! You glanced at her breasts!" Phil and Anna begin to laugh. Anna looks surprised he had, but likes it. "That is very good! But you must only look at her eyes. You may look at her breasts with your peripheral vision only! You may look at her eyes and tell her you strongly desire to look lower, to look at her whole womanly body." Phil and Anna still have laughter in their eyes, but something else is growing, Phil thinking about breasts and Anna feeling desired, feeling as irresistible as chocolate sauce. This is good.

I go off to dance alone, leaving Phil and Anna to dance and create more sexual tension.

At promptly eight o'clock, I turn the music down lower. "You will practice together every night at this time in the living room of the house you shared. You will be alone for this time. No one else may be in the house. There will still be no talking. None. No talking at all! Phil, you will ask her to dance with your eyes and your body. Anna, you will submit, and you will enjoy it. You may not make love. You may not even kiss. Only dancing. One hour only. You will return here in six nights. I will teach you very sexy moves in six nights. You will be trembling. You are very good dancers. Now go home."

They shake my hand again and go.

Phil on Goodnights and Changes

WE DROVE HOME in silence. I parked, got out to open Anna's door and walked her to her tree house. This time she knew what I was doing and let me open the door for her. I gently guided her to the ladder with a hand on her lower back. She walked a step in front of me, where I guided her, and I let my eyes fall to look at her derrière. Womanly. I remembered how it looked when she did those low tango steps, swishing back and forth, full and beautiful. I wanted to let my hand fall as my eyes had done, but I refrained. She started up the ladder, but turned to look at me before continuing. There was a smile in her eyes, and a little one on her lips. There was perhaps a little spunk in her eyes, too, and maybe, just maybe a hint of desire.

I looked at her. Even above me, she looked small and delicate, though really she was neither, unless in comparison to me, which I guess is the essence of being a man and a woman. I wanted to take her face in my hands and kiss her as I had not in two decades. I remembered Martina's adamant instructions, and so did not kiss my wife, my wife whom I had grown to feel entitled to. Perhaps she saw desire in my eyes. Perhaps that is what made her continue to smile.

I return to the house through the French doors that lead to the kitchen and pour myself a glass of Silk soymilk. I miss whole milk. So many things have changed since my heart attack, big things and little things—little things like milk. Silk is actually quite good, but I just hate the fact that I had to change.

Even bigger than that, I hate the fact that everything had to change. In the beginning, I welcomed change. I sure didn't want to stay poor. But then there was a point where everything was perfect, when I had it all, when my kids were little, my wife was happy, and I was successful. It didn't last long enough. It changed.

I walk into the hall and study a family portrait from the seventies. We all look happy. I study Anna's expression closely. Yes, she really was happy—that's not her fake smile.

I think back to the births of each of my children. You know, they didn't let us in the delivery rooms in those days. I wanted to protect Anna from that experience. I wanted to carry that burden for her. The moments you experience when your wife is in childbirth are among the most powerless a man ever experiences. After the birth of each child, I was so relieved to find Anna alive and reasonably okay, that the sight of her and each new child made me vow to spend more time with my family. Each time I didn't follow through on my vows. I walk down the hall and look at all the pictures. Most of them are of moments I missed.

I return to the kitchen to put my glass in the dishwasher, turn, and begin to walk back out, when Anna's painting catches my eye. I love her old paintings.

Anna and I were in the same art class in our senior year. I was frustrated and she was focused. I tried so hard. I really wanted to impress her. Mrs. Bergstrom stood by me one day and said quietly, "The expense of effort is awareness. Sometimes awareness will get you further." I didn't understand her then, and by and large I still don't, but I do recognize that I sabotage myself when I try too hard. Awareness is the hard part of that statement for me to understand.

I think about learning to play the chanter, about how when I'm really aware of my fingers, of the music, it flows, whereas when I really want to make Al think I'm the best student he's ever had, I mess up.

I wonder if there's some parallel with that in my marriage. The more I tried to fix things, the more pressure I put on myself, the more stress I was under, the more nervous I became, and the more nervous I became, the worse I made my marriage. The moment I gave up on my ability to save my marriage, something changed.

I don't know. I still don't completely understand. I always thought effort was good. Clearly though, sometimes I do get in my own way. I think about the heart attack that could have killed me. Was that a result of effort? Yes. But then I look at other times where I thought effort got me where I wanted to go. Was that effort? Is there a difference between effort and determination? What did Mrs. Bergstrom mean by effort? Overexertion? I don't know. Maybe effort is like first gear— good to get one started, but not something one wants to drive in all the time.

Tonight there was a moment when the dance no longer took effort, when I could be aware of how Anna felt in my arms, how she smelled, and how sometimes her hair would brush my face and tickle it.

Forrest on Blowing it

I SEE JADE OUTSIDE her house, sleeping. When she's asleep, there's no waking her. I let myself inside and take a shower. I rub the bar of Dr. Bronner's Peppermint Soap on my T-shirt and scrub it in with my hands, then take my T-shirt off, rinse it, and drop it on the floor. I do this to each article of clothing. My socks take the longest. Then I wash my body. The soap rinses off onto my clothes. I step on them repeatedly to give them a second wash. I turn off the water, step on my clothes a few times to wring them out more, and wrap myself in Jade's towel. I reach under the sink where Jade keeps some Comet and a scrub brush just for me. I sprinkle some Comet on the shower floor, scrub, and leave it on so it can continue to bleach my stains and kill my germs.

I carry my wet clothes in one hand as I sift though her drawers in search of some sweatpants. I find some old gray ones that will do and put them on. Then I walk out her back door and hang my laundry on her fence.

When I walk back in, there's a huge man in her room,

turning down her bed.

"Who are you?" we ask each other in unison.

"Jade's brother," "Jade's friend," we say simultaneously.

"Oh, Peter Lemonjello," he says.

"In the flesh," I reply. "My main house burned down today." I gesture toward the forest fire. "I just got out."

"Wow," he says, and waits for more of the story. I don't tell it to him though. Instead, I just blurt out, "Oh, you're Nisa-Josh," as I put two and two together.

"I'm Josh," he says, confused. "What does Nisa mean?"

Uh-oh. "She didn't tell you."

"Tell me what?"

"She remembers you from before."

"From before what?" he asks.

"From before this life."

"Na-uh," he says. That's my out.

"Yeah, you're right. I was just messing with you. Please don't kick my ass."

I must not have been very convincing because then he says, "Wait, you were serious, weren't you? What did she tell you?"

"Hey, do you have any clippers?" I return to Jade's bathroom, find her scissors and start to cut off my dreadlocks and hack back my beard. I make a pile on the counter so I can donate it to the birds for their nests later.

"What's Nisa?" he asks again as I chop away.

"Who," I correct. "*Who's* Nisa. Nisa is Jade's old best friend from some place in Africa—I don't know how long ago." He looks both amused and skeptical. "Look. If she thought you really wanted to know or thought you were ready to hear it, she'd have told you. It's not really my place to tell you anything. But if she ever tells you anything, believe it. She found me when I ran away thirteen years ago. I could have been anywhere. I was in the middle of nowhere and she found me. *I* didn't even know where I was. Jade knows stuff."

Now Nisa-Josh looks uncomfortable.

"But, she doesn't know everything . . ." This isn't helping; he still looks concerned. "Hey, just forget about it. I mean, besides skating around in a superhero cape and refusing to wear shoes, she's totally normal." I go to the kitchen for a used lunch bag, return to the bathroom and put my hair in it. "I'm just going to take this and go," I tell him, and leave with my bag of hair.

Man, what a day. I return to the chairlift tree house and sleep for fourteen hours.

The Moon on Aretha

THE MOON ABOVE sees it all. It understands Aretha is like a new moon, something that is there but cannot be seen, something that is simply between phases.

The moon sees Jade's strong fingers sinking into the abdomen of her massage client, releasing the psoas muscle which causes Linda, or Hip Problem Lady as Jade calls her, so much pain. Linda breathes, Jade waits, Grace lays her hands on. The moon sees this, and the moon sees something these three cannot.

Outside, the moon sees Lula, Linda's Doberman, sniff the fence. She runs along the fence until she reaches a knot hole in one of the boards, and sticks her nose through it. It meets the nose of Orca, a gigantic black lab with a white star on his chest. Orca smells Lula and finds her irresistible. He paws the fence. He stands up against the fence, but cannot see over the top. He sizes up the six-foot tall wooden fence, and remembers jumping such a fence when he was just two, but he is older now. The smell of Lula drives him crazy. He's determined. He shifts his focus from the top of the fence to the bottom, and begins digging. He digs zealously, until at last the hole is just large enough for him to crawl through.

The moon sees Aretha waiting for the gametes from Lula and Orca to come together in that miraculous, life-creating union. Aretha condenses her spirit until at last, the moment is right for her to jump into the body of Lula. Here, her new body will gestate, until it is time for her new journey, this time in the body of a dog that lives to swim and fetch. It will be an exciting, new experience.

The full moons of each month look slightly different. The moons of late summer appear larger and richer in color and warmth, yet it is in fact the same moon. So it is with the spirit of Aretha, appearing slightly different in each incarnation, but recognizable as the constant it truly is. The moon knows, dogs have a way of finding the people with whom they want to spend another life, and has no doubt it will happen. It will be a new chapter, an opportunity for new experiences, lessons, and perspectives. And in the way no moon cycle is really better or more valuable than the moon cycle preceding or following, so it is with each chapter in Aretha's existence.

Jade on her Astral Dream with Aretha, Complementary Colors, and Secrets

I DREAMT LAST night I was petting Aretha's soft, soft fur. My senses were heightened, making Aretha even softer to me. So soft. Soft like I had never felt soft before. *And I thought I'd never do this again.* I laughed at myself for being so silly, for thinking death was permanent.

I was so happy to be with Aretha, to have found her. I began to lead Aretha home.

But when I reached home, Aretha was no longer with me. Where had she gone? Where had I lost her?

My room was still dark when I woke. Grace was sitting in my rocking chair. "Oh, you silly girl. God, you'll try anything, won't you? Aretha can't come back here with you like that."

So it was real.

In my divorce with God, where God seemingly got custody of my dog, I at least got visitation privileges it seems. Oh, Gracious God.

And with that low-vibration thought, Grace disappeared.

Josh was behind me, spooning me. The first night he slept here, I was shocked to wake up with him next to me. While he slept, I studied him. His features were so different from mine, his brow, his cheeks, his lips. His upper jaw is pronounced. There's nothing angular or sharp about his face. It is so beautiful, soft, but not delicate.

Each night I fall asleep in the gravel hole where Aretha sunbathed, where I can stare at the stars and imagine her flying among them, and in the middle of every night, I wake up next to Josh, both of us still in all our clothes. I stare at him for a while, then go back to sleep, and when I wake up again, he's gone. We haven't talked for days.

I look at where his arm and my arm cross. The two of us are at opposite ends of the color spectrum. I think we're beautiful. When I was little, and coloring while Mom painted, she showed me that blue made orange look more orange, and that orange made blue look more blue. She explained that if you put each color of the rainbow in a circle, blue and orange would be on opposite sides, as would yellow and purple, and red and green. She showed me how opposite colors bring out the beauty in each other. They are called complementary colors. That's what our skin reminds me of—complementary colors.

I flip over under the weight of Josh's arm. Instead of

studying his face tonight, I just embrace him. I don't know why he feels compelled to stay with me, but it's nice. It's comforting. I'm thankful. He's not as soft as Aretha, but still nice to hold onto after a disturbing dream. I give him a little squeeze. He makes a lovely, low "Mmm" sound, shifts his arms on my back, but doesn't wake up. I rest my head on his chest and give him another little squeeze before I fall back to sleep. As I drift off, I feel him kiss the top of my head, and I melt.

"Are you awake?" he whispers.

"Mmm," I answer.

"I met Peter Lemonjello tonight."

Now that got my attention. I hope Forrest wasn't too frightening for him.

"He slipped and told me about Nisa . . . well, not everything."

This isn't happening. "And you believed him?" I murmured. "Peter Lemonjello has spent the last thirteen years in self-imposed solitary confinement." I really don't want to have this discussion.

"He told me you found him in the middle of nowhere."

I don't reply. Rule number one: It's okay not to tell the truth, but it's not okay to lie.

"It got me wondering if I even know who you are."

"You haven't known me that long . . ." *in this life anyway.* "How well do you expect to know me at this point?"

"Your brother says you know things," he says.

"Yeah, big deal. You know things, too. He knows things.

Everyone knows things."

"Jade, why won't you just be honest with me?"

"I haven't lied to you. I never lie."

"That's not the same as being completely honest."

"I just lost Aretha, Josh. I don't want to lose you, too."
What's the point? I think I already have.

"Why do you think you'll lose me if you're completely honest?"

Well, he would have found out eventually and when he did, he would use his free will to opt out of our agreement. It's out of my hands. I might as well come clean. "Okay. Fire away. Ask me anything."

"Tell me all about Nisa."

I break away from Josh and lie on my back. I miss his arms around me already, but I might as well get used to it starting now. "Nisa was like a sister to me."

"Nisa was a girl?" See, I'm rocking his world already.

"Yes. We sat on a hill looking down at a village of huts below. We were African and wore lots of beads around our neck and not much else. I don't know what tribe that is. Nisa told me her father arranged for her to marry a man from the south, which meant she would be moving. She told me she wished one of us was a man so we could marry and never be torn apart like this. I asked her who would be the man, and she volunteered."

"And why do you think I'm her?"

"You have the same eyes."

"How do you know that's not just chance?"

Shit. Do I tell him about Grace? "Look Josh, I really don't see why this is so important. It's today, this lifetime. You always have free will. You can always think this is too much and get out of any agreement you've made. You can believe in past lives or not believe in them. It won't really change the present. This is real, right now, you and me. And the sense of connection we have is real. Does it matter why we have it?"

"Did you really find your brother in the middle of nowhere?"

"Yes, and if you were lost and needed help, I could probably find you, too. And if I needed help investing, you could help me. The stock market is way more complicated and mysterious than finding people."

"How did you know where to find him?"

I look at him, defeated. I wish so much he would stop asking questions for which he's really not prepared to hear the honest answer. I'm going to miss him so much. I waited so long for this reunion. "Does it really matter?" I ask.

"I want to know," he answers.

"There are a couple ways I know things other people often don't. Other people could. It's not like this information is only available to me. I don't know why I seem to be the only person listening. First, I can feel yes and no in my body. Yes feels like strength. No feels like weakness. It's as simple as that. Like when you've eaten lots of brownies, but you love brownies, so you go to eat another, but just holding it makes you feel weak. Your body is telling you no. Or like when you eat something healthy you've been craving and it makes you feel stronger. Your body is telling you yes, thank you, it needed that, and yes, that was a good choice."

"And the second way?"

I wince. Grace appears and sits behind Josh where I can see her. I look at her, and she nods at me. Okay, here it goes. "Ever since I was a little girl, I have been able to see my spirit guide. She tells me things."

"Spirit guide?"

"Right. All of us who come directly from Heaven into this life, whether we recognize it or not, have a spirit guide. It's a friend from Heaven who floats between the Heaven dimension and the Earth dimension to advise us, protect us, and help us keep our agreements."

"What does she look like?"

"A person. Black, cornrows."

"What kind of things does she tell you?"

"Um . . . she tells me about problems my massage clients have mostly and helps me to help them more. She often tells me if I'm in danger. She tells me to stop burning my food, but hey, who doesn't? She told me where Forrest was, and she told me I was going to have fun with you. I thought it was going to last longer than this though."

"Can you see my spirit guide?"

Oh, God, let this end. I look over at Grace, who has her arm around a short smiling Japanese man. He waves at me. "He's a short Japanese man. I just saw him for the first time. He smiled and waved."

The little Japanese man speaks to me, "When he was little, he stole his brother's red toy car. He never told a soul he did it. He hid it in the kitchen, in a punchbowl. Tell him I said to give it back the next time he's home." He laughs like this is fun.

Oh shit. "Okay, your guide says you stole your brother's red car and that you hid it in the kitchen in a punchbowl and he wants you to give it back the next time you're home."

Josh looks like he has seen a ghost. Yep, this is going exactly the way I thought it would. This bites.

"I need to go," Josh says.

I close my eyes for a second, then look down instead of at him. "I know," I say, more than disappointed—crushed. I really liked him.

He gets out of bed and lets himself out. I lie on my side and Grace sits next to me as I cry myself back to sleep.

Pearl on Getting What She Wants

WHILE BEATRICE IS away on a special shopping trip to Rapid City to get more yarn for baby sweaters, baby booties, and baby blankets, I take down all my snake skins. Twenty-one in all. I roll them up and put them in a burlap sack, which I strap to the back of my bicycle. I take one of the strawberry pies Beatrice and I made yesterday and put it in a box to take to that sweet Andrew Mabey at the Post Office. I also take my blue ceramic piggy bank.

I start toward town. I wave at Julie, Sasha, Erika and Rod along the way. Julie is working with a new horse, an Appaloosa, which is a surprise being that all her other horses are Morgans. Sasha, of course, is still in her garden, and Erika and Rod are fixing their turkey fence. Hopefully they'll deal with their geese, too. If you've ever been chased by a gaggle of killer geese when you're on your bike, you know nothing is scarier, not even George Stewart's pit bulls. I wonder if a gaggle of geese has ever killed a bicyclist. I'll have to ask around.

I drop off Andrew's pie first, and get my mail. I do believe I made Andrew's week. No good mail. Just advertisements. I throw them away. I continue a few doors down to Wallace's Boot Shop. My snake skins plus twenty-five dollars in change get me the red cowboy boots I've been dreaming of. Maybe I'll wrap them up and give them to myself for Christmas or my birthday with a tag that reads, "To Pearl, from the Rattler Family." Beatrice would be incensed. Yeah, better not. She wouldn't see the humor in it, and that would make her hate my boots. Nah, maybe I'll just ditch the box at the post office and pretend like I've had the boots a long time.

Jade on Massaging Lana Jones and Dreams from Other Lives

I STAND ON Lana Jones' doorstep. I know there must be security guys watching me, so I go ahead and ring the bell even though I'd like to just stand here for a minute and try to center myself. I'm not up for this. I'm totally not up for this. I hear pitter-patter footsteps approach from inside, and then her daughter answers the door.

"Hi!" She greets me with a big smile. She's about ten with great brown curls. She's followed by a small, black dog with short hair and a long nose. She guides me back to a quiet room where I unzip the bag around my massage table, unfold the table so the legs pop out and lift it upright. "What's your name?" she asks me.

"Jade."

"I'm Elle."

"Hi Elle. I like your dog." Elle is sweet. She has a nice

spark. I take extra padding and some sheets out of the pocket of my bag. I unfold the pad and put it on the table.

"Do you have a dog?" she asks.

"My dog just died," I answer. My eyes start to water, but I hold back my tears.

"I had a dog that died once."

"It's hard," I say.

She nods. "It's hard." She studies the pad on my table. "That's really old."

"Yep. It's been with me a long time." I put on the sheets. The dog begins to bark.

Lana walks in and puts the dog on the massage table. The dog stops barking. "She gets really excited about massage tables," she explains with a dazzling smile. "I'm sorry I'm running late. I'll be right with you."

"No problem," I say.

"Elle, may I please speak to you in the other room?" Elle follows her out and gets a hushed scolding for not finishing her homework.

Lana returns. "I'm ready," she says with a deep exhale. She looks me right in the eye. I recognize something about her. I step out to let her get on the table in private and return when she calls me.

"Will you open that cupboard and hit the play button?" When I turn the music on, I hear the beautiful voice of Ayub Ogada. I get a flash of a memory where I'm fishing in a boat with my little sister, rocking with the lapping waves just off the shore. I take a good look at the little sister. She's dark black, almost purple-black with hair cut very close to her head, and she has Lana Jones' eyes. She holds a little black dog in her arms. We sing in harmony at the top of our lungs. Little sister, good to see you again. I want to sing along with Ayub Ogada loudly now to see if Lana will sing with me again and remember me, but I don't. It would be bad for business. Instead, I just enjoy listening to the beautiful African music in the presence of my beautiful sister whose dog now sleeps between her ankles. Grace appears and sings along loudly. She notices Lana, recognizes her and jubilantly begins to shout greetings in Swahili. Grace must have been in that life with us, too. I silently thank my sister, Lana, for reminding me death is not the ending we think it is. Such a beautiful soul she is.

I come home, lie in Aretha's gravel hole, look at the stars, and fall asleep.

In my arms, I hold the body of a rottweiler I loved in that life. In the distance, I see a castle. I work for the people who live there. This dead dog belonged to them, but I was the one who loved her. I lay her down in a trench I dug and take a few moments to touch her fur for the last time. Tears drop from my eyes into the dirt I shovel onto her. I am a man, and thankful to be alone grieving for a friendship few would understand.

I wake from my dream and recognize the dog in the dream as Aretha.

I'm alone. It seems Josh moved me indoors and decided not to stay. I didn't even expect him to move me inside.

I miss my dog. I miss my dog so bad. I want her back. I yell it at God, "I want my dog back!" I am so incredibly not pleased with God right now.

I've had enough dreams about Aretha, dreams from other lives, to know our friendship is as old as time, and that we'll always weave in and out of each other's lives, but I don't want her back later. I want her back now.

I feel extra sorry for myself tonight because I don't even have Josh anymore. I have nothing.

Olive on Effort and What She Lost

I STUDY GRANDMA Pearl and Beatrice as they approach me. Beatrice sways and swishes through the orchard in a lime green dress and work boots, while Grandma Pearl struts like the force she is. They are so beautiful to me, like an extension of the earth, Beatrice dancing out of its surface with the flowers and wheat, and Grandma Pearl . . . well, she is more like a small buffalo.

My eighth six-inch layer is nearly finished. Before I start my next layer, I'll need to insert my window bucks.

"It's really starting to take shape!" Beatrice says with a hint of amazement.

"Yes, Scott McPhereson is coming out tomorrow to trench my waterline and dig and install the septic. I can't believe it's really happening!"

"You're really doing it, Olive!" Beatrice is impressed.

"It's nice to move at this pace," I say. "I really have time to get lots of ideas and consider all of them carefully . . .

where I want nooks and shelves . . . things like that."

Grandma nods approvingly, then switches gears. "You got a letter from Matt." She hands it to me. "Meatloaf sound good to you?"

I nod, then open the letter. The weather, yeah, yeah, yeah. How are you, blah, blah, blah. Then there it is: "I've fallen in love again. Her name is Alise. She moved into the rental across from the snowboard shop. It was effortless. We're moving to Mexico. I don't know what else to say. I thought it would be best for you to know."

"Are you okay?" Beatrice asks. I read the letter aloud.

"*Effortless,*" I say. "Of course it was. If it had taken any effort, it wouldn't have happened."

"Yeah, God forbid any woman be worth effort," Grandma Pearl says.

"I'm better off without him, you know. You don't have to feel sorry for me," I tell them. "It's a blessing to me to have that bridge burnt."

"Sometimes people aren't suited for each other and are better off apart. It still hurts like hell," Beatrice says, and puts her hand on my back.

When she said that, I don't know, the dam just broke. I began to sob. They both took me in their arms, one stroking my hair, and the other stroking my back. "I loved him," I said through my sobs. "I loved him so much. I really thought it was forever."

"Oh, Olive Oil, life is really painful sometimes," says Grandma Pearl.

I jump back, pulling out of their embrace, startling Beatrice and Grandma Pearl. "Oh my God!"

"What is it?!" they ask in unison. Beatrice's eyes bulge and Grandma Pearl searches her side frantically for her gun.

"Did you feel that?!?"

"Feel what?" shouts Beatrice, looking all around like I'm referring to an earthquake.

I take one of each of their hands and place them on my belly, then take a deep breath . . . "There! That!" Grandma Pearl sighs in relief and Beatrice puts her other hand over her mouth as her eyes well up.

"This baby's got something to say," Grandma Pearl tells me.

"You know, Olive, it just might be time to close old chapters," says Beatrice. "You're about to start a whole new one and you can't be carrying a lot of baggage into this one."

"She shouldn't be carrying all these heavy building materials, either—at least not by herself," says Grandma Pearl. "Tomorrow, we're gathering the Thunderellas together for a very important meeting—we've got work to do."

I take one last look at the letter in my hands. "Grandma Pearl? Beatrice? Want to go with me to put something in Dean's barrel that's really worth burning?" But before they can answer, I feel it again—another kick . . . and then another. "On second thought, I think I'll make my own little fire. Put together a little burn pit right here for when I have goodbyes to say."

"That's my girl," says Beatrice.

"You be sure and send the smoke over Dean's way," says Grandma Pearl as she and Beatrice turn to leave.

Jade on the Third World Planet

TONIGHT, WHEN I wake, Josh is in my bed. I'm stunned. I rest my hand on his precious face and lay my head on his chest. I adore him.

He stirs, gives my back a couple strokes, makes a couple "Mmm" noises and whispers, "Are you awake?"

Oh, no. "Yes," I reply.

"Are you okay?" he asks.

"I'm all right," I answer. "It's a nice surprise that you're here."

He doesn't acknowledge the other night. "Are you going to be okay?"

"What do you mean, like one of these nights am I going to fall asleep inside?" I clarify.

"Yeah," he answers. "I don't really see you bouncing back yet. I just wonder if you're going to be okay."

"Yeah," I answer. "Yeah . . . it's just really hard being here sometimes."

"What do you mean here? Here with me, or here in your apartment, or here in Cottonwood, or here in life . . . ?"

"Earth. I mean Earth."

"What are you saying?" His arm gets rigid and stops rubbing my back.

I prop myself up on my elbows. "Josh, I'm not suicidal, if that's what you're thinking. I already tried that in another life. It didn't work. I was just shuffled right through to a new life, and had to start all over again. No, I'm definitely not suicidal."

"So what are you saying?"

I pause for a minute to try to think of how to explain this. "I went to massage school with a woman who served in the Peace Corps in Africa. She had amazing stories. I think Earth life is like her trip to Africa. You know, when you're back in your comfortable life in the States, Africa seems like a great adventure. You know it's going to be hard sometimes, but you sign up anyway because it sounds so interesting. Then you go there and wonder, *What did I get myself into?* You're not sure you're going to make it. Flies are in all your food and you finally get hungry enough to just go ahead and eat insect larvae. There's no toilet paper, so what are you going to do? You have to wipe your ass with your hand, and then just wash your hand. When it's finally over, you go home to your friends and family in the States, show some slides, tell stories which by that time seem funny about how you ate grubs and wiped your ass with your hand, and everyone, including you, sees your adventure as one big fascinating success. You talk about how much you learned and how grateful you are for that experience. Maybe a couple of your friends run right out and buy tickets. Same with Heaven and Earth."

When Josh chuckles uncomfortably, it's clear he doesn't know what to think or say. That's okay. He doesn't see or hear his guide, so I can't expect him to know what I know.

"I'm just going through a hard time right now is all. Metaphorically speaking, I'm wiping my ass with my hand. But just like if I was in Africa, tomorrow I could be in a fascinating market or listening to some great marimba and feeling really happy I chose to come on this great adventure. Life is like that. The good times don't last and the bad times don't last, and before you know it, your third world adventure is over. You get to go home to where there are hot showers, fresh food, and all the toilet paper you could ever want. While you're in Africa though, it really is better for your peace of mind if you don't think about the States too much—if you just give in to the experience and be present in Africa. I know all this, but I don't know that it makes it any easier. Actually, I know for a fact, it doesn't." Life is like the news. More understanding and awareness about current events don't make watching the news more enjoyable—only more interesting.

Rather than say anything, Josh just rubs my back.

"That's nice," I say.

"My backrub?"

"Yeah, it's like the marimba music I was waiting for."

He kisses the top of my head, holds me tight, and goes back to rubbing my back.

The Moon on Phil and Anna's Waxing Love

THE MOON SAW it all, and the moon understood. Just as the moon gets a little fuller each night when it's waxing, so did the hearts of Phil and Anna.

On the first night, Anna showed up at the house at seven o'clock. Phil put on music and extended his hand to her. Anna took it. They danced. It became more smooth and natural. At eight o'clock, Phil looked at the clock apologetically. Anna walked to the back door and smiled to tell him she had a good time. He smiled back and then walked her to her tree house.

On night two, Anna showed up at seven o'clock. Phil was better dressed than the previous night. He put on music, extended his hand, and she took it. With a small but clear movement, he spun her into him. She put her hand on his shoulder. He looked down at her, inhaled deeply, smelling the perfume she had dabbed behind her ears. He danced with greater confidence. She danced with greater confidence. At eight o'clock, he looked at the clock, but didn't say anything. She saw him looking, though, and noticed it herself. She took his hand and walked to the door. She gave it a little squeeze before she let it go. With his eyes, he told her he knew she had caught him not wanting to tell her it was time to stop, and laughed at himself for this violation. Then he opened the door and walked her all the way to the ladder. She watched him walk back to the house. He looked back at her before going in, and she gave him a sexy smile.

Anna showed up at six fifty-five on the third night. Phil offered her a glass of red wine. She accepted. Phil put on music and held his hand out to her. She took it and moved into him like a breeze. She caught her breath. They danced, moving toward each other and away from each other, push, pull, push, pull, twist and step, twist and step. Their knees, bent, low to the ground. Big steps. Legs seemingly entwined, but well within their boundaries, complying with the agreement made. The hour seemed very long this time as their desire for each other grew. She watched the clock closely, a little flushed. Phil didn't know how much he could take. At eight o'clock, she stopped, put her hand on his cheek, and looked deeply into his eyes. He looked at her lips. He wanted those lips. He began to move in for the lips, but she ran out of the house and closed the door behind her. This is when Phil knew he had her.

On the fourth night, Anna showed up at six forty-five. Phil offered her a glass of red wine and she accepted. She drank it quickly and had another. Phil put on music. He held his hand out and she walked right into his space, right into that space where, like magnets, people are attracted to each other or repelled. He was attracted. She took a long, desirous look at him before taking his hand. He let the hand on her lower back creep a little lower at times. She let her hand on his shoulder creep up to his neck and play with the hair at the nape of his neck. He was aroused. She was aroused. At eight o'clock, she walked out the door to the tree house with him still holding her hand behind her. She turned and looked at him one more time, but before she could start up the ladder, he put his hands on her face and looked at her with the kind of desire she hadn't seen since they were teenagers. He wanted to kiss her so badly. She smiled and shook her head, afraid to disobey Martina, Martina who had brought them this far in only a week. But, oh, the tension. She could not stand it. She pushed him away, ran up the ladder, and watched him strut back to the house.

Phil came home at six o'clock on the fifth night. The music was already on. Anna was dressed in a black linen shirt with the top four buttons left unbuttoned. She had made linguini puttanesca. He loves linguini puttanesca. He spun his fork in the noodles and brought them to his lips. A few broke free, so he had to slurp them. Anna leaned forward enough to give him a peek down her shirt and watched his lips. He sipped his wine and locked eyes with her. She sipped her wine and held his gaze. With his eyes, he told her this was the most delicious meal he had ever eaten. This is where she knew she had him.

At seven o'clock, he held out his hand to ask her to dance. She took it. He pulled her in to him. She assumed the dance position. He pulled her closer. They tangoed low across the floor. Though their faces were only a couple inches apart as they danced, they did not kiss. Their eye contact was broken from time to time when one of them looked at the other's lips. *I want to kiss you,* this glance said. *Oh, I want to kiss you.* But they trusted Martina's wisdom in the ways of love and refrained. The sexual tension built as they danced and danced. It built and built and built. Neither of them looked at the clock to see it was eight o'clock. Or nine. Or ten. Finally, Phil rested his palm on her cheek, looked at her regretfully, then turned and walked to the door. She followed him. As he reached for the door, she slid her arms under his from behind, and wrapped them around his chest. He put his hands on hers and caressed them. He spun around within her hold and placed his palm on her cheek again, looking so deeply into her eyes, he thought they were surely merging. She put a hand behind his neck to pull him closer to her. He inhaled her smell. Intoxicating. He wanted so badly to kiss her. But they should not. Martina told them not to. Martina had gotten them this far. Oh, but her lips, her eyes, her smell, her magnetism. He could not stand it any longer. He kissed her like a soldier going off to war. My God, they had passion again.

Forrest on Jade's Birthday

IT'S MY FAVORITE day of the year—Jade's birthday. It's the only day of the year I take a break from oats, grouse, and rice, and indulge in chocolate cake. And this year, Taj Mahal is playing at the outdoor concert. Chocolate cake and Taj Mahal. Life is good. Below, Jade approaches with a backpack and Nisa-Josh. "Hey!" she calls out. "I brought Josh!"

I throw down the harness. She helps him into it and clips him to the rope. He looks scared. I see her point to places up the tree. I toss the other end of the rope already through the figure eight safety down to her so she can belay and help pull him up. He looks thick and awkward to me, like he would be a terrible climber, but he does pretty well. He's a strong climber. He pulls himself up onto the deck of the tree house, laughs nervously, and exhales.

"Watch this," I tell him, as I throw the harness and rope back down to Jade. She clips in and scrambles up the tree like it's nothing. "All that massage makes her a wicked climber." Josh doesn't dare look down.

"Ya, Petah Lemonjello, it is da birthday girl, Helga," she says in a fake accent and begins to sing, "Hort fer das laben, hort fer das laben, ich meinen kochen." Very loosely translated: Happy day, happy day, eat my cake. We couldn't remember the happy birthday song from high school German class, so one day we just made one up.

I greet her by putting a crown of Indian paint bush, lupine, and balsam on her head. "Helga, what a happy day it is. I am now ready for my four-hour butt massage," I say in my Peter Lemonjello voice. She slaps my butt instead with a newspaper.

"Look at this, hero" she says, holding the newspaper. The first headline says, "Fire Crew Makes Narrow Escape." Good. The first crew to respond managed to run around the fire to the south. The second headline says, "Man Saves Ranger." It's an interview with Lightning Bob talking me up. Oh come on, Lightning Bob, I didn't do anything anyone else wouldn't have.

I scan the article and reach the part where investigators have no suspects, but offer a thousand-dollar reward for information leading to an arrest. I hope Matt likes Mexico. I hold it for Jade, point to that sentence, and say, "I saw this. It was *Bear Bait.*" I don't want Josh to pick up on what we're talking about. I know Jade can keep a secret. Her eyes get really wide. "I'm only sharing that in case you want to let *the perfect one* know." She looks unenthusiastic about that. "I know. Tough call."

At the end of the article is a plea for me to contact

Lightning Bob at the Forest Service office. Hm. Okay. I study the map of where the fire burned. Yes, that includes the location of my main house all right. I had no doubt it would burn. I nod my head and put down the paper like it's no big deal.

"That was a pretty amazing story," Josh says to me.

I nod.

"So is this your sign?" Jade asks.

"Yeah," I say, amazed. "Hasn't quite sunk in yet."

"Hey, he's starting!" she announces as Taj Mahal comes onstage. Jade and I dangle our legs over the edge of my tree house while Josh nestles back by the trunk of the tree. "Are you okay?" she turns back to ask Josh.

"I'm great," he answers and scoots forward a little more. She puts her hand on his ankle to reassure him.

"I have a surprise for you," I tell her. "I know how you like to feel the earth under your feet, and I know there are times when you have to wear shoes whether you want to or not. I made these for you." I reach into a paper bag and grab the moccasins I made for her.

She gasps with delight.

"Oh, Forrest!" she exclaims as she tries them on.

They go all the way up to her knee for when the snow is deep. At the top, I made fringe. She loves fringe.

"Look at this!" she marvels and touches the quills I beaded on. "Oh, so beautiful!" She stands up and hops around to admire how the fringe moves. This makes her smile. She turns to Josh and explains, "He made these!"

Josh doesn't strike me as the kind of guy who can appreciate a good pair of moccasins, but he tries.

She sits back down next to me and puts her arm around me. She rests her head on my shoulder and says, "This is the best gift ever."

Josh creeps a little closer to the edge.

"Cake?" I ask them.

Jade reaches into her pack for forks. "Yahoo!" she answers. "Maybe we should skip birthday candles this year."

I dish her up a piece onto a napkin. While below Taj Mahal sings "Blues Ain't Nothin'" I join in the tune, replacing the lyrics with those of "Happy Birthday." Josh joins in.

"You still get to make a wish," I tell her. She looks at Josh, winks, turns back to me, and says, "Done."

When the concert is over, they prepare to rappel down.

Jade says, "Let me know what happens at the Forest Service office."

I assure her I will. I belay as Jade rappels down first. I pull the harness back up and toss the other end of the rope down to her so she can belay Josh. I give him some instruction, assure him Jade won't let him fall, and watch him go reluctantly over the edge. He really hates this. He must really love Jade.

Olive on her Housewarming

VIGAS ARE THE hardest part. I pick up one end of the long narrow log and walk toward the other end, walking with my hands also, so that the end I first picked up gets higher and higher as I approach the other. When the pole is straight up in the air, I'm able to walk toward my wall, and slowly let it fall to rest against the wall. Here's the hard part. I have to pick up the low end and push it over the wall, high enough that it clears the other wall. Since I'm going to have a living roof, I need many vigas. When all my vigas are up on the walls, I mix another batch of mud, climb up my ladder, anchor my vigas in place, and fill the gaps between them with mud. I can't believe it. Tomorrow or the next day, I'll be ready to begin my roof. I'll lay planks on my vigas, then layer special industrial strength plastic over my planks, throw dirt up there, about a foot of it, and plant it. Or at least I'll do what I can. Each week that goes by makes it more difficult as my baby grows inside me. Not only is the physical protrusion of my belly an obstacle, the Thunderellas are becoming more and more adamant that I need to be careful, that lifting heavy things could send me into labor. They're a wise group of women, so even though I want to do as much of this on my own as I can, I heed their advice often. These days I'm doing more directing than lifting —and a lot of laughing. The Thunderellas will do that to you—nothing they do is without a certain flair.

My planks have come from the Methodist Church in Ione that burned down. Most of the floor boards were in good shape. They smelled smoky, but I sanded them, and they've been sitting out in the air for a few weeks now, under the tarp I put up to shelter my tools and materials. Not only were the floor boards a good find, but they left me feeling like I was supported, and I was going to be okay.

Hazel had an old shed on her land that had fallen down. For safety reasons, she was happy to help me tear it down and take the materials away. I used the old boards for a small deck, and will use the rest for a couple interior doors. I continue to fill in the spaces between my vigas and reflect on my gratitude for having enough—no more, no less, just enough. I'm thankful for every bit of it.

As the sun gets low, I enjoy the silence of sitting alone outside my almost complete house. I think about what to plant on my living roof. I'll probably go with Grandma Pearl's suggestion—strawberries and thyme. Maybe next year I'll plant taller things, I don't know.

I see the Thunderellas meandering toward me. Grandma Pearl pushes a wheelbarrow. They are quite a sight, a mix of colors and movements. I told Grandma Pearl I felt the need to skip tap night tonight because my feet are too swollen to fit in those shoes.

"We brought you a party!" Beatrice calls out as they arrive. Fiona hooks up some white Christmas lights and some party lights with horses on them to a car battery in the wheelbarrow and drapes the lights over my vigas. Beatrice and Hazel unpack cold pizza, some potato salad, wine and sparkling cider on the small deck. Grandma Pearl sorts out everyone's tap shoes, except mine, and sets up the radio.

"It just didn't seem like tap night without you. Since you couldn't come to us, we decided to come to you," says Grandma Pearl. "Fiona, it's time!"

Fiona, beaming with pride at the role she's been granted, hands me a pair of new flip-flops. I feel truly blessed.

We eat, drink, chat, and then Grandma Pearl turns on the music and gets the party going. The only station we get out here is NPR, and tonight, it's the Thistle and Shamrock Show. We squeeze onto the deck together in a row, everyone in their tap shoes and me in amazingly comfortable flip-flops.

"Okay, everybody, palms up and Riverdance!" We laugh hard, hold our palms up high so they touch the palms of the woman next to us, and follow Grandma Pearl doing the regular old time step, holding our upper bodies more straight and still—our own rendition of Irish Step Dancing.

I turn to my right where Hazel is doing her best to look stiff and Irish, and I start laughing harder. To my left, Beatrice is laughing behind her cat glasses and gives me a joyous wink. Stomp, hop-shuffle-step, flap, ball-change, laugh.

Martina on Phil and Anna's Third Dance Lesson

I CRACKED THE door to see Phil guiding Anna up the stairs with one hand on her back. They wear small smiles. "You have not talked?" They shake their heads. "You have practiced every night?" They nod and smile a little bigger. "You have not made love?" They shake their heads and laugh, a little embarrassed this time. Embarrassment. A good sign. Lovemaking is taking root as forbidden. They are embarrassed because they want it. "You have not kissed?" I watch their reactions closely. Anna smiles and blushes. Phil looks sideways and toward the floor. "You have kissed!" They look guilty. They look ashamed. They do not look sorry. I am pleased.

"Phil, Anna, assume your dancing position. Take a step, step, step, step, now here, you are going to dip her like this. Firmly. Let her know she is in good hands. Before you pull her up, look at her. She is vulnerable. She is in your arms. She is trusting you. She is yours. Look at her. Isn't she beautiful?

She is yours. Now pull her up to you, keeping her close as you do this. Now step, step, step, step, and Anna, wrap your leg around him. No man can resist that. Do you know what that does to him? You are a tease. You love it. Phil, dip her again, but like this, this time. You have turned the tables. She teased you, but you are telling her turnabout is fair play. And back up. And step, step, step, step, now Anna take your hand off his shoulder, with palm open wide. Run your hand up his cheek and up, up, straight up and hold. Phil, pivot her like this and this. Anna, you are going to look away. Look here and here. Now back to eye contact. Step, step, step, step. Phil, swing her out like this, and swing her back tightly. Hold her for a minute. Notice how small she is in your arms. Now step, step, step, step. Good. Now, Phil, you may choose any of those variations and ask Anna to follow with clarity in your hands. Savor each one. Let the tension build."

I tango off to a corner of the room by myself, leaving Phil and Anna to entwine and untangle themselves over and over. Entwining, untangling, entwining, untangling, like a pull-start motor.

At eight o'clock, I turn down the music. "Tonight, you will go home and sleep in the same bed. You will burn a red candle all night. You will not talk. You will not make love for a week. You may do everything else." I do not truly expect them to abstain, but give this instruction to prolong the inevitable, to let the sexual tension build until it consumes them, to make their love decadent, not obligatory. In truth, I know we are finished. I have taught them the ways of love.

Phil on Kissing

ANNA AND I ran out of the studio and stumbled down the stairs as we kissed, frenzied. I held her soft, delicate hand as we ran to the car. We kissed in the car while I put the key in and started the engine. We kissed like we had not kissed in decades. I sped home as she kissed my neck, my ear, my cheek. I parked and kissed her. She crawled onto my lap. Oh. I opened the door, and stood with her still clinging to me, kissing me. She put her feet down and ran into the house, to a drawer in the kitchen where she found a red candle left over from Christmas. She held it up victoriously. I took her other hand, hurriedly ran to the bedroom, and lit the red candle.

Jade on Root Beer Floats

"YOU KNOW WHAT the world needs," I say as Josh and I wander the aisles of the grocery store after the concert, "more ice cream."

"Root beer floats," Josh specifies.

"I love root beer floats. In fact, I think I'd like to take a bath in one."

"And you could just drink and drink and never run out."

"Out of Crazy Straws. I love Crazy Straws." It's nice to almost feel like myself again. Josh has been an incredible friend, just as amazing as Nisa ever was. I love him.

"That sounds like a birthday wish," Josh says. He goes back to the front of the store to get a cart and then returns to the ice cream aisle. He puts seven boxes of vanilla ice cream into the cart. I smile. If he's doing what I think he's doing, he truly is the man of my dreams.

"It's nice to see you smile again," he says softly near my ear. I love his voice. The sound of his voice makes my cheek-bones tickle.

A Hefty bag containing the unfolded ice cream boxes and empty pop bottles sits on the floor. Cubes of ice cream float in the bathtub. Two cases of root beer don't go nearly as far as you'd think. The actual float is not very deep, but the foam threatens to spill out over the top.

Josh and I laugh hysterically as he hands me one of two Crazy Straws. It's our first time naked together. It's a little awkward. We hold hands and step into the root beer float bath.

"It's cold," he says, still laughing.

"Really cold!"

"I missed your laughter." He melts me.

I never thought anyone would melt me. In his presence, I'm just like this puddle of woman. I give him a hug. "You're my best friend," I tell him. While I hug him, I indulge in a moment of really taking in his body. I've seen a lot of bodies. I have massaged between two and three thousand bodies. I've never seen one like this. "And a fine, fine hunk of eye candy," I add and explode into laughter. I wish I could be serious and sexy, but come on, we're standing in a giant root beer float. I go to break away, but he doesn't let go.

"What did you just say?" he asks, and laughs in disbelief. "Did you just say 'eye candy'?"

"Maybe," I say self-consciously, still giggling, but feeling my cheeks heat up. Shit, I know they've got to be fuchsia by now. If I had beautiful dark skin like his, no one would ever know when I was blushing. Man, that would be nice.

"I love you," he says with a smile that will keep me a

puddle for the next year.

I place my hand with the Crazy Straw behind his neck, and my other on his cheek, then kiss him. "I never thought I'd feel this way about anyone," I tell him. "I love you so much."

He kisses me again and gets *that look*. You know the look. That's when I knew I was in trouble, but didn't mind. "Let's get in," he whispers mischievously.

We squat down awkwardly, still kissing. "Who's going to be on the bottom?" I ask, starting to laugh again.

"You are!" And before I know it, I am.

I laugh and shriek. "Wicked cold!"

"Okay . . ." He rolls us over. "Oh yeah," he agrees, laughing, "that is definitely not okay."

We go back to squatting. "Foam feels kind of good," I say. I scoop up a handful and lick it.

"Really? You like it?"

Now I feel embarrassed again. I look down and reach up to kind of cover my face with my hand, not thinking, until I become aware there is root beer float clinging to my forehead.

"Oh, let me get that for you," Josh says. He kisses and licks the root beer float off my face. It felt nice. It felt *very* nice.

I scoop up more root beer float, dribble some on my neck, and then dribble some on his shoulder. "Oh, no," I say. "Look what I've done."

Pearl on Why Good Guns Make Good Neighbors

THAT BASTARD DEAN fires up his '68 Mustang, which sputters and roars interchangeably. He revs the engine. He is going to wake up both Olive and Beatrice. I put on my boots and Carhartt jacket and trudge over there.

"Dean," I shout authoritatively over the sound of his decrepit engine. He ignores me. He knows better. "Dean! It's late! Turn that son of a bitch off!"

"Hey Pearl, it's 9:50. Legally, I still have ten minutes to be noisy, so blow it out your ass."

Now Dean really shouldn't have said that. I take out my trusty .44 Ruger, put a hole in two heater hoses and one in his radiator. I thought I was being nice by sparing his engine. Water began spurting in several directions. Dean picked up a jack handle as if he was going to come after me with it, as if I wouldn't blow a hole in him large enough to crawl through. Fool. Before turning and walking away, I take another look at my watch. "According to my watch, Dean, it's five after ten.

You're in violation of the law for disturbing the peace. I could also haul you in for threatening an officer, but I feel nice today. I feel downright charitable, Dean, so I'm going to give you yet another chance to develop some manners."

I return home. As I walk by Beatrice's room on my way to the bathroom, I hear her. "I heard shots, Pearl," Beatrice accuses in a loud whisper.

"I saved Dean's life," I whispered back.

"Really?"

"Yes, I was going to kill him, and then I changed my mind. Dean lives."

Anna on her Art Show

THERE HANGS MY life: In the beginning, the emerging fruit, the raisins, and last, the majestic cottonwood trees. On the portable walls in the middle of the gallery, my Goddess-like daughters, the next generation, part of the cycle of life. In my paintings, I see my own summer and winter, and my own rebirth. My branches blossomed, leafed, and then my leaves fell. I grieved for my leaves and thought I'd never have leaves again. That was the raisin era. In the spring, my branches grew fuller and grew new leaves. No, they weren't the same leaves as I had before; they are the leaves of a new era. It is a new time. I am going to be a grandmother.

The paintings of my daughters are not for sale, though you wouldn't believe what I've been offered for them. In fact, none of my paintings but the raisin ones are for sale. They are snapshots of good times. I'm keeping the originals and only selling prints.

I've been asked by a couple women if I would paint them on commission—if I would help them see their own beauty and perfection in the context of nature. This era of my life is not about doing things for other people, but that cause does seem worthy to me. I'm thinking about it. Each woman who does not recognize her own beauty contributes to the collective belief of all women that we are not good enough, and it hurts us all. Perhaps painting one woman at a time could cause a shift, even if it's only slight.

It's funny. I've wanted my whole life to have my work's worth recognized, and now that it finally is, I don't care. I look at all the paintings I love and think about my kids. My work is, and always has been, priceless.

Olive on Childbirth

FLAP-TOE-HEEL. Ouch. Yeow. What's that? Flap-toe-heel. I hold up my giant belly and keep dancing. Shuffle-ball-change, shuffle-ball-change—splash. Splash? I look at the puddle on the floor, and then look up at Grandma Pearl and the other Thunderellas.

"Come on ladies, it's showtime!" Grandma Pearl shouts to the others. "Hazel, you have the biggest car, can you drive?"

"I can drive," Hazel answers. "How far along is she?" I hear her whisper to Grandma Pearl.

"Only eight months," Grandma Pearl whispers back.

Outside, snow and dried leaves flurry in the air. Yowza! There it is again! I work to breathe in the strong wind. Fiona gets in the front of the Impala with Hazel, while Beatrice and Grandma Pearl guide me into the back between them.

"Punch it, Hazel!" Grandma Pearl calls out. Hazel hits the gas and off we go.

Yow-yow-yow-yow-YOWZA-YIKES-YEEHAW!!! That

hurt!

"That was two minutes," Fiona announces.

"Oh dear. Look at that," Hazel says as she stops the car. She parks it and gets out. I can't see what is going on.

"Hazel! What are you doing? We don't have time for this! We have places to go, Hazel!"

Eee-eee-eee-eee-EGADS! Christ on a bike!

"One minute, forty-five seconds," says Fiona.

Hazel comes back with a duck in her hands. She hands it to Fiona to hold. "Be careful of her wing." Then she turns to Grandma Pearl and explains, "She has places to go, too. Someone shot her wing. She wasn't able to migrate. She needs us."

"Just GO!" Grandma Pearl shouts.

Ja-ja-ja-ja-JUMPIN' JAHOSAVITCH!

"One minute, thirty-five seconds," Fiona says.

"This baby's coming fast. I don't think we're going to make it to Rapid City," Beatrice says.

Hazel begins to sing a song in Lakota.

Ah! AAAAHHHHH! I bend over with the contraction and feel all kinds of hands on my back. I start to rip off my clothes.

"Here Olive, lean back on me and let your Grandma deliver your baby," Beatrice says while stroking my hair. I breathe in short puffs.

Hazel stops singing. "Olive, you will have an easier time if you squat on that seat and brace yourself against the front seat. Let gravity help you."

I put my feet up on the backseat and grab the front seat as my next contraction hits. I curl into myself and try to hush a scream. The duck squawks when I quietly scream. I start to cry. I don't think I can do this.

"One minute, twenty seconds," says Fiona.

"Beatrice, there's a blanket behind you. Put it under Olive," says Hazel. Beatrice wedges a fleece blanket between my feet. "Pearl, squeeze the tops of her hips. It will help the bottom of her pelvis open and relieve some pressure."

Holy-holy-holy-holy-HOLY SHIT! I am going to rip in half! The duck squawks a little louder this time.

"One minute five seconds," Fiona tells us.

Hazel begins to sing again. The snow starts to fall harder and Hazel has to slow down, unable to see the road.

OH DEAR JESUS MAKE IT STOP! Squawk-squawk-squawk-squawk. I really feel the baby move with that one. I whimper and try to bend over to see if I see a baby yet.

Beatrice gently rubs my back as Grandma Pearl gets down on the floor to try to get a look. "Fiona, is there a flashlight up there?" Grandma Pearl asks.

"Glove compartment," Hazel interjects in the middle of her song.

With one hand, Fiona holds the duck and with the other opens the glove compartment and digs out a flashlight. I take it from Fiona, hand it to Grandma Pearl whose still on the floor, and let out a whooping scream. The duck screams too.

"She's crowning!" Grandma Pearl shouts.

Hazel stops singing again. "Olive, listen to me. Your body

knows what to do. That baby knows what to do. When you have contractions now, sing out, 'Come on, Body!' I am singing to Great Spirit and to your baby. I am asking Great Spirit to help and I am telling your baby this is a good place."

COME ON BODY! COME ON BABY! OH MY GOD, COME ON BABY! COME ON BABY!

"We have a head! One more big one, Olive!" Grandma Pearl coaches.

COME ON BABY! COME ON . . . baby. I feel the baby slip out and I reach down to catch her, but Grandma Pearl's hands are already there. Beatrice holds me tightly. I watch my tiny baby in Grandma Pearl's hands and can't believe my eyes. She's alive. Overwhelmed with relief, I cry and cry.

"BOY!" Grandma Pearl shouts to a chorus of cheers. Fiona looks back, her eyes as big as saucers, while the duck begins to squawk softly with my little boy's soft cries. "And you thought it was going to be a girl!"

OH! OH! "What is this? I thought it was over! AAAH!" I shout.

Hazel quickly turns around and explains, "Placenta."

Beatrice takes the blanket from under me and wraps it around me as Grandma Pearl hands me my tiny boy. I hold him close, looking down to study this new person. My heart overflows and I begin to cry again, this time not from my body ripping open, but from my heart. Beatrice pulls me back onto her so I can lie back a little and rest while Grandma Pearl messes with my placenta.

"Pearl, keep that placenta attached until we get to the

hospital. That baby's pretty early." Then Hazel looks at me in the rear-view mirror and says, "You did good, Olive."

"Hazel, crank the heat, will ya? We have to keep this little baby very warm," orders Grandma Pearl. I hear the noise of Hazel cranking the heat up a notch.

The car is quiet as we drive slowly in the snow flurries the rest of the way into Rapid City.

When we finally reach the hospital, Hazel pulls up to the ER entrance. First, Grandma Pearl, drenched in sweat, gray straight hair sticking to her forehead, gets out. I hear the click of her tap shoes on the concrete. With Beatrice's help, I scoot over and out (ow!) wearing nothing but a blanket and my flip-flops, baby wrapped up tight inside my blanket. My hair must have looked as bad as it felt. Fiona got out at the same time, sweaty, with a suspicious bump under her navy pea coat, and a beak sticking out between two buttons. Hazel put on her hazard lights and got out with Beatrice. The five of us thunder into the ER, trying not to slip on our own dripping sweat in our slick, noisy tap shoes and flip-flops, click-click-click-click, with Grandma Pearl shouting, "We've got a babeeeee!" and Fiona leaving a suspicious trail of duck feathers behind her. I feel the assurance of my little boy moving a little, and peek down my blanket to admire him. A nurse rushes over to me with a wheelchair and whisks me away.

Forrest on Probation

"HI," I SAY to the Forest Service secretary. "I'm looking for Lightning Bob."

"Forrest? Is that you?" I hear his voice call out from another room, and then watch him hobble in on crutches. "Good to see you! Good to see you! Look at you! You got rid of your hair! Hey everybody! This is Forrest!"

"Hi, Forrest!" everyone calls out. I want to run out of there.

"Let's go outside," Lightning Bob suggests to my relief. I'm still not particularly comfortable indoors. We sit on a bench by a juniper bush. Lightning Bob rests his crutches against the bench next to him. "I have something I want you to consider. I've been looking for a new tower to work in since mine burnt down. There are not many of these positions. There are two rangers retiring this year. One in western Montana and the other in the Idaho panhandle. You're good at observing. You're good at predicting fire. You keep your cool in emergencies. You're a good poet. I think you would make an excellent fire lookout ranger. New people generally have to walk on water to get one of these positions, and you've essentially done that. I don't know much about your life, but I think I know enough to suggest this might be a really good thing for you to consider. I already talked to the district ranger in both places about this. You could take your pick, and I'll go where you don't. The towers are within a day and a half drive of each other. We could still get together for a game of cribbage now and then. You'd have to get your GED before next summer."

Hm. A lookout tower would be a great halfway house for a person like me on probation. A lookout tower would be a great way to maintain my lifestyle, but still integrate back into society a little. "I'd like that," I tell him.

"Super! Super!" he exclaims. "The ranger in the Idaho tower actually wants to leave in two weeks, so that position opens up sooner. My ankle won't be healed up by then. There are ways we can work around this, but if you wanted to start as early as two weeks from now, it's waiting for you."

I nod that yes, I'd like that. I'd like a place to go. I'd like a helpful job.

"Super! Super! Let's go inside, and I can walk you through some paperwork and call the district ranger up there. Oh hey, before I forget, I wrote a poem about you." Of course he did. I smile.

"The Fire" by Lightning Bob
Sparks flew,

Wind blew
My friend and I we ran
The flames
Insane
Hot as a frying pan
We fled
So not to be dead
As the fire licked our back
Flames stoked
We choked
My friend carried my pack
I slipped
I tripped
It looked to be all over
My friend
Did tend
He put my arm over his shoulder
We got down
To town
Fatalities were zero
Now I shall
Thank my pal
Who will always be my hero.

After Lightning Bob helps me with paperwork, I head off to find Jade.

I knock, but no one answers. I let myself in to write her a note telling her that I'm going to be a lookout ranger. It's funny, I feel proud. It's a new feeling for me—this happiness. Wow, I can't remember the last time I felt like this. I think about my future with happiness now, not mere acceptance. Wild. "Dearest Helga," I start to write to Jade, but her phone rings and interrupts my ability to put my thoughts together.

Her answering machine kicks on and I hear Grandma Pearl's voice. God, I haven't heard that voice in thirteen years. "Jade? It's time! Olive had her baby! It's early. She's at the Samaritan Hospital in Rapid now and will probably spend a couple days here. If you can come, I know she'd be happy to see you! Love to you!"

Wow, I became a ranger and an uncle all in the same day.

Pearl on Fences and Integrity

NOW, IT'S ONE thing if Dean's cows get into my sunflowers and wreak havoc, but I can't have them getting into Olive's safflowers and flax next year. I feel like Anna's just waiting for her to fail and I'll be darned if I'm going to let that happen. I load up a couple hundred yards of coiled barbed wire, a few new T posts, and some tools into the bucket of my tractor. It's too heavy to carry. Phil and Anna are bringing Olive and the baby home today; I want everything to be perfect. I sure don't want Dean's damn cows running all over our gathering.

This tractor makes my butt hurt. It needs to be said. Plus, it really puts my old lady bladder to the test.

There goes Dean on his stupid four-wheeler. I hate listening to that damn thing. Look at him, riding around like some kind of idiot instead of fixing his fences so that an old woman doesn't have to. What kind of poor excuse of a man makes an old lady fix his fences to keep his cows out of her livelihood?

I watch him and imagine using him for target practice. I have lots of time to imagine on the long, long ride out there.

You know, I don't think Dean has ever done a thing to maintain these fences. In fact, I don't think these fences have been touched since Martha Peterson lived here. If there's one thing I absolutely cannot stand, it's a lazy farmer. Dean is lazy. I take the fence post driver, put the cup over the top of my T post, grab both handles and start slamming. When it hits the top of the metal T post, my whole body rattles. Jesus, what kind of man makes an old woman jar herself all up like this? I hate him. I really try not to hate anyone, but I sure hate him. I spend all day repairing his negligence, all damn day, when I should be home with Beatrice, preparing cookies and cider, and later, supper. Dean is a waste of my time. I pound in more T posts and think about all I should be doing at home to prepare for the arrival of everyone. That was a lot to dump on Beatrice. I start to feel guilty and decide to go back.

I get back onto the torture machine commonly referred to as a tractor, and begin the jolting ride back home on the little road that follows the fence line, as if jarring myself to death pounding T posts all day wasn't enough. I should have peed before I started home. The seat belt hits me right in the bladder. I return to thinking about all that needs to be done at home and flip the tractor into fourth gear to hurry back. I really have to pee. I start to look for the house, but can't quite see it. I wonder what Beatrice is doing. *Oh shit!* I realize how much I jerked the wheel when I hit that last bump, and feel the tractor begin to go over. Oh shit oh shit oh shit!

"Miss Pearl! Miss Pearl! Miss Pearl!" I hear Dean's panicked voice. Miss? Since when does Dean call me Miss? Oh Jesus, I must be dead. Wait, I can't be dead. My arm hurts too much . . . Unless I'm in Hell, which would explain the arm pain and the presence of Dean. "Miss Pearl!" I open my eyes. There's Dean jumping off that four-wheeler I hate so much. "Are you okay?" Do I look okay? What a stupid son of a bitch. "You're pinned. I'm going to go get my tractor and call you an ambulance! I'll be right back!" Everything gets fuzzy and dark, so I just close my eyes and give in to it.

The ground rumbles, and I hear a loud noise. "Now Miss Pearl, don't you worry. I'm going to get you out from there! You just relax!" Relax? Dean revs his tractor engine and the chain on the bar near my ear clinks as it tightens. I feel the tractor go up, up, and back upright. He jumps up in my cab, puts down a roll of newspaper, and takes off his flannel shirt. Ew, wish I hadn't seen that. He puts the roll of newspaper next to my arm and makes a sling out of his shirt. "Now don't you worry, Miss Pearl, you're going to be okay. The ambulance is going to meet us here." A breeze hits me just right and I'm aware that I have indeed peed on myself. Oh, Dear God, please take me now, I just can't bear the indignant experience of Dean seeing me with pee all over myself. He's going to tell everybody. What's worse is he's going to love telling everybody.

"Dean," I whisper.

"Yes, Miss Pearl?"

"Dean, I am embarrassed," I just say.

He looks me right in the eye and says, "I have no idea what you're talking about."

"Dean, I believe I have peed all over myself."

Once again, he looks me square in the eye and says, "I have no idea what you're talking about."

Could it be? Could it be that there is a gentleman in Dean who would not acknowledge my condition? Clearly, I am hallucinating.

"The ambulance will be here any minute, Miss Pearl. Just you hang on."

I hear the ambulance drive up the field, stop, and a man yell, "Is there a gate nearby? We need to get through the fence!" The pain in my arm is so intense, I start to go gray again, but not before I hear the crushing of the fence under Dean's tractor. Thank you, Dean, for I have now just crushed my arm for nothing.

The next time I open my eyes, the paramedics are stabilizing my arm and lifting me into the ambulance. I immediately pass out again.

Anna on Reunions

PHIL AND I pull up to the farm with Olive cradling Kelly in the back of our car. "Now remember," I say to her, "you always have a home with us. You can always change your mind."

"Welcome!" Beatrice hollers to us, "I just made some sweet rolls!" I take a deep breath and prepare to try my hardest to be nice to one of the two women who are working to prevent my grandchild from having a father in his life, and who enabled my daughter to have a medical crisis without medical insurance. I honestly don't know if I can. Considering the euphoria I feel looking at Kelly, I'm surprised with myself, but I just can't ignore how Olive's setup here terrifies me.

Beatrice bubbles over with enthusiasm at our arrival. "Olive, honey, I made you two beds, one indoors and one on the back porch, so you can take your pick."

"Thanks, Beatrice. I've been dreaming of being on the back porch for days."

"I don't know where Pearl is. She went off to fix some fences earlier today and I haven't seen her since. I'm sure she'll be back any minute. Anyway, come on, come on around to the back porch, and unwind from that long drive."

We shuffle in, get Olive and Kelly settled, drink juice and eat a sweet roll. It's awkward. I really don't have anything to say to Beatrice.

"Um, so Phil, I understand you've been picking up the bagpipes this summer," Beatrice says to try to fill the silence.

"Yes. I was going to play in the Trailing of the Sheep Parade this weekend, but seeing my first grandchild was more important."

"Yes," Beatrice agrees, and then there is that awkward silence.

I hear a car, and then Jade calls out, "Where is everybody?" She rounds the corner and finds us. Her hair looks pretty and smooth, and her burnt orange sundress is uncharacteristically tasteful. Josh stands behind her, smiling warmly at us, wearing a very nice white shirt, slacks, and some shiny black loafers.

"Welcome, dear! My goodness! How long has it been?" Beatrice greets Jade.

"Gosh, I don't even know!" Jade stops to think, but just shakes her head. "You haven't changed a bit though! Beatrice, Olive, this is my love, Josh."

"Welcome! Welcome! Have a sweet roll, Josh!"

He accepts. "Thank you," he says. "Delicious!"

"Olive!" Jade's face breaks into a huge smile as she walks

over to Olive, rests a hand on her shoulder, and kisses her on the top of the head.

"Want to see your new nephew?" Olive asks, then pulls the receiving blanket to the side so Jade can see his face.

Jade's eyes well up. "Good job, sis."

"Beautiful," adds Josh, with a self-conscious smile.

An ambulance screams by and most of us peek around the corner to see which neighbor is experiencing misfortune. It turns up the old Peterson place. "Maybe Dean finally got his," Beatrice says. "That would make Pearl happy." As we turn to return to our seats, Beatrice trips over a pot of flowers. For a second, she is completely airborne. In a split second, Josh darts toward her projected landing spot and catches her. First, her orange juice hits him, and then her full weight. He doesn't flinch. For a second, we all simply stare, amazed.

Phil breaks the silence. "Great catch!"

"She is a great catch, isn't she?" Josh jokes.

"Thank you," Beatrice says, blushing. "Oh, look what I did to you," she fusses as she assesses the quantity of orange juice all over his pants. "I can put those in the wash for you."

"Thanks, but the airline lost my luggage. I have nothing else to wear right now."

"Then you must wear my overalls. I'll feel horrible if I have to look at an orange juice stain on you all day."

He looks at Jade as if asking her for help, but she just shrugs and smiles. "Oh, Josh, I think you'll look very nice in Beatrice's overalls."

"Mom, would you like to hold Kelly for a while?" Olive

asks me. Would I like to? It's been all I can do not to snatch that baby from her!

"Oh, precious, there, there you go," I say as we awkwardly exchange him. "Are you feeling okay?" I ask Olive.

"Oh, yes," she answers. "Just a little tired. I might rest my eyes—only for a minute though."

"Why don't you go in and lie down?"

"I don't want to miss anything," she explains, and then shuts her eyes. This makes me smile; I remember those days.

Josh steps out onto the back porch wearing Beatrice's overalls over his crisp, white shirt. The overalls are significantly too short—almost up to his knees. His black socks and shiny loafers stand out. He looks at Jade for encouragement.

"Sexy," she says, completely entertained.

Beatrice stands, looking across the field. "Oh, no. Dean's cows have come through the fence again!"

"Beatrice, I'll get them out. I've got just the thing," Phil offers. He stands up, walks to our car, takes his bagpipes out of the trunk, and begins to march out into the field.

"Come on," Jade says to Josh. "Let's go help."

The three of them march out, Phil in front in his khaki slacks and plaid cotton shirt. He refrains from playing the pipes until he gets close to the cows and away from Olive. Josh slips here and there in his loafers. Jade's dress swishes with her sassy walk, and I'm sure her tall moccasins are warding off the cheat grass better than Josh's socks are. They are a funny picture, all of them. They continue to walk until they are specks. I hold Kelly in my arms and follow Phil with my eyes. My heart is full.

The phone rings, and Beatrice jumps up to get it. "Oh my God . . . Oh my God . . . Okay, thank you." I go inside. Beatrice is pale and shaken. "Your mother had a tractor accident. Dean found her. She's been taken to the hospital. Her arm's broken, and she has a little concussion. Do you want to go to the hospital with me?"

"Is she okay?"

"Sounds like it, but I want to get over there right away," Beatrice says.

"I think I better wait until Phil gets back. I'll be right behind you, though."

"Okay, I'm so sorry to leave you all fending for yourself." She shuffles off to her room to pack a bag. "She'll need fresh clothes to come home in." I don't know if she's talking to me or to herself. "Okay, I'm off." She flies out the front door as fast as her legs will take her.

"Tell Mom I'll be right there," I call behind her. Beatrice peels out in her old Ford LTD.

I decide I better go out and find Phil and the others so we can get going to the hospital. As I walk in the direction where I last saw them, holding Kelly in my arms, I notice the most beautiful house I've ever seen. I'm immediately drawn to its simplicity. I hesitate to go closer, knowing I should really find the others, but I feel a pull from it, like it's gently beckoning me. "We'll just be a minute," I whisper to Kelly as I carry him over to the house. When I'm at the threshold, it hits me—this is Olive's house—this is what she came here to create, and my heart fills. I feel overwhelmed, so many emotions coursing through me. Regret. Sadness. Joy. Hope. And love. I hug Kelly closely to my body and whisper in his ear, "You're lucky, little one. You picked a good mother." And as I pull myself away from this house I don't want to leave, I share one last secret with Kelly: *"And not a bad choice in picking those two crazy ladies you'll be living next to. Not bad, Kelly . . . you're going to be just fine . . ."*

Realizing it could take me too long to try and catch up with Phil and the others, and that Olive will worry if she wakes with no one there, I return to the back porch where she continues to "rest her eyes." I hear bagpipes in the distance playing "Amazing Grace" over the sound of bleating cattle. I notice the sound of bagpipes getting closer and can see specks where Phil, Jade, and Josh had disappeared. Good, they're on their way back. A cat darts across the yard, and my eyes follow it to where it stops. A young man stands by the garden, staring at me. He wears long, green shorts and a tan T-shirt with a tree on it. He has a terrible haircut and little nicks on his face. Who is he? Why didn't he come to the door? Why is he just standing there? I stare back. I wish Aretha was here. I feel vulnerable with a sleeping daughter and a baby in my arms. He slowly walks toward me, and I survey the patio for things I could hit him with if I had to. I look up again, and oh . . . those eyes. I take a moment to really look at those eyes. Forrest?

"Mom?" he asks.

"Forrest?" My eyes well up.

He doesn't say anything back, but walks around and up the steps of the back porch. I stand. He approaches, throws his arms around me, careful not to squish the baby, and sobs. "I'm so sorry," he says over and over.

I want to ask him so many things, but nothing comes out. I can't take it all in. It doesn't seem real. It *can't* be real. I've been waiting for this moment for thirteen years. I often thought this moment would never happen. Now, here it is, and I feel completely unprepared. Here it is and I don't know what to say.

With one arm cradling Kelly, I put my free hand on my heart. "Thank you for the tree house and the beautiful poem."

He pulls back, purses his lips together in a self-conscious smile and nods. He looks happy.

"You want to hold him?" I ask. He hesitates, and then nods. He holds out his arms, and I place Kelly in them. He opens his mouth to say something, but nothing comes out.

We sit in silence for a couple moments, and then I ask what I have wondered for the last thirteen years. "Forrest? Why did you go? What did you do that was so bad that you didn't think . . . ?" I don't know how to finish my question.

Forrest looks toward the old Willa Meyer place. Then he stands and hands Kelly back to me. "I'm sorry, Mom. I . . . I . . . I just . . . I just can't . . . I can't explain." He doesn't look me in the eye, and it's as if my mothering instincts—dead for so long—have kicked in again. I sense the distress in him, can almost taste it. Before I can say anything though, he starts to walk away.

After thirteen years, I get him back for five minutes and then lose him all over again? "Forrest, wait. Please . . . I can't lose you again. I can't bear losing you again."

He pauses and turns around. This time he looks me in the eye. His eyes tell me how sorry he is. Then he shakes his head and says, "You're not losing me." He reaches up and leaves a folded up piece of paper on the porch railing, then walks away. Despite his words, my heart wrenches, feeling grief all over again. I feel I've just lost him again.

I awkwardly stand with the baby in my arms and juggle him so that I can reach the paper. I sit back down and unfold it with one hand.

> *Like a salmon leaves*
> *Its home waters*
> *To experience the sea*
> *As it experiences*
> *What is not home*
> *I have experienced*
> *What is not home*
> *What is not light*
> *What is not God*
> *Like the salmon*
> *Is driven hard*
> *To swim upstream*
> *To jump cliffs*
> *And even dams*

To return to its
Origin
I find my way home too
By a force so strong
I swim up against
The very force that washed me
Down
against sin
And jump fear
To return to my
Essence
My light,
My divinity, my
Home

—Forrest
Bald Peak Lookout Tower c/o USFS,
Bonner's Ferry, ID 83394

Phil on Being Young

ANNA AND I sneak off to the old swing, holding hands. We almost trot down the dirt road that runs along the fence bordering the field. Near the end, I pull one strand of barbed wire up and step on the next strand down so Anna can crawl through. "Here you go, Grandma," I say.

"Thanks, Grandpa," she says and returns the favor.

From there, we almost skip as we cross the neighbor's field to the old tree.

Yes, the swing is in disrepair, but I've come prepared with new materials. I dismantle the old swing; I'm beginning to understand that sometimes things have to come to a complete end before they can see a new beginning. At the same time, it just doesn't make much sense to throw it all away. I pick up the old wooden seat and smile. "It's still good."

Anna smiles, too. "I didn't think there would be anything salvageable," she says.

I go right to work throwing new ropes over the old branch and threading the old seat onto the new ropes.

"I loved this swing," Anna sighs.

I hold it for her to test out.

Instead of sitting in it, she says, "You know, there's something I always wanted to do . . ."

"Yeah?"

"You sit first."

I sit on the rebuilt swing. "Are you going to push me?"

Instead of answering, Anna kicks off her shoes, pulls up her skirt, sits on my lap, and wraps her legs around me. My jaw drops, but I recover, kick off the best I can, and as an entwined pair, we slowly swing.

"Are you sure this seat isn't going to break?" Anna asks. "I mean, it must be pretty weathered by now."

"It might break, but if it does, we'll just fix that too."

I know time can never go back. The past can never be revisited. At best, I can take elements I enjoyed in the past and recreate them in the present. I am no longer in a state of retirement; I am in a state of reinvention.

Anna takes one hand off my neck, places it on my cheek, and kisses me.

The Moon on the Divinity of Second Chances

THE MOON ABOVE sees it all. It sees Pearl in her La-Z-Boy recliner, holding Kelly in her good arm, while Beatrice sits on the arm of the chair, filling in for Pearl's weakness. Across the coffee table from them, Olive sleeps soundly on the couch. Beatrice rests one arm behind Pearl's neck, as she quietly whispers in her ear, "We came into each other's lives too late to have a family together. I've watched a lot of your family grow up, and I have loved them, but I never really felt like they were my family, too—until now. Now," she glances down at Kelly, "we have a family together."

"Indeed we do," Pearl replies. Careful of her injured arm, she gently leans into Beatrice and rests her face against Beatrice's shoulder.

Outside, a little ways away, Dean burns a couple tires. The toxic smoke drifts into Pearl and Beatrice's house. The two women exchange looks. "Why don't you let me handle it this time?" Beatrice asks, and gets up before Pearl can argue.

She goes to the kitchen, packs a half dozen strawberry tarts into a lunch sack, slips on her boots, and walks with her normal bounce across the field. She stops at the trees, practices a few of her best wheezes, then continues up the little rise to Dean's burn barrel.

"Why hello, Miss Beatrice!" Dean smiles at her. "How is Miss Pearl doing?"

Beatrice wheezes and replies, "Oh, she's doing all right, thanks to you, Dean." She pauses to wheeze some more, and gasps for air. "You are not only a good neighbor, but a hero. Here, I brought you some strawberry tarts I made today. It's such a small gesture for the gratitude I feel in my heart."

"Oh, Miss Beatrice, I didn't do anything anyone else wouldn't have," he says. But the Moon, like Beatrice, can see that Dean rather likes that word, hero.

"Us old women are vulnerable you know, so it warms my heart to know we have such a good, kind soul living next door looking out for us." She gasps for breath and coughs.

Dean blushes. "Miss Beatrice, you have a terrible cough. Are you sick?"

"Actually Dean, it's your burn barrel. You see, I have terrible asthma. When smoke from your burn barrel comes and fills our house, I can't breathe. I noticed Olive's premature baby is having trouble breathing tonight, too. But don't worry about us, Dean. I know you are just doing what you have to do. In fact, I actually wanted to apologize. Usually, since I can't breathe, I know Miss Pearl comes over in her most confrontational way. I apologize for all her rude behavior.

Sometimes people have to burn, Dean, I understand that. I just came over tonight to deliver these tarts and thank you for saving Pearl's life." Beatrice pauses to wheeze some more. "I saw your mother at the post office today and told her what an exceptional young man you are. Of course, word had spread all around town before the ambulance even drove away with Pearl about what a hero you are, so I didn't have to tell her. She is so proud of you."

"Aw, shucks, Miss Beatrice." Dean picks up his hose and walks over to the spigot to turn on the water. "I am so sorry about my burn barrel. I'll have to pay more attention to the wind when I burn. Please forgive me. You know I'd never mean to cause you harm."

"Of course I know that, Dean. You're a good boy. We're lucky to have you for a neighbor. I better get back to help with the baby." Wheeze. "It was sure nice talking with you, Dean."

"Always a pleasure, Miss Beatrice!"

Beatrice smiles to herself as she walks back to the house, up the porch stairs, and in the back door. She strikes a victorious pose, hands on her hips. "Pearl, you catch more flies with honey," she whispers.

The moon above understands something about the part of its face that is seen depending on where the sun shines its light. And from above where time and time again it is in its own way anew, the moon sees second chances everywhere.

It sees Phil and Anna doing the tango by candlelight late into the night at the Starlight Motel in Summerville. Other guests can see their silhouettes dancing back and forth between the red candle and the curtain.

It sees Forrest in the back of a hippie couple's pickup truck with a new used guitar, hitchhiking to his new home, and putting his poetry to music. He thinks about Kelly's new life, all he is about to embark on, and makes up a lullaby:

Beautiful Boy
Go to sleep
Let your mind rest
Count the sheep
Go to the place
Where the dreams are
Go to the moon
And stars
And know that you're loved
For all that you are
And this love you'll keep
I'm singing
You to sleep.
Beautiful Boy
Close your eyes
Travel
To the skies
And know that you're safe
Wherever you are
You are watched
By the stars

And know that you're loved
For all that you are
And this love you'll keep
I'm singing
You to sleep.

He thinks maybe, just maybe, he'll sing that song to his own kids one day. He doesn't know, but for the first time he's open to it.

The moon sees Josh and Jade finish Olive's roof, dump the last of the dirt up there, smooth it out, then plant the strawberries and thyme. It sees them rinse off dirt and sweat by running through the irrigation sprinklers. It sees them hold hands as they walk back drenched, hang their clothes over the porch furniture, then fall asleep under a blanket on an air mattress on Pearl and Beatrice's back porch, entwined, their limbs like the stripes on a beautiful zebra.

And the moon sees Aretha grow in the body of Lula, preparing to reunite with Jade in a few short months.

The moon knows that just as it must wax and wane, just as another full moon is inevitable, so are second chances in humanity below.

Acknowledgments

THANKS, OF COURSE, to my editors, Elizabeth and Chris Day, who help me stick with it when my attention span is shot, who edit without telling me what to write, but improve my awareness about where the holes are. Thank you, Nancy Burke, for providing the avenue to make my dreams reality. Thanks to everyone at DayBue Publishing, Chapter One Books in Ketchum, The Book Store in Wenatchee, and Sunflower Books in LaGrande—I appreciate all you've done to promote my writing. Thanks to my high school English teacher, Bill Hawk, who had high expectations and the skills as a teacher to help us meet them. I learned a lot from him. Thanks to Mary Hoeksema and Tess Haddon for great feedback and perspectives. Thanks to Barb Julian and Diane Honsinger for reading a very early draft a couple years ago and encouraging me not to go in that direction. Thanks Mom and Gram for tons of encouragement, and for always believing in me. Thanks to both Dad and Mom, who are happily married, for instilling in me the belief that I am capable of anything. Thanks to all the book groups who invited me to discuss my first book, *Church of the Dog*—I am a better writer for the awareness you gave me. Thanks to everyone who let me know *Church of the Dog* touched them. Some of my most productive days were spent at the homes of Leanne Webster, Andee Hansen, and Mari Wania—thanks for inspiration and clarity I couldn't find at my house. Thanks to everyone in the Wood River Valley who helped or cared when I lost Tasha Good Dog and spent three months searching for her. Love comes in so many forms; to everyone in my past, present, and future who radiates it in my presence, thank you for the strength, encouragement, and inspiration it gives me.